Praise for

ALYS MURRAY

"A feel-good summer novel."

—Buzzfeed on *The Magnolia Sisters*

The Perfect Hideaway

ALSO BY ALYS MURRAY

The Magnolia Sisters
Sweet Pea Summer

ALYS MURRAY

The Perfect Hideaway

FOREVER

New York Boston

Forever
Hachette Book Group
1290 Avenue of the Americas, New York, NY 10104
read-forever.com
twitter.com/readforeverpub

Originally published in 2020 by Bookouture in the United Kingdom
First US edition: January 2024

Forever is an imprint of Grand Central Publishing. The Forever name and logo are trademarks of Hachette Book Group, Inc.

The publisher is not responsible for websites (or their content) that are not owned by the publisher.

Forever books may be purchased in bulk for business, educational, or promotional use. For information, please contact your local bookseller or the Hachette Book Group Special Markets Department at special.markets@hbgusa.com.

Library of Congress Cataloging-in-Publication Data
Names: Murray, Alys, author.
Title: The perfect hideaway / Alys Murray.
Description: First US edition. | New York : Forever, 2024. |
Series: Full bloom farm ; 3
Identifiers: LCCN 2023036569 | ISBN 9781538756836 (trade paperback)
Subjects: LCGFT: Romance fiction. | Novels.
Classification: LCC PS3613.U7567 P47 2024 | DDC
813/.6—dc23/eng/20230818
LC record available at https://lccn.loc.gov/2023036569

ISBN: 9781538756836 (trade paperback)

Printed in the United States of America

LSC-C

Printing 1, 2023

For everyone who has ever agreed to watch a black-and-white movie with me, even when you didn't want to.

The Perfect Hideaway

Chapter One

Annie

"I can't believe I did it. I can't believe it's finally happened."

After almost a year and a half of planning the nuptials of her brother, Luke Martin, to her dear friend, Harper Anderson, the day had finally come. The restored wood cabin dance hall high up in the Northern California hills surrounding the wine-and-cheese town of Hillsboro was the perfect place for a wedding reception. It was an oasis of warmth and love from the dark, cold, wooded mountains beyond its walls. The Anderson family, famous around the country now for their flowers, had filled the entire place with open, lovely blooms, which caught the light and filled the dance hall with color. The wooden beams of the ceiling captured every glinting glimmer of candlelight and flashbulb; the atmosphere—a simple and delicate blending of rustic and chic—seemed to envelop its guests, drawing them into the intimacy of the space, welcoming them onto its dance floor and giving a perfect backdrop for the bride and groom as they took their first steps together as a married couple.

Annie wished she could say that the wedding had been perfect. She wanted nothing more than to be dancing in the center of the floor, her mind blissfully clear of spreadsheets and mood boards and itemized lists that had been haunting her since she first found out about the engagement.

Instead, she stood at the fringes of the night, watching from the sidelines as everyone else enjoyed the fruits of her meticulous planning, unable to get the little details out of her head. Things no one else would have noticed, things she knew weren't important in the grand scheme of things. A loose thread in the hem of her best-woman dress. A dangling petal on Harper's bouquet. The slight, awkward pause when Luke couldn't get the ring box open quickly enough during the ceremony. The champagne coming out a full minute behind schedule once the reception began in full swing.

These little details loomed impossibly large in her mind. But she knew it wasn't the real reason she was struggling to relax into the party she had planned.

The fresh glass of champagne in her hand grew warm as she waited there, turning over the day in her head, just as Rose—the eldest and most statuesque of the three Anderson sisters who had welcomed her into their lives since she and Luke arrived in Hillsboro two years ago—swanned up beside her, the edges of her soft, purple gown brushing against the tops of her dyed-to-match shoes. Tonight, she'd traded out her usual cat-eye glasses for contacts, but even without her signature look, she was easy to spot in a crowd. Just behind her, Annie could see the youngest Anderson sister, May, fleetingly back in town for the wedding with her boyfriend, Tom Riley. Annie caught his eye and gave him a happy wave. Her own engagement to Tom was the reason she and her brother originally moved to Hillsboro, and she and Tom had remained friendly ever since their amicable parting.

They hadn't officially become family until today, when Harper and Luke had said, "I do," but Annie adored the Andersons as if she had known them her whole life.

"You don't look so good," Rose said, her words slurring slightly. Poor thing was such a lightweight when it came to alcohol.

Annie forced a laugh. "Thank you, Rose, for your brutal honesty. What do you mean?"

"You're wrinkling your brow. I was under the impression internet stars didn't wrinkle *anything*."

It was true, as a social media influencer and brand promoter, Annie spent hours of every day cultivating her social media image—editing out flyaways, smoothing any lines at the corners of her eyes or patches of cellulite on her slender frame—so she could land brand deals and promote the hottest nail polish or clothing brand of the minute. It was exhausting, and, apparently, useless under the astute gaze of a close friend.

Finally taking a sip of her champagne, she tried not to think of the throngs of cameras stationed in the corners of the room. Reporters from as far as Europe were documenting the night not just for Luke and Harper's sentimental value, but also because, well, with Annie's career as an influencer and her brother's place at the top of the tech world, the pair of them were something like celebrities. Digital Age darlings. And no one was going to miss this wedding.

If things had gone according to plan, she wouldn't have minded the photographers. Despite the fact that Luke had serious issues with the press, Annie reveled in the spotlight. There was something nice about being looked at and admired from a comfortable distance; cameras brought people close enough to look, but not close enough to actually *see*. But there was a downside to internet fame and now, with the laundry list of wedding mistakes burned into her mind, she couldn't help but think about how every photograph would be nitpicked by the faceless trolls online, about how they might turn the happiest night of her brother's life into something to be dissected and ridiculed.

She made a mental note to turn off notifications on her social media apps before going to bed tonight. The last thing she needed was to be hungover *and* have to deal with internet mobs making fun of her mistakes.

"Seriously. What's going on with you? You're in the middle of the most beautiful wedding this county's ever seen and you look like someone put mud in your shoes."

Annie sighed and tossed her blond hair over her shoulder with one manicured hand.

"The most beautiful wedding? I can name about fifty things that went wrong today. That's my brother and Harper up there. I wanted everything to be perfect."

"Oh, Annie, I don't think perfect matters much, at least not tonight. I mean, look at them. Have you ever seen two people looking happier?"

Annie dragged her gaze to the couple twirling in the center of the room—her brother and her new sister. They held each other as though letting go would mean the end of the world, and they laughed as though they wouldn't care if it did, not so long as they had each other. For so long, she'd rooted for the two of them to get together, fought for it, even. But now, as she looked at them, her joy couldn't seem to make the journey from her mind to her heart.

Luke was married now, and for the first time in her entire life, she and her brother would be apart. He'd been her entire family for most of her life, her best friend and the person she counted on above everyone else. Now, she would be alone.

Alone. That word echoed, bouncing back to her again and again and again. *Alone. Alone. Alone.*

Rose had the kindness not to mention Annie's mental distance, *and* to change the subject.

"So, what are you going to do with all of your newfound freedom? No more wedding to plan, no more brother to look after? I have decided I'll be turning Harper's bedroom into a crafting room."

"I'm finishing up moving into my new house first thing in the morning. And after that...uh..."

Her own blood chilled as she realized she didn't have an ending to that sentence. For the first time in her entire life, Annie Martin didn't have a full calendar ahead of her. Not a single thing to look forward to. Not a single thing to distract her from that word. *Alone.*

Suddenly, it all made sense. Her inability to shake off the wedding's small mishaps. Her sudden distaste for the cameras all around her. Those mistakes felt like *her* mistakes. She worried that the cameras were going to capture just how empty she suddenly felt.

In one big gulp, she threw back all of the champagne settling in the bottom of her flute. It did nothing to calm her nerves, but it did give her enough bubbly strength to muster up one of her blindingly fake smiles.

That was what she always did in moments like this. Fake it until she made it.

"You know, I'm sure something will come up. It always does."

Tomorrow, she would worry about the towering question mark that was her new life. Tonight, she would do literally anything to avoid it. Scanning the room, she found the perfect distraction on the dance floor. As couples twirled and laughed, cuddled and swayed, Annie turned her attention to the woman standing next to her.

She was going to make Rose Anderson her new project.

"What about *you*, hmm? Is all of this wedding stuff helping you catch the love bug?"

Rose laughed, clearly relieved to see the smile on Annie's face and her seeming return to her usual bright and chipper persona. "With all due respect, Annie, I'm pretty sure my high school health class warned me against catching love bugs."

It was the closest sweet, demure Rose—with her gentle smile and soft tone—would ever get to an innuendo, and Annie couldn't help the giggle that escaped her. Just like she couldn't help the certainty that the sweet, demure, beautiful woman standing next to her deserved all of the love in the world.

"You know what I mean! Come on. I think there are some pretty eligible bachelors out here tonight who'd be lucky to get even a dance with you."

Without waiting for any kind of verbal agreement to this sudden turn of events, Annie started off across the reception hall, making a beeline for the small bunch of groomsmen lingering at the farthest end of the room, closest to the bar. If there was one thing Annie knew about people, it was that very few could stand an unfinished conversation. Want to guarantee someone will follow you? Start walking away in the middle of an exchange.

Just as she suspected, Rose followed close on her heels, using her long-legged strides to somehow pass through the crowd like a serene swan gliding on a pond instead of a slightly panicked woman trying to keep up with a matchmaking friend.

"Annie," Rose said, her voice taking on the distinct lower register of a disappointed teacher—the closest she ever got to sounding truly upset. "We've talked about this."

Sure, they'd talked about it plenty of times. No matter how often Annie assured Rose that she could find her the perfect man, one who would simply worship and adore her, the eldest Anderson sister always rebuffed her. *I'm not interested in a relationship right now*, she'd always say, *I like being single.*

Annie had heard every excuse in the book. Most people she knew found matchmaking and cupid-ing secretly insulting, as if Annie wanting to help them find the loves of their life somehow implied they weren't capable of doing it on their own. But the truth was . . . she liked being useful. She liked helping. And tonight, she was going to start by finally helping Rose.

Carefully maneuvering her way through the crowd of tipsy wedding-goers, Annie spotted her target across the room—Rishan, the tall, lanky senior developer at AppeX, her brother's tech company. From everything she knew about him, he was kind and respectful, easygoing and reserved. Just the kind of person who'd be the perfect test subject for Rose.

That was the thing most people didn't know about helping people find love—test subjects were almost always necessary. Rishan would show Annie just what kind of man Rose actually liked and responded to, which would only make the task of actually finding the man of her dreams easier.

"One of Luke's groomsmen is over there. He's a little shy, but he's an absolute genius when it comes to tech stuff and he's very sweet. Let me introduce you."

"Wait—"

But Rose's protestations fell on deaf ears. Even if Annie had bothered to listen, she was already tapping Rishan on the shoulder, drawing his attention away from his phone and back to the land of non-digital interaction.

"Rishan!"

"…Yes?"

The poor guy couldn't have looked more confused if she'd just asked him to pick colors for a Spring Lookbook. His bearded jaw dropped slightly when Annie stepped aside to introduce her friend, who hung back an awkward step behind her.

"This is Rose. Rose, this is Rishan."

"Nice to meet you," Rishan said, though his tone hinted at some hidden terror at the realization that a beautiful woman seemed to be talking to him.

"Yeah, you too."

For a moment, Annie waited for conversation to spark naturally, for the two to hit it off like she'd secretly hoped they would. No such luck.

"Rose here was just telling me how much she wanted to dance."

"I wasn't—" Rose turned her wide, apologetic eyes on Rishan. Annie didn't exactly see sparks when their eyes met for the first time, but it was early still. Anything could change on the dance floor. "I *really* wasn't—"

But Annie slapped a hand on Rishan's shoulder, drawing his bewildered gaze her way. Annie answered that look with a pointed one of her own. In her experience, guys who worked with computers all day weren't so good at taking hints without a wink and nudge—sometimes, literally.

"And I'm *sure* you wouldn't want her to dance alone."

"Of course not—" Rishan stammered.

"Great," Annie said, before anyone could object or change their mind. Stubborn people always needed a little push in the direction of love, didn't they? "Have fun, you two!"

Perfect. Now time to find a table, find a waiter with canapés, and watch from the sidelines to see how this one goes. Maybe I could even—

"But what about you?"

Rose's voice practically grabbed Annie by the shoulders and spun her around. Even her most composed, amused smile couldn't hide her confusion. "Me?"

One of Rose's eyebrows quirked upwards, the smallest hint that this was not, in fact, a friendly question asked out of curiosity, but a challenge.

"You're not going to dance alone, are you?"

"No," Annie choked out, knowing she couldn't back down now. "Obviously not. As it happens, I already have a dance partner."

"Is that so?"

It would have been very easy to just tell Rose that she was going to sit this one out and rest her feet or something, but Annie's pride bristled at the prospect. *Think of something. Think of someone. Come on, Annie. You can do this.* Desperately, she searched the faces of the room for someone without a partner, someone who wouldn't possibly turn her down.

Then, she spotted him. Sitting down in the dining section of the hall, squeezed between two happily drunken couples, sat a man in an obviously borrowed tuxedo, looking more handsome—and more miserable, given the set of his shoulders—than any man had a right to. She could just barely make out his profile, but dark, curly hair crowned his head, with its sharp, scruffy jawline, and he stared out absently at the dance floor. His tie had been undone and his shirt—slightly rumpled, was unbuttoned at the top. Though his suspenders were still in place, giving him the appearance of a man who'd stepped out of a time machine or a black-and-white movie, he was eminently disheveled… and definitely the most intriguing man in the room.

Looking at him was like catching sight of lightning striking an electrical grid. All sparks.

Annie's heart stammered. Or maybe that was just the drums from the wedding band suddenly starting a new song. She wasn't sure.

No, she *was* sure. It hadn't been her. Annie Martin wasn't the kind of woman who got all moony-eyed over any guy, much less a stranger.

And certainly not this stranger. Because in the split second after those sparks had extinguished, the man turned his face towards her, giving her a better view of his strong jaw, rich chocolate eyes, and curving lips, and she realized that this wasn't the first time she'd seen him. Oh, no. This was George Barnett. George Barnett, the snoop who worked for the *Hillsboro Gazette*, the one who Annie had once had to chase—in her bathrobe, no less—away from her house with nothing but a croquet mallet when she'd caught him trying to spy on the place with a telescopic lens.

The sparks she'd felt a moment ago fell to the wire-ends of her brain and caught fire. What was *he* doing here? She certainly hadn't put him on any guest list she'd written.

"Annie?" Rose prompted, a small smirk on her lips. "Who're you going to dance with?"

But before the question had even been asked, Annie was already walking across the dance floor, her fake smile firmly in place. She was going to dance with George Barnett. And then, she was going to kick him out.

Chapter Two

George

Under normal circumstances, George Barnett wouldn't have been caught dead working the *Hillsboro Gazette*'s society beat, much less *asking* for it and then trading a free month of coffee to Shannon Park, the Society Editor, for it. He was into gumshoe reporting and scandal, the kind of hard-boiled detective work that won people Pulitzers, not the kind of carefully crafted PR wizardry that appeared on the newspaper's sixth page.

But these weren't normal circumstances, which was how he ended up with an invitation to Hillsboro's most exclusive wedding of the century and a slightly uncomfortable rented tuxedo. Tonight wasn't just any nighttime wedding in the swankiest venue in the county. This was the wedding of Hillsboro royalty—Harper Anderson, future owner and operator of her family's flower farm, if the rumors were to be believed—to Luke Martin, one of the nation's youngest tech moguls.

But he wasn't here to celebrate. The thing about George Barnett was that he believed in finding and exposing the truth, no matter the consequences. And men like Luke Martin, men with deep pockets and tight-knit social circles that rarely ever leaked, were the worst kind of trouble. A man like that—and his family—could get away with a whole lot and bring a whole mess of trouble upon people without the resources to fight them.

Ever since the Martins had descended on Hillsboro two years ago with their L.A. cars and oversized sunglasses, George was convinced that there was something fishy going on. And he was going to expose it no matter what. And if it meant getting his big career break and a chance at the nationals, well that would be a win-win scenario as far as he was concerned.

Even if it meant being here. In the middle of this wedding. The last place he wanted to be.

His idea of a good Saturday night was hanging out with a few beers and his faded VHS copy of *All the President's Men*. Dancing and drinking with Californian society elite wasn't his idea of a perfect night. Still, he'd always believed that a good reporter was something like a good spy—ready to go undercover and slip into even the most dire of situations at a moment's notice—so, he put on a brave face and tried to collect any intel he could from his safe place at the far end of the room. He might have been a good soldier-for-the-truth, but he wasn't going to go so far as to dance at this thing.

"So," he said, trying to cut into the conversation to his left, where a graying man and a slender woman in their fifties chatted animatedly. "Do you know the bride or the groom?"

A leading question, considering he'd grown up in Hillsboro and knew for a fact that this man probably knew neither of them well, but a necessary one. Gathering background information like this always required a soft touch; no one wanted to feel like they were being interviewed.

"Groom," the man responded, his voice a jovial grumble, like one might expect out of Santa Claus. George made a mental note of that, in case he ever wanted to use it in a story someday. "I've known Luke Martin since he came to work at... Darling, have you had some of this wine? It's very good."

His wife nodded, placing her now-empty glass on the table before her. "You know, I think it's from a local vineyard. They were at the Food and Wine Festival—"

No luck with that conversation. George turned his attention to the couple on his left, an even older pair who seemed as though they'd be much more at home in a suburban L.A. country club than here in Hillsboro. Inclining himself to the slender, regal woman in the pair, he tried to turn the charm up to maximum, flashing her what he'd sometimes been told was a winning, heartbreaker of a smile. Charming women wasn't something he did on the regular, but when a story was on the line, he would do just about anything. And he *needed* a story about Luke Martin. So, he batted his long lashes and tried to make this spindly older woman feel like the only person in the room.

"So, you know the groom I take it? I'm a friend of the bride—"

"Well, yes, I know the groom. Lovely ceremony." Apparently, his charm bomb was a dud, because she immediately returned to her husband, leaving George in the conversational dust. "Didn't you think so, dear? I thought the reading from *Star Trek* instead of the Bible or the Torah was a bit gauche, but—"

George opened his mouth to speak, to interject that he thought the *Star Trek* reading was actually pretty badass and something he would have done if he got married—which, in fairness, he didn't ever plan on doing—but the sound died in his throat when a soft hand touched his shoulder. Slender fingertips barely, accidentally, brushed the skin of his neck, sending electric shockwaves down his entire body, waking him as though he'd been splashed with ice water in the middle of a deep, foggy sleep.

Then, a voice sliced through the din of the party, clearing away all of the background noise until he only heard her soft, warm tones. She—whoever she was—spoke to him with the familiar charm of old, reunited friends, but he couldn't for the life of him place who she was.

"There you are!"

Not by voice, anyway. Because when he turned around and followed the sleek, classic design of the purple bridesmaid's dress up to the eyes of the stranger, he realized she wasn't such a stranger after all. From this angle, given the way she stood over him as he sat at the table, he was forced to look up at her like a worshipper at the feet of an angel. Given the way she looked, it was almost appropriate. Blond and beautiful, delicate and blue-eyed, she was one of the most striking women he'd ever seen.

They hadn't ever technically met. Oh, they'd had an encounter once—which mostly amounted to him sprinting away from her while she, clad only in a floral print bathrobe, chased him with a giant wooden hammer on a long stick. Not his proudest moment, and one he deeply regretted—but they'd never introduced themselves.

Still, he knew who she was. Annabelle Martin.

The groom's sister. The internet celebrity. The human embodiment of everything George thought was wrong and dishonest about the world. In his research for this profile he'd been wanting to write on Luke Martin—a piece he'd been trying to pull together since the first days of the Martins' time here in town— he'd spent plenty of time scrolling through Annabelle's Instagram feed and online lifestyle magazine. That scrolling rewarded him with bitter glimpse after bitter glimpse into this perfect stranger until he almost felt he knew her. Everyone in town spoke about her as if she was this perfectly lovely darling, a sweet saint with a heart of gold, but he knew better. No one who hawked facial cleanser and thousand-dollar sunglasses on the internet could be good deep down. Despite having never spoken more than a handful of words to her, he'd developed a kind of caustic dislike for her, one that should have been strong enough to last up until this moment.

But when he looked up and met her piercing blue eyes—blue as the first clear day of spring after a terrible, terrible winter—and her pink lips tilted upward, revealing a slight, imperfect dimple in her left cheek, he couldn't help but feel some of that slip away.

It was always harder to hate people in person than behind a screen.

No sooner had he discovered himself softening under the warmth of her crystalline eyes than he steeled himself again. She was a subject, wasn't she? Part of a large, grand story George wanted to tell about the richest man in town and how he'd brought big-city "values" to this small town. He couldn't afford distraction. Couldn't afford softness. Couldn't afford to get lost in her blue eyes or dwell on the way his stomach tightened at the feeling of her soft hand on his shoulder.

But he *could* afford to play along as though he knew her. At least that would get him somewhere.

"Uh...yeah," he said, holding out his arms to present himself. Hopefully, this wasn't some kind of trick. He could only assume she cared about appearances enough to refrain from chasing him with a mallet again. "Here I am."

"I've been looking for you everywhere. Have you been sitting here this whole time? Come on. Let's go."

Okay, of all the things he was expecting Annabelle Martin to be—spoiled, impetuous, snobby—he wouldn't have ever guessed *infectious*. To his surprise, he didn't even mean that in a bad way. Her commitment to this charade or mistake or whatever it was made him want to play along, too. Her smile tickled his lips, begging him to copy her even though it was against his better judgment. And when she took his hand and led him away from the table, he followed without even a second thought.

The warmth of that hand in his sparked something in his chest, but he dismissed the sensation as nothing more than the result of too many Saturday nights alone. Her confident steps carried him through the party, but her sudden silence now unnerved him.

"I'm not sure you've got the right guy," he said, letting her maneuver him through the throngs.

"No, I've got the right guy. You were about to drown out there. I saved you. But..." Very suddenly, she paused on her high heels and spun on him, a move that came so suddenly he barely had time to stop himself. Their noses almost touched; she made him aware of every line of her body. "I want something in return."

"And what is that, exactly?"

Her eyes sparkled. "I need a dance partner."

With that, she squeezed his hand again and pulled him once again towards the dance floor, where now the band was in full partying mode, drawing life and rhythm from everyone near it. The muscles in George's body tensed at the thought of joining them, of drawing attention to himself. He'd thought that an incognito search and report scouting night would have been the ideal way to go about things. This was supposed to be a simple fact-finding mission; dancing with the most beautiful girl in the room—his subject's sister, no less—was not how he had envisioned the evening going.

"I don't dance," he lied, ignoring the five years of ballet and ballroom he took during his days as a young football player.

"Of course you do. Everyone dances. Haven't you ever seen a musical?"

"Yeah, but I don't live in one."

Soon, they came to the dance floor's edge, where he dug in his heels and refused to be dragged along any further. No way was he going to let himself be cajoled or manipulated into dancing with Annabelle Martin. Absolutely not.

Though, as soon as that thought came to mind, she turned her flaring eyes upon him, raised a smirk, and said—too loudly, drawing the attention of nearby revelers, "It was *so nice of you* to ask me to dance."

George drew himself in closer to her, hissing, "What are you doing?"

She hissed right back, triumphantly setting her shoulders. "Making you look like a jerk if you suddenly run away."

Again, George had underestimated her. He'd been beaten, and badly. Apparently, that realization had been apparent on his face, because Annie's smile once again returned and pulled him again towards the sea of dancing couples, just as the band began their transition into a slow, languorous big band ballad.

"Come on. It's easy once you try."

Knowing he had no choice but to obey—not with all of the nearby eyes watching their every move—George joined her, and allowed himself to pull her close. One hand in hers. One hand at her waist. His body flush against her own.

He was aware of every inch of her, of her breath against his neck, of the soft scent of her poppy perfume; he was also aware of his natural—and inconvenient—desire for more of all of it. Straightening his spine and trying to put at least a little distance between them, he tried to let the bitterness he'd sometimes felt while scrolling through her Instagram feed (something he usually did while eating grilled cheese . . . his ultimate struggle meal at the end of the month when the rent was due and his student loan payment had taken the majority of his paycheck) infect his heart.

"But what is Annabelle Martin doing dancing with a nobody like me?" he asked, dipping his lips down towards her ear. The words were a slight, smiling taunt, and he felt her breath catch when they reached her.

"And what is an investigative journalist doing at my brother's wedding, hmm?"

Oh, he'd fallen for it. He'd fallen for her pretty girl act and her niceties and her smile and now, he was stuck here, in the center of the dance floor in her arms, so she could interrogate him about how he'd managed to sneak his way into this wedding.

Great. Just great. After almost two years on the Martin Family beat, he'd finally gotten as close as he was ever going to get...and he'd blown it.

"Well, Annabelle Martin—"

"Annie. I go by Annie. Not Annabelle."

Her dainty and friendly exterior was gone now. The command was so sharp, so harsh, and so choked by pain that, despite his desire to chip away at this woman's facade, he couldn't help but immediately and without reservation agree.

"Sorry." He swallowed. "Annie Martin."

They danced in silence for a moment, an awkward silence that left George feeling confused and conflicted. Sure, he'd meant to get under her skin—she was, at least in his eyes, a frivolous person who probably hid some dark secrets he wanted to uncover—but he hadn't meant to hurt her by saying her own *name*.

Curiosity tugged at him; his journalistic instincts told him there was a story there. Before he could pull on the thread, though, Annie tossed her head and took control of the silence.

"So, what are you doing here? And how did you get here?"

"What is this, twenty questions?"

"Well, it's a long song. And I don't know anything about you. Except that you're a terrible dancer, a guy who tries to spy on people in their own homes, and a snarky reporter, which is three strikes against you."

"Snarky," George scoffed, but noticed a pang of relief in his heart as she returned to something like normal. At least he hadn't hurt her too badly. "I prefer sharp-witted."

"You'd have to have wit to be sharp-witted."

How did she manage to smile as though they were having a perfectly pleasant conversation and dance while simultaneously burning him like a piece of forgotten toast? He had to hand it to her, the woman had skills.

"And here I was thinking that the rumors about Annie Martin being the nicest, sweetest girl in town were all true. Glad to see some of my investigative reporting paid off tonight."

"I'm usually a delight, when I'm around better company."

"Then why did you ask me to dance?"

"Because I needed to keep you away from everyone else. And so I could keep my eye on—"

She stopped herself short, biting down on her lower lip in such a way that George couldn't help but let his eyes fall to them. Pink and perfect and kissable. One of her top, front two teeth was chipped, a small imperfection in an otherwise outwardly perfect person. Somehow, it made her even more beautiful. But it was her sudden trepidation that truly captured his interest.

"Keep your eye on what?"

"I'm not telling you anything, you snoop. After this dance is over, I'm going to make sure someone sees you out."

"Why? Because you think I'm a party crasher?"

"No, because you're a terrible newshound and we don't talk to reporters."

Now, she had his complete attention. It was as if the rest of the room didn't even exist. *This* was the kind of thing he'd come here tonight to learn, and he'd stumbled into it. It was like winning the lottery because someone accidentally gave you the ticket.

"Did your brother teach you that?"

"No, years of living in America taught me that. I mean, *real* journalists are great. Protecting democracy, alerting the public to problems, ranking the cats from the musical *Cats*. But you aren't a real journalist."

He was surprised by the intensity of his reaction to that. Heat flared along the back of his neck; his stomach dropped.

"What am I, then?"

"The guy who tried to spy on me in my own house."

"I didn't mean to spy on you. Just your brother. Unless you have something to hide...?"

"I don't have anything to hide from you. You're just an ego with a laptop. A persistent thorn in my brother's side."

Very, very guilty. It'd been almost two years on the Luke Martin beat and he hadn't so much as talked to the guy. But that didn't mean he didn't try. Often. The man's poor secretary spoke to him so often that last year she'd sent him a card for Hanukkah.

"I wouldn't have to keep bothering you or him if he would just give me an interview."

"Well, I'm very sorry, but he doesn't do interviews," Annie said, using their interlinked hands to suddenly lead him in the dance. George's dancing instincts took over, and he tried to fight the sudden loss of leadership, but Annie was not having it. Her eyes flashed. "And neither do I."

"Are you—" Still, she pulled and tugged him where she wanted to go. And he'd thought the dancing part of this interaction, at least, had gone well. "What are you doing?"

"It's none of your business," she retorted, though she didn't stop trying to twirl him where she wanted to go.

"It's my business if you're going to keep throwing me around like a rag doll."

"Off the record," she stressed the words and shot him a pointed look before darting her eyes across the dance floor once again, "I'm trying to set up my friend Rose, and I need to see how things are going."

"So, the internet celebrity spends her time meddling in her friends' lives."

Her shoulders stiffened. The muscles in her cheek tightened. And even after those blatant tells, she still smiled and tried to pretend that he wasn't getting to her. "I don't meddle. I find that characterization offensive."

"You can *find* it however you like. Find it with a map for all I care. But that doesn't change the facts."

She raised one eyebrow, and pulled her gaze from over his shoulder. "Which are?"

Shrugging as much as he could while still keeping their dancing position mostly intact, he casually flicked through all of his memories of her and of her online presence. Figuring out someone like this wasn't incredibly difficult. Even an amateur newsprint sleuth could have deciphered her in a heartbeat. "That you're bored and the internet has isolated you and so you try to get a little piece of self-value from messing with the lives of everyone around you."

The music swelled and ebbed around them, just like the light in Annie Martin's eyes. Strangely, George didn't feel the rush of victory he'd expected to feel at the sight of her defeated. Instead, he felt like a perfect jerk.

Not that he was going to let her know that. In his profession, feeling things for anyone—including yourself—made finding the truth all the more difficult.

Annie bit down on her lip, and when she recovered enough to speak, she stared down at his lapel. "You think you have me all figured out?"

"I'm a pretty good judge of character."

A wry laugh. Then, she leveled her gaze at him. So intense, so fiery, so undeniable, so inescapable that he wondered if she could see his soul somewhere buried in the depths of his eyes. "I try to find my friends love because they deserve it. Because I believe that everyone good in this sad, lonely world deserves someone who gives them back all of the love they put out there. And whether you like it or not, Mister Cynical, I believe that more love in this world is *always* a good thing, even if it takes a little meddling to get there."

For the briefest of split seconds, she'd almost moved him. He could hear the ring of truth as she spoke, and it rattled something within him that he hadn't felt in a long, long time.

But then, he glanced over her shoulder, trying to escape her eyes, and realized that he'd been a fool. Of course she believed in goodness and romance and the power of love; she'd probably never faced much adversity at all. However, once she saw what *he* saw, maybe she'd be less certain.

"You might want to reevaluate that belief, matchmaker."

"And why should I do that? Because your dark heart can't take it?"

"No, because your friend just tossed her dance partner's phone into the punch bowl."

Chapter Three

Annie

The rest of the night was as much of a damage-control disaster as Annie could have ever fought against in her nightmares. Of course, with a little bit of luck and her iron fist, Annie was able to keep Luke and Harper from even suspecting that anything was out of the ordinary, and the two of them went off to their honeymoon together without knowing that Rose had destroyed an AppeX corporate phone, causing the groomsman in question to storm off, but not before filling his pockets with as many party favors—sugar candies and soaps created by May Anderson—as he could possibly carry. So much for respectful and easygoing.

Eventually the last of the guests had faded away and after helping the wait staff with clearing, Annie returned home to the empty Martin house, where the silence around her echoed every time she so much as breathed. Exhausted, Annie crawled into bed with a throbbing headache, a dress still stained orange with rum punch, and a heart full of silent prayers for a long, deep, dreamless sleep.

She didn't get her wish. Mostly because she couldn't stop thinking about that reporter, George Barnett.

Had she come home, tried to sleep, and, failing that, immediately opened up her laptop and started extensively google-searching him? Yes. Had she now read every article he'd written for the *Hillsboro Gazette*? Also yes. Was she proud of that? No. Not exactly.

But she couldn't help it. He'd somehow managed to wrangle the wedding invitation Annie had sent to Shannon Park, the *Hillsboro Gazette*'s Society Editor—a very kind, very tiny, seventy-something who perpetually wore shocking yellow eyeglasses and an expression that told you she knew about a million and a half things you didn't—and weasel his way into their celebration.

Usually, she wouldn't have minded something like that. Annie really did believe in *the more, the merrier*, and that alcohol and food, like good times, were meant to be shared. Yet, whenever she thought of him—his arrogant smirk, his seemingly firm belief that he belonged there, his brazen flirting or teasing or whatever it was... his hand around her waist—a maze of goosebumps ran up and down her spine.

Why, of everyone in the world who could have shown up out of the blue last night, did it have to be *him*? Why did it have to be someone who provoked such a reaction out of her? Why did it have to be the one man in the world with the power to destroy her?

Annie tried not to think about her secret very often. She tried to hide from it as best she could, locking all of her memories of That Time and That Experience in her life in a trunk in the back of her mind. But George's sudden appearance last night—and his damnable persistence that promised her he wasn't going to quit until he got something from them—reawakened those ancient feelings... and the fear they brought with them.

She couldn't be exposed. She couldn't let him find the truth, no matter how much he searched for it. If people knew... her life would be ruined. Her brother's reputation... It would all go up in smoke.

By the time she pulled up to 121 Second Street at nine the next morning, Annie was *still* thinking about him. Oh, she had a million other things that she should have been thinking about. After all, she was moving out of the house she'd shared with her brother so that when he and his bride got back from their honeymoon, they'd have the palatial mansion up in the hills all to themselves. And she needed to call her assistant in L.A. and see that the boxes she'd shipped to the apartment she still kept in Hollywood for work engagements had all made it. But no. She was still turning *him* over in her mind. Still haunted by the threat of his very existence. Still haunted by the ghost of his hand on her waist and the forbidden, ridiculous feelings that stoked in her.

Monster, her mutt puppy—well, not so much a puppy anymore, but she'd always be a puppy to her—with big eyes and a perpetually wagging tail, glanced up at her from her place in the passenger seat. Annie didn't know much about animal psychology or how much pups like Monster knew about human emotions, but she couldn't help but think the animal's tentative lick on her wrist was supposed to be encouraging. *You can do this*, the warm bundle of fur seemed to say.

If only Annie could feel as brave now as she'd been last night when she faced down George Barnett. Even half as much courage would be nice. But as she stared up at the darling little farmhouse-style building that would be her new home here in Hillsboro, Annie couldn't have felt less brave. When she collected her things and Monster's leash to stand outside of the small, two-story structure, she'd never felt as small, either. The house, cozy as it was, seemed to minimize her until she felt small enough to step on.

This was her big future. The first step into the rest of her life. For every part of her that wanted to believe she could do this, there were about a million other parts whispering, hissing, that she'd never be able to make it.

Not that she had much of a choice. Luke was gone; he'd found someone perfect to love, and she would never resent him for that. In fact, she'd been the one to encourage it. But now that the ramifications of that choice settled all around her, she couldn't help but wonder if she was up for the challenge.

Her thoughts were mercifully interrupted by the crowing sound of a man's voice as he came out from the house's front door. Her viewing of the property and the signing of the lease had been done through his assistant, but still, she recognized him from his business card and his website—tall, dark-skinned, and portly around the middle, he had an irrepressible smile that made her like him instantly.

Someone whose smile was contagious even at a time when she felt so miserable? That was a person she could really like.

"You must be Annie Martin!" The man rushed forward and took her hand in his large one, a comforting, sweet gesture that, for the briefest of seconds, made her feel really quite at home.

"In the flesh," she agreed. "You must be Mr. Abalos."

"Every day except Sundays, when I become The Singing Cowboy at the Bronze Boot's Open Mic Night. Have you ever seen me perform? Oh, of course not, I would have seen you. Ah, hello, pup! What an adorable little creature." He spoke a mile a minute, his eyes sparkling. Taking her suitcase from her left hand, he ushered her and Monster inside. "Come in, come in. I'm sure you know how all of this works. I'm sure you've done this a million times."

Following close behind him, Annie walked into the small house she would now call home. When she'd been searching for a place to move to after her brother's wedding, Luke had first sent her listings for large, palatial villas, the kind of place you'd expect someone with "internet celebrity/influencer" on their business card to live, but after the first showing, when she could hear nothing but her own heartbeat and the solid echoing of her heeled boots against the barren wooden floorboards, Annie knew she needed something more modest, a place where she wouldn't be constantly confronted with the emptiness she now felt inside.

121 Second Street fit the bill perfectly. Weathered and aging, small and cozy even for just one person and a dog. Here she'd be so preoccupied with fixing chipped paint and not knocking into her furniture every ten seconds that she'd probably never have time to be lonely.

"Actually…this is the first time I'm renting a place. I've never done this before."

"Really?" Mr. Abalos asked, not unkindly, as he reached for an accordion folder he'd previously brought in here with him. "At your age?"

"I've lived with my brother most of my life. He just got married, so…"

"Of course!" As Mr. Abalos flipped through the folder in search of something, his mouth went off to the races once again.

"Congratulations. The pictures in the paper this morning were so darling. I was telling my husband and our son about it over breakfast. Of course, Tomas—my thirty-year-old son who we make far too comfortable at home so he'll never leave—couldn't have cared less, really, but even he had to admit that the flower arrangements were beautiful. That was after a few mimosas, you understand, but still. Quite the accomplishment. You must be so proud."

"Yeah. Yeah, I'm really proud. They're so happy, you know. That's what matters."

If that was what mattered, then why did she feel so alone?

Shaking the thought from her head, she returned to Mr. Abalos and tried her best to smile like a normal person when he handed her a key and a thick envelope with her name and her new address inscribed on the green cardboard.

"Absolutely. Now, everything is in the lease, but I wanted to be the first to say... Welcome home, Annie Martin. I hope you enjoy your time here and if you need anything, anything at all, please feel free to call me. I'm never very far from my phone."

Thanking him and promising to eventually make her way to the Bronze Boot for one of his Singing Cowboy performances, Annie ushered him out of the door and closed it behind her. Monster had already made herself quite comfortable on the threadbare couch in the living room, and as Annie leaned her back against the now-closed front door, she breathed a long, clarifying exhale.

This was all a matter of perspective, wasn't it? She wasn't *empty*. She just... now had vacancies in her life for new things. She wasn't *lonely*. She was... available for new adventures and new people to love. She wasn't nothing and no one without people constantly around to distract her from herself. She was...ready to build herself up.

"Oh, God, I can't do this."

She couldn't start over. She didn't know how. No, what she needed was a distraction. Yes, she was going to have to throw her entire self into something, some new project that would make all of the voices in her heart quiet for a while.

More than that, though, she knew that there was only one way to really make herself happy again. It was the way she always made herself happy when she fell into one of these emotional valleys of hers. And that was to make *someone else* happy. Annie had been all over the world, tried more distractions and diversions than she could count. But still, there wasn't anything that made her so happy as knowing she'd made someone else's life a little bit better.

There was enough darkness in this world. Annie had felt it. So, she wanted to do her best to bring some light wherever she could.

Rose. Rose would be the perfect place to start. Finding Rose someone to love was a worthy use of her talents and the perfect thing to help her get past this sudden rut in which she found herself. Reaching into her pocket, Annie fished out her cell phone and Mr. Abalos's business card.

"Mr. Abalos? Your son, Tomas...Would he be interested in meeting the woman who made those beautiful flower arrangements?"

Annie had everything set up perfectly. All she had to do was wait. The thing about contrived plans to help people fall helplessly in love was that they usually required extensive planning, monitoring, and maintenance, the kind at which Annie excelled. Like a great heist, if even one piece of the puzzle was a second too late or too soon, if a door stuck or a car backfired nearby, everything could be thrown into chaos. Ruined. And Annie couldn't allow that to happen. Not when this was the one thing keeping her going right about now. Complicated planning gave her mind somewhere to go besides the empty rooms of her house. She could make Rose happy, and that would make her happy, wouldn't it?

As Annie stood in the Hillsboro Town Square, which bustled around her as tourists and locals alike ran their morning errands—bouncing to and from the various bakeries and coffee shops, the bank and the printer's place—she ran through the sequence of events one last time. In exactly five minutes, fifty-four seconds Rose Anderson would arrive to open up her store. Annie had parked in Rose's usual spot, so she would have to park at the north end of the square, then walk directly across the park towards the florists' boutique where she spent her days, at which point, Tomas—who didn't know exactly *who* his father had set him up with—would meet her in the center of the square. Annie had given strict instructions to the shopkeepers around the square *not* to let Tomas or Rose linger in their stores, and Annie had made sure that all of the usual dog walkers who made the town square part of their morning routine re-routed this morning towards the park down the street. So, when they inevitably crossed paths, Tomas would invite Rose to lunch, which Annie had suggested during her phone call with Mr. Abalos. Rose would probably blush and decline, but Tomas would insist that he'd seen her flowers in the paper this morning and want to whisk her away to some long, languorous meal where he could see the true romantic behind the wedding flowers, and then they'd have such a good time that the two would probably elope this very afternoon and run away to have lots of beautiful babies and buy a cat and—

Okay, maybe Annie was editorializing a bit there at the end, but the fact remained that if Tomas had come all the way into town at his father's request that he meet a mystery woman in the center of the square at exactly 10:13 in the morning, then he would probably insist on some kind of real date. And then, Annie's work here would be complete.

Well, it wouldn't be complete until they officially made that date and Annie had to go spy on—no, *chaperone*—that, too. It was hard work, finding true love for someone else, but she would bear the burden happily, as long as it eventually made someone else happy too.

Keeping her eye on the square, Annie walked the south end of the street, careful to scan the horizon for any potential distractions.

The problem was that the most dangerous distraction wasn't across the park; it was walking in her direction, and it *also* wasn't paying attention. A solid, strong body crashed into Annie's, and as their figures met, a Styrofoam cup crushed between them, covering her in warm coffee. The figure backed away immediately apologizing, his face going drawn and contrite.

George Barnett stood in front of her, and for a moment—brief as it was—he looked at her as though he was genuinely sorry for something. The look disappeared almost immediately, but there was something strangely comforting about the idea that he had real feelings buried somewhere deep down inside of him.

"Excuse me, miss, I—Oh, it's you." George's face fell, and his eyebrows knit as he frowned. Somehow his frown made him slightly more handsome; he'd clearly perfected the dark and brooding thing. "Sorry. I didn't realize I'd bumped into royalty."

"I knew it was you right away," Annie said, daintily brushing the droplets of coffee away from her black coat. "You're pretty good at being in exactly the wrong place at exactly the wrong time."

"What?" George raised an eyebrow as he helped himself to a seat on her favorite bench, the one that sat at the corner of the square and faced both the place where the puppies liked to meet *and* the ice cream shop. "You're not going to cry over your thousand-dollar coat?"

"I got this coat at a thrift store eleven years ago. It's seen worse days and yet, somehow, it's still here."

"Like you?"

Annie's heart hitched. He hadn't said it unkindly; in fact, if she didn't know better, she might have suspected him of trying to sympathize with her, as if he'd seen past her mask. Unfortunately, she did know better. This guy had been sniffing around her brother for a story for a long time now, and she knew that he wasn't trying to get on her good side. He was trying to fish for information.

"Comparing me to an old coat. Be still my thundering heart." She glanced down at him, where he sat in her spot and fished through a brown paper bag for what she could only assume was his breakfast. Normally, the sight of a handsome guy sitting in her seat wouldn't have stirred her in the slightest, but him? He wasn't allowed. Annie's eyes darted back and forth, surveying the crowd of usual morning passersby. The familiar faces—of Mrs. Monroe, who carried her twin kittens in her purse, of the Khazin brothers, who hung up flyers advertising their latest business venture, a food truck that only sold various forms of cheese fries—were the only things keeping her from fully losing it on him. "Would you please get off my bench?"

"*Your* bench? I have my breakfast on this bench every morning and I've never seen you on it."

Oh, he was impossible. No wonder her brother had been going out of his way to avoid him. "In about two minutes, Tomas Abalos is going to run into Rose Anderson and if I'm not watching carefully and *discreetly*, I might miss it."

George's dark eyebrows scrunched. "Didn't you subject her to enough last night? And why would you want Tomas and Rose to meet up, are you taking bets on the cage match?"

"I beg your pardon?"

"Tomas and Rose were straight-up rivals in high school. One time, he even spent a night in lock-up because he stole the tires off her car for a 'prank.' They go out of their way to avoid each other and you know that's hard in a town like Hillsboro."

No. No, no, no. She couldn't have possibly screwed up *two* meet cutes in less than twenty-four hours. It simply wasn't possible. There had to be some sort of mistake, a misunderstanding—

"But...but his dad said—"

"Richard Abalos doesn't have a mean bone in his body. You think he was going to turn down even the most harebrained scheme if it meant his son making amends with someone?"

Right. There *was* a misunderstanding. And it was on her part.

Not that she was going to admit that to him, obviously. Folding her arms across her chest, she tried to keep her absolute frustration at his casual, devil-may-care demeanor at bay. A task that proved almost impossible as he smirked up carelessly at her.

"You know what I think?" she began hotly.

"No, but I'm hanging on your every word."

He was trying to get under her skin. She wouldn't let him. Not now, not when she clearly had the high ground. He'd proved it last night and again this morning.

"I think you're a cynic. You don't think *you* can be happy, so you go to extremes to convince others that they can't be happy. That's not going to happen here. Tomas and Rose are going to reconcile, and you're going to—"

SPLASH! Every muscle in Annie's body went taut as the sound of a body crashing backwards into water smacked her ears; carefully, she turned around to see Rose standing over someone Annie could only guess was Tomas, who was currently struggling to pull himself out of the fountain in the center of the town square.

Mercifully, only a handful of teenagers were around to document the moment with their phones. Annie groaned; she could practically hear George's smirk growing with every passing second.

"You were saying?" he asked.

Annie blinked as she stared at the scene before her. "What is it with this girl and water features?"

By the time Annie turned around, George was halfway through slathering his bagel with schmear. The arrogant jerk somehow managed to look glowingly gratified, despite the fact that this entire scenario was categorically terrible.

"Like I said." He shrugged, apparently unfazed by Annie's stern look. "Enemies."

"Enemies can sometimes become lovers. Haven't you ever read a book?"

He snorted. "Not the kind you read, apparently."

Dismissing the cringeworthy jab at romance novels—typical unimaginative cynic—the wheels in Annie's head were already turning. She couldn't give up on her task, not now, not with an empty house and the quiet life waiting for her there.

"Okay," she said, taking the seat beside George and trying not to think about how good he smelled. Or how this close proximity reminded her of their dance last night. "Who else can I set her up with?"

"Why do you need to set her up with anyone at all?"

"I just do, okay? It's..." She wasn't going to tell him the truth; she didn't think she would tell *anyone* the truth. Folding her arms over her chest, she tried as best she could to defend herself without giving him any insight he didn't deserve. "It's what I'm good at. And everyone should do what they're good at. Fish gotta swim, birds gotta fly, you've got to be in my way and ruin everything—"

"Ruin everything? If you'd listened to me, you might have saved Tomas from nearly drowning."

Annie rolled her eyes. Men. Always with the dramatics. "People don't drown in fountains six inches deep. Now, as much as I'd love to sit and chat, I have to find someone else—"

"And I'm sure that will go just about as well as your last two attempts have."

Okay, so he wasn't going to let her run away from this confrontation. Great. Annie stood and turning on her heels back to face him, pointed one pastel-painted nail in his direction.

"What do *you* suggest I do then?"

"Seek medical attention. Go to therapy," he said, dryly.

So infuriating! What a...a...Well, she didn't know if there was a polite way to put what she thought of him, so she focused on the sudden heat she felt rising up in her cheeks. Annie was the kind of person who thrived on sincerity, on kindness, on optimism and honesty. This man had none of those virtues at his disposal.

"Look, if you're not going to help me, then you can just...sit there and eat your bagel."

But for what felt like the thousandth time this morning, she stopped herself short before she could completely leave his presence. A light bulb illuminated in her mind.

"Wait...That's not a bad idea."

"I know," he grumbled. "I've been trying to eat this bagel for ten minutes but *somebody* keeps interrupting me."

"No, it's..." How to articulate this without getting completely shut down by Mr. Cynical here? "*You* could help me. You're a reporter. You know this town. You must have known Rose at school, you could help me find someone for her."

George's lips pressed into a thin line. "I don't do freelance work."

"Not even if I could get you an interview with my brother?"

She hadn't meant to say that; mostly because she didn't mean it. Her brother was never going to give this guy an interview, no matter how much she promised him one. But her mouth ran away without her, writing verbal checks that were surely going to bounce. Still, it was enough to give George pause. His jaw hung loose and limp; he eyed her skeptically.

"You wouldn't do that."

Annie wasn't a liar; she couldn't even pretend to be one for the time being. How could she make the promise without actually making the promise? Was it possible? She could at least attempt it. "If you help me, I would encourage him to explore the possibility, which is better than nothing."

George didn't look convinced. The cold fingers of desperation clenched around Annie's throat. She couldn't keep failing and she couldn't go back to her lonely house. Not now.

"Please. I need this. I need help."

"Even from someone like me?"

He glanced up at her from under his long eyelashes. Her heart stammered. How had she not noticed how beautiful his eyes were before? Why did she suddenly care now?

She nodded her head.

"Yeah. Even from someone like you."

Chapter Four

George

One of the first things they teach you in journalism school: *Distance provides perspective. Just like a camera needs some space to put a picture entirely into focus, so too does the journalist need some space to put a story into its full, clear context.*

In other words, don't let yourself get too close to your subjects. That should have been an easy rule to follow, especially where Annie Martin was concerned. They were completely different people from completely different worlds. The last time they'd spoken, she'd verbally laid him out, questioning the core of who he was at the most fundamental levels. She was an infuriating, beautiful, mystery box of a woman who was deeply involved in the story he believed could make his entire career. Keeping her at arm's-length not only should have been easy. It was *imperative*.

Yet when she looked at him with those wide, blue eyes, her lip trembling from the effort it took her to hide her emotions from him, his heart involuntarily clenched.

"Okay. I'll help you."

Not out of any sense of duty or anything altruistic like that. But because there was a story here—he could sense it in the small ways she moved, in the tiny gestures that gave her away—and he would endure a little matchmaking if it meant finding it. George knew the way people looked when they were hiding secrets, and he was willing to wait out the truth.

Would it be mind-numbingly boring? Yes, probably. Would he regret agreeing? He already did. Was this the most harebrained scheme he'd ever devised for sniffing out a story? Without question. But he'd been chasing the Martin siblings for the last two years; he wasn't going to let them slip through his fingers now, especially not when Annie's lips gently parted in surprise and she looked at him like that.

Like he'd just given her the stars.

"You will?"

Approaching the subject carefully, as he always did, he re-wrapped his bagel and shoved it in his messenger bag before rising to his feet and considering the woman before him. "Yeah. But if your brother says no, then I want an exclusive interview with you."

Something shifted in Annie's expression, but George couldn't read it. She brushed invisible dust away from the bold floral print dress currently hugging her slender, lovely form. "Me? What would you want an interview with me for?"

George considered his options. If he wanted this story—not just Luke Martin's story, but hers—then being close to them was better than anything he could have hoped for. Traditional interviews were stuffy and guarded. This... this would be real access. A real insight into these people and the secrets that they held. A chance for justice, if there was any to be found. If he couldn't have the brother, then Annie would be the biggest break in this story. He was sure he could uncover at least *some* of their secrets through her. "Because it's better than nothing. Do we have a deal?"

"Yeah. We have a deal."

"Good. Let's go."

No time to waste. He headed off down the block, his feet carrying him along the familiar street as his mind raced. Annie, though, hung back, her eyes wide in confusion.

"Go? Go where?"

"I'm a reporter, Annie," he said, flatly. "I need coffee and I need it ten minutes ago. Let's—"

But before he could encourage her to follow him again, the slightly shrill, extremely tense voice of Rose Anderson cut like a knife across the town square.

"Annie Martin! I need to speak with you!"

Annie ducked into him immediately, turning around so as not to face the approaching Rose. "Hey, pretend like we're having a good time."

George couldn't resist a quip. Better than feeling any real emotions, that was for damn sure. "I don't think I'm a good enough actor for that."

"Shut up," Annie grumbled, just in time to spin once more—how wasn't she getting dizzy with all this spinning?—and beam up at her friend, who glowered as if someone had just stolen the tires off her car. "Hey, girl! How are you? Wow, you look...you look so good this morning. Is that new lipstick? How are you feeling after that champagne last night? I noticed you had, like, two whole glasses. That's usually enough to—"

But Rose—sweet, kind Rose, the one Anderson sister who everyone in town could agree that they liked—was not in the mood to listen to any of Annie's fawning rambles. She cut straight to the chase. "Did you try to set me up with Tomas Abalos?"

Annie blinked, so innocently that, for a moment, even George almost believed her. "Who?"

"Do not play dumb with me. You are way too smart for it."

"I may have *mentioned* to Mr. Abalos that you had done the lovely flower arrangements for the wedding and he may have *mentioned* that Tomas was a fan of your work. That's all. Why? Do you think he's cute?"

"You're impossible."

Annie tossed her head defiantly, sending her blond curls dancing and catching the morning sunlight. "I'm just trying to help!"

The discussion between the two women picked up in speed and intensity, and suddenly, George felt unbelievably out of place, standing here between them like a forgotten recording device. His fingers itched for the notebook in his pocket, but given the current vibe, he couldn't bring himself to risk the ire of either of the women standing in front of him. Rose heaved a great sigh, resting a hand on Annie's shoulder.

"Annie, you know that I love you so much. You're like a sister to me. But if you don't stop with the obvious ploys to set me up with someone, I'm going to lose it. Okay?"

The Martin woman opened her mouth once, then twice. Against his better judgment, George's eyes followed those soft, pink lips. He swallowed hard as Annie recovered. "Yes. Of course. I'm so sorry."

"Look," Rose said, dropping her voice slightly. "I understand that you're upset about losing your brother. And I know you're probably just...I don't know...looking for an outlet of some kind. But maybe you should focus on you, you know?"

Annie blinked too fast. Her smile was too bright. Too wide to be comfortable or honest. None of those small quirks escaped George's notice. "You're right. Don't worry. I'll find something."

From his point of view, Rose didn't look entirely convinced, but eventually, she relented, offering Annie a kind smile and a reassuring shoulder squeeze. Strange. Rose had been angry with Annie not five seconds ago and now she was trying to take care of her? George didn't think he'd ever understand friendship like that. "Call me if you want to have lunch or something, okay?"

"You got it."

For as much as George liked to think of himself as a good study of character, he couldn't quite figure out what had just happened. Or why Annie now had a far-off look in her eye that proved impossible to decipher. When he and *his* friends fought—which was rare, considering how few of them he actually had...keeping friends was a difficult endeavor when one spent most of their waking moments working—a disagreement like this usually sent them to their separate corners for a few days at least; it did *not* make them want to still help each other.

Everyone said that for all their virtues, the Anderson sisters were weird. George, who'd gone to high school with all three of them but spent most of his high school days locked in the student newspaper office, was starting to believe the town gossip. The second Rose left, George slipped straight into reporter mode.

"What was that about?"

"She doesn't want me to play matchmaker, obviously," Annie said, as she watched Rose's retreating form draw further and further down the sidewalk. George watched her too, thinking that, as he watched her go, he was also watching his opportunity to monitor the Martin siblings go too.

"So, you're going to stop."

Annie's scrunched-up face told him that was the most ridiculous assumption he could have made. She even scoffed at him to punctuate the point. "What? No, obviously not."

"But you said—"

"No one wants to think they need help finding love, and *everyone* is wrong about that." Annie tossed a long streak of hair over her shoulder, letting it catch the morning sunlight and temporarily blind him. How did she manage to get it so soft, so shiny? Why did he have the sudden urge to run his fingers through it? "She'll be thanking me once this is over."

"It didn't sound like that to me."

"Well, no one asked you how it sounded, did they?"

Pushing it was a bad idea, the worst, but his curiosity—as ever—got the worst of him. As Annie fumbled in her bag for a pair of oversized sunglasses he'd sometimes seen her sport around town, he drew closer to her, inspecting her face for any betrayal of what was going on inside that beautiful head of hers.

What? She *was* beautiful. That was not a sentimental note, but a journalistic fact. Nothing more.

"And what was all of that about losing your brother? What did she mean by that?"

"I'm not your interview subject. You can stop it with the interrogation."

George shrugged, trying to keep it as casual as he possibly could, considering that he was clearly trying to pick at a barely scabbed-over wound. "I just think that if we're going to work together, we should get to know each other. That's all. If there's a reason you're all tied up in knots about finding Rose someone to date, then maybe telling me would help make my job easier."

There. There it was. Annie may have been able to conceal her eyes from him with those glasses of hers, but she couldn't hide the sight of one side of her mouth tightening into a grimace as the other desperately fought to smile. There was something else going on here; it was written in every line she tried to hide.

"You don't need to worry about me. You need to worry about Rose and the various men of this town who might be her perfect fit, okay?"

"But—"

"We can talk later. I've got some errands to run. See you around!"

Before he could protest, she was gone. Leaving him more confused, and more intrigued, by her than he'd ever been before.

Later that day, despite the fact that it was his day off, he returned to his small cupboard of an office in the *Hillsboro Gazette* offices just above the pie vault on Main Street. The entire building had once belonged to the *Gazette*, but as time and media changed, their offices and their staff grew smaller and smaller, forcing the paper's owners—the Hackett family—to subdivide and sell the space off in parcels until only a few small offices in the center of the building's upper floor remained. As a consequence, the confined space of George's office, with its pinstripe papered walls and dark wood accents, remnants from the paper's profitable glory days, always smelled intensely of butter, sugar, and fresh blueberries, a smell he usually loved.

Today, though, he was too distracted to drink in the scent of ever-baking pie, too distracted to so much as glance at his emails, and too distracted to do much of anything besides think about Annie Martin. He'd hoped that work would drag him from thoughts of her, but that turned out to be impossible.

She didn't make any sense. George loved a puzzle, sure, but he wasn't sure she was a puzzle at all. She felt like an ancient carving whose codex has been lost to the sands of time. He'd always assumed she was as vapid and spoiled as her public image suggested, that she had bewitched everyone in town with her pretty smiles and her Los Angeles decadence. But their interactions over the last couple of days threw a few shadows onto that perfectly logical picture of her he'd been painting all of this time. He'd seen flashes in her—brief moments of crystalline clarity—that told him she wasn't who he thought she was. She had depth. Complexity. And she wasn't interested in sharing it with him.

So, he'd have to do what he always did in a jam like this. He'd have to do some legwork and find out the truth for himself.

An hour into his musing, he noticed a slim envelope in his in tray. George noted the slender handwriting on the front of the eggshell paper, and somehow knew Annie was behind it. Tearing into the missive, it began:

Dear Mr. Cynical,

Below, for your reference and convenience, I have outlined some rules for our work together. Please be advised that any breaking of these rules will result in immediate termination of my end of the bargain, regarding an interview with the Founder and CEO of AppeX Industries.

Warm regards,
Annie Martin

This whole thing should have infuriated him. *She* thought she could dictate the way that *he* worked? While he was doing her a favor? Under any other circumstances, he might have fumed and ripped up the paper right then and there. But instead, as George imagined Annie storming into her house with the fury of a thousand hurricanes to write this note, his lips pulled into a smile.

He'd gotten under her skin.

1. *Please keep all discussion and correspondence—in person and via both classic and new media—to the subject of the work; distracting inquiries should be kept to a minimum.*
2. *All conversations should be kept off the record unless otherwise, specifically, denoted.*
3. *In the course of undercover work, vis-a-vis the matchmaking of (1) Rose Anderson to (2) heretofore unselected gentleman, the art of subterfuge may be employed. Please remain professional*

in these regards, and keep all physical contact to professional, business touching only.

4. *All personal questions should be submitted, in writing, to Annie Martin's publicist.*

George read the scrawled handwriting once, twice, and then a third time before they really began to sink in. He hadn't just gotten under her skin, it seemed. He'd rattled her from the inside out.

Good. It was nice to know she found herself as thrown by his presence as he was by hers.

A knock on his office door pulled him from his thoughts. He didn't answer it, but Erica Kane, his editor, opened the door anyway so she could look down at him, eyebrow raised in confusion.

"What's that?"

He considered how to answer that for a moment before responding, "A lead."

"Are you going to pursue it?"

His eyes traced the words again; he smiled. Maybe Annie Martin wasn't a puzzle. Maybe she wasn't an ancient riddle. Maybe she was a trap. And maybe he was about to fall head first into it.

"Weirdly...I think it's going to pursue me."

Chapter Five

Annie

Annie Martin felt ready for battle as she walked up the two flights of rickety, almost certainly *not* up-to-code stairs leading to the *Hillsboro Gazette*'s offices. When she'd woken up this morning after her first night of sleep in her new house, it had taken her a full minute to realize and remember where, exactly, it was that she found herself.

Right. New house. New chapter. New life.

Her phone displayed thousands of new social media interactions, but upon further inspection of her messaging apps, she found... exactly zero messages. Nothing from her friends. Nothing from her brother. Just the silent emptiness of the phone screen, staring judgmentally back at her, reflecting her own tired eyes.

Not a problem. It wasn't like Annie *cared* or anything. No, she didn't have time to care, not with everything else she had going on. First thing, she took Monster on a nice, long walk. Then, breakfast, which she took at a busy café on the square and not at home as she probably would have when Luke was around.

After that, she decided to get some work done. There was no shortage of cutesy Instagram shots and poses to be done in Hillsboro, and once she'd filled her camera roll with a couple dozen usable shots, she turned her attention to answering emails and reading over contracts. Many people might have thought she was just a pretty face, only good for promoting yoga mats online, but contract negotiation was where she really excelled. When Luke started up AppeX, Annie had been his first employee, checking over proposed business contracts and, as the company grew, new hires. Sure, the whirlwind life of social-media stardom had taken over most of her attention now, but she still used those skills to her advantage.

But there were only so many emails and so many contracts that someone could read before their eyes went cross, so eventually Annie made her way over to the *Hillsboro Gazette*.

The office might as well have been ripped straight out of an article in *Elegant Shabby Chic Monthly*. Exposed brick and beams contrasted with aging, antique furniture. The walls were punctuated with framed, yellowing clippings from smash news pieces. Declarations of Peace hung alongside news of Coronations and Funerals, Scandals and Victories.

For a brief, fleeting moment, Annie considered what an article about *her* would say. What would someone like George write about her? He was elbow patches and long-past-five-o'clock-facial-scruff; she was social media and floral prints. She was gossip fodder; he was a serious journalist. She wasn't sure what he thought he was going to find in her; she only knew that her gut told her it wouldn't be anything good. But it was looking like it might be either that or throw her brother to his mercy.

Swallowing hard she grabbed the strap of her purse and approached a small front desk overloaded with packages and letters, and coffee cups and wrappers. From behind that pile, Annie could barely see the top of a woman's head, late twenties with two matching top buns and a pair of fire engine red, geometric glasses perched upon a pert, cute nose. Her nameplate was actually covered in masking tape, and upon that was written *Mynette Chen—Administrative Assistant/Professional Badass.*

Mynette Chen did not look, in even the slightest sense, amused by or interested in Annie's presence here. Beyond her, the small newsroom of about fifteen people bustled with activities—phone chatter and typing, mostly, but the occasional coffee slurp or text alert—but Mynette sat as the stoic center of the storm.

"Hello, yes," Annie said, her usual smile in place but her usual bravery not rising to meet it. "I'm here to see George Barnett."

"Do you have an appointment?"

Annie's smile wavered. She'd been expecting her charm to liven Mynette up a bit, but that didn't seem to be happening. "Uh, no, not…not exactly, no, but he'll want to see me. We need to see each other."

Mynette touched her index finger to the tip of her tongue and used it to flip a page in an oversized date book. Annie didn't even know people still *used* date books. How cute! She made a mental note to get one for herself later, and if she found it worked, do an Instagram post about it. "And what is the nature of this appointment?"

"We're working on a story together." Mynette raised one eyebrow. Annie's faith that the small fib would work didn't pan out. She edited her statement with a little self-deprecating wince. "Kind of."

For a moment, Mynette continued to stare into the depths of her date book, but then, she raised her chin and looked—really looked—at Annie for the first time. Her withering stare traced the lines of her face, searching her for something Annie could only hope she gave. Then, without fanfare or excitement, she intoned:

"You're Annie Martin."

"Yep. That's me."

There was always an awkward silence after introductions like this, introductions to strangers who knew her too well. It was in that brief pause that Annie's entire self-esteem hung in the balance. *Please like me. Please, please like me.*

The jury was still out on Mynette. Using the tip of her black ballpoint pen, she pointed down the hall and to the left, where the furthest doorway stood, resolutely shut. "He's not in his office, but you could go in there and wait for him."

When it became clear that Mynette wasn't going to say anything further, Annie thanked her and gave an awkward, bow-curtsy-supplication gesture as she tripped in the direction she'd been pointed. Heat blossomed around her neck; she chewed at the inside of her lip.

Mynette hadn't liked her. What had she done wrong? What mistakes had she made to so thoroughly destroy her relationship with a person she'd just met?

Annie's stomach plummeted. Here she was, really on her own for the first time in her life, and she was already screwing it up. George didn't much like her. Mynette didn't much like her. Of course it would be like this.

With every step she took down the hall, further and further from this stranger and her judgments and her silence, Annie wanted nothing more than to turn tail and run, as fast as she could, in the opposite direction. This happened to her sometimes. When she wasn't the perfect, glistening goddess they all wanted her to be, when her persona wasn't crafted carefully enough, when she slipped from grace, people always turned on her. People always left.

That's why she never—*never*—allowed anyone to catch her at her worst. Smiles and quips and perfect hair... It was all the price she paid for people to like her.

Somehow, today, she'd failed with Mynette, but hopefully, she'd get another chance to befriend her. She couldn't stand the thought of someone out there not liking her.

Once in the small office at the end of the hall, Annie flicked on the light and began inspecting. She'd always thought of newspaper offices like the clean, modern, and sleek presentations you saw in romantic comedies, with white walls, big windows overlooking the Empire State Building or the Golden Gate Bridge, and oversized photographic mood boards for everyone to brood over and toss out at the climactic moment when the hero had a breakthrough.

George's office... it wasn't that. It wasn't that at all. A window-less cell of a space made even darker by the tinted, aging brick of the walls, every available surface was covered in stacks of paper—receipts, notes, dossiers, completely disorganized and nonsensically arranged. If George had ever bothered to use the rusting filing cabinet in the corner, Annie couldn't tell.

Breezing around small stacks of paper at her feet, she approached the walls and inspected the bylines printed and hung there. Pieces from the *Hillsboro Gazette*, from a college newspaper she'd never heard of, even a small Letter to the Editor from *The New York Times*.

An exposé on recent tariffs' effects on local winemakers. A profile of an activist fighting for native rights. A puff piece on a miniature horse farm.

They were all admirable and well written, but Annie's attention kept going back to the miniature horses. Why, among all of these noble and detailed pieces of journalism, was *this* hung up on his wall?

She was still staring at the framed piece when the door slammed open behind her, signaling that she was no longer alone in her inspection. Now, she couldn't just speculate about the man. She had to actually deal with him.

People were right when they said nothing good could last.

George huffed, gasping for air as if he'd just finished an Olympic sprint without training for it. "What are you doing here?"

How weird that he managed to look more handsome now, with his cheeks slightly pink and his chest heaving with the effort it had taken to run in here. Annie bit her lip to hide her amusement.

"I'm working," Annie intoned, leaning in to get a closer look at the article's photograph, where a group of smiling children chased after a pack of stampeding miniature horses. She smiled for real this time, not bothering to hide it. She couldn't help it. The pure joy on the children's faces was enough to counteract the sour presence of her co-conspirator in this matchmaking scheme. She turned to face him. Once again, he was thoroughly disheveled, but this time, his shirt clung to his chest, giving her a clear outline of the strong, solid muscles there. She swallowed and picked up a piece of nearby paper, examining it blindly. Anything to distract her from his body. "Which seems to be more than *you're* doing."

"Really? Because it looks more like snooping to me. And, for the record..." He snapped the paper from her hands. She jumped back in surprise. "My time sheets are none of your business."

"I'm not snooping. It's not snooping if you're reading the wall art." Once again, she went back to the hanging pieces, pointing out one series in particular about some people called the Winslow Family. She'd never heard of them. "You really have a thing for toppling family dynasties, don't you?"

"People who hold too much power for too long, especially those who don't earn it, are more likely to think that they can get away with anything. I'm just a study of human character."

"And that's what you think my brother and I are, huh?"

In the reflection of the glass, Annie tried to get a read on him, but he might as well have been behind a brick wall. He kept his face neutral, emotionless, even as the strain of keeping her own mask in place wore her down.

She needed him. And she wanted him to like her. But that didn't mean she had to like him.

"I don't know what to think about either of you yet. I haven't gotten to *talk* to either of you, not really."

"Yeah, and you're totally not the man to jump to conclusions, are you?"

"No. I don't jump to conclusions. I study the evidence carefully and eventually, like a great detective giving a long speech about justice and truth, saunter, with much due diligence and checking of sources, towards conclusions."

Annie spent plenty of time in Hollywood and she knew plenty of insufferably arrogant people. Usually, she knew how to handle them—a few cutting remarks wrapped in faint praise, like feeding a heartworm pill wrapped in bacon to a dog—but George Barnett's arrogance had so infected him, she didn't think any amount of tough love would break through. He even had the audacity to smirk at her.

"And what direction are you *sauntering* towards where I'm concerned?" she asked, turning around so she could lean on the room's only passable piece of furniture, the arm of an otherwise completely covered couch.

George didn't answer. She didn't miss that. "You know I have a job, right? Not all of us just get to sit around and take pictures of coffee and cookies for a living."

It was Annie's turn to smirk. People making fun of her job was nothing new. "No. Some of us have to wear ugly shoes and take pictures of those, too."

"You really shouldn't be in here, is what I'm saying."

"But we have so much work to do," she protested.

"Yeah, *after hours*. I can't do your matchmaking mess on company time."

Coming here, she'd known that this would probably happen—he'd try to resist the beating drum of matchmaking progress, she'd have to use all of the tricks in her arsenal to get him on board—but it would be worth it when Rose was finally with the man of her dreams.

Annie tried not to think about what she would do *after* that.

Anyway, she wasn't leaving until they made some real progress. If her abandoning her post until five o'clock, when it was convenient for him, was what he wanted to discuss, then she'd just have to change the subject.

"Was that why your administrative assistant didn't like me very much?"

"Mynette's just a tough nut to crack, that's all."

"What's her thing? Does she have a thing? Flowers? I could send her some flowers. Or is she a candy girl? You can't not like someone who sends you candy."

George retreated to the space behind his desk. Unfortunately, his chair was covered in papers and a handful of Amazon boxes, so he couldn't sit, but he leaned against the back in what Annie guessed was supposed to be a power pose.

"It was probably a ten-second interaction that she's already forgotten."

"I don't want her to not like me."

"Why do you need to be liked?"

"Why do you need to play armchair investigator all the time?"

"I'm not an armchair journalist, I'm an *actual* journalist. And I'm not one all the time, only during work time, which you're still interrupting."

Annie threw up her hands. Men! When would they learn to just let her have her way? Why waste his breath arguing and messing about when they all knew her plan would eventually be done? "You're impossible."

A voice, deep and feminine, rose above the sound of Annie's pounding heart.

"Don't I know it. Who are you?"

A tall, black woman in a pressed pantsuit leaned in the doorway, with one raised eyebrow cast curiously in Annie's direction.

"Erica. Er, this is Annie Martin. She's...we're..."

Ding! A light bulb went off in Annie's head. George wanted to do work? Fine. They could definitely appear to be doing that.

"We're working on a story together."

Erica's eyebrows *both* shot up this time. "You are?"

"Yes. It's a very important story about the isolation and heart-break that can come from living in a small town."

"...I'm listening."

"You know. It's a small town. The numbers game isn't in your favor, dating-wise. Imagine how hard it is to find the love of your life when you've known everyone since the time you were a kid. Look at poor George here. Imagine how hard it must be for him to get a date when everyone already knows how annoying he is." She gave them her sweetest smile.

George and Erica shared a look.

"And what do you propose?" Erica asked.

Annie was fresh out of brilliant, lightning-strike idea moments. She shrugged. "We're letting the investigation take us where it leads. We don't want to predict the piece before we have all of the facts, of course."

"And your name would be on it? That could really be a boon for the paper."

Nope. Absolutely not. Because it doesn't exist and won't exist. I'm not going to sell my friend's love story to a newspaper. How heartbreaking. Annie faked a professionally enthusiastic smile, the kind businesses bought when they paid her to endorse a product she hated. Also, she got the impression that George wouldn't like her suddenly stealing his thunder with a byline. "It's a possibility."

The muscles in Erica's face didn't move as she considered the proposition. Then, she pointed at George with one long, red-painted fingernail. "I want a proper pitch from you at our meeting on Friday, Barnett."

"You've got it, boss."

Annie followed her out, taking the left where she took the right and trusting George to follow her. They were on assignment together now, after all.

"What did you think you were doing back there?" George hissed as he followed up behind her.

"You said we couldn't work together during the day because it wasn't work. Now, it *is* work. Come on. Let's go."

"Go where?"

"Aren't you an investigative reporter? Why don't you investigate and find out?"

His steps faltered, but didn't stop. He muttered under his breath, "Impossible woman."

"Infuriating man."

Together, they moved to the front of the small office, drawing the attention of everyone in the reporting pool. But it was Mynette who was the first to say something, just as Annie had gotten her hand around the knob of the stairway door.

"Where are you two going?"

"I'm taking him—"

Mynette stared disinterestedly down at her crossword puzzle. "I wasn't asking you."

"We—we're going on assignment together," George answered, his face paler than Annie had ever seen before. "Erica's orders."

With a wave, Mynette dismissed them, and Annie hightailed it for the stairs.

"See what I mean?" she asked, whispering as if Mynette could hear them even here. "So, what do you think? Chocolates or flowers?"

"From the way she treated you, I'd be shocked if even diamonds won her over."

"Shut up."

But even as she shoved him with her shoulder and tried to hate him, she couldn't help but feel, strangely enough, for the first time since her new life started, that she wasn't completely and totally alone.

Chapter Six

George

Despite the fact that the little house on Second Street was only a stone's throw away from his own, it wasn't exactly what George had in mind when he first imagined Annie's place. During his investigations of the Martin family, he'd visited the house she shared with her brother once. Well, seen the outside of it. Through a telescopic lens. It was a palatial mansion built into the side of a hill, the exact kind of *Lifestyles of the Rich and Famous* place he could picture her slouching around in.

But this . . . this place was positively run-down. More charitable interpretations might have called it *rustic* or *cozy*, but when compared to the house she'd *been* living in, a more accurate descriptor would have been "a total dump."

Even more surprising? She loved it. It was clear in the gentle, easy way she reached for her key, the little shake of happiness her shoulders gave when she stepped over the threshold and welcomed him inside.

"Alright. I think we have a lot of work to do, so I want to get started right away. Especially now that our work is sanctioned by the *Hillsboro Gazette*. Do you think I'll get a per diem for this? Or one of those fedora hats with the little piece of paper in it?"

"I don't think reporters wear those anymore."

George followed her into the house. He craned his neck to drink in every little detail. The place was mostly still in boxes and suitcases for the moment, but there were little flairs and touches that reminded him of who she was. A Veuve Clicquot bottle used as a flower vase. Pieces of fine jewelry hanging up on the coat rack by the door. Annie wandered into the kitchen, but George lingered in the entryway and living room, only half-listening to her as he approached the fading, aging couch against the far wall, where a shaggy mutt of a dog was currently staring up at him with all the hope of an animal about to get ear scritches.

"Of course they don't! If they all dress like you, then it's clear they have no real sense of fashion. Can I get you a drink or something? I have…uh…Wait! Don't sit down."

Too late. But his body tensed up anyway.

"Why not?"

"Grocery store. We need to go to the grocery store. I need pens, and paper and sticky tape and an assortment of meats and cheeses to offer you. I mean, you are my guest, after all, and I don't want to be a bad host—"

George relaxed into the couch. Shabby as it was, the thing was damn comfortable. He couldn't see her in the kitchen, but the frantic rustling told him that she was as distressed as she sounded. Not knowing the first thing about being a Woman of High Internet Society or whatever Annie called herself, he hadn't realized how a little thing like no cheeseboards would cause such a commotion. "I don't think that's necessary."

A cabinet slammed shut. "Come on. Let's go."

"I'm afraid that will be quite impossible."

"Why?"

She emerged from the kitchen, looking positively windswept, with strands of hair out of place and worried eyes.

Clearing his throat, George pulled his gaze away from her and motioned to the small animal in his lap who'd cozied up to him the moment he'd sat down.

"Because I now have a puppy in my lap and I can't move. Those are the rules."

"Oh." Annie smiled and approached so she could give the pup a little *boop* on her nose. "That's Monster."

"Hello, Monster." Adopting a teasing tone, George rubbed at her soft ears. "*You* don't mind if we don't have an assortment of meats and cheeses and overpriced water bottles, do you?"

And thus, the moment of Annie's tenderness vanished. Her daintily biting snark returned. "Monster doesn't speak English, and Monster doesn't understand the importance of a well-placed charcuterie board when it comes to making friends."

George stumbled over the use of that word. He raised a surprised eyebrow.

"Friends?"

"Workplace colleagues. Uneasy allies. Whatever you want to call us. Now, are you coming?"

Moments later, they found themselves on the cracked sidewalk path that would lead them to the nearby grocery store. At first,

Annie had wanted to get into her car and drive all the way to the other side of town to go to the big, chain grocery store—apparently, she and her brother had been ordering grocery delivery from there for a while now, a real travesty as far as George was concerned—but he'd managed to persuade her to give the local grocery, Barnett's Place, a try. She'd asked him if there was any relation, like if he was endorsing his family's business, but he assured her it was nothing of the kind. Just a coincidence.

Annie held an umbrella over her head, despite the fact that there wasn't rain anywhere in the seven-day forecast. She'd tried to convince George to join her, or to at least put on a baseball cap, but he'd flat-out refused. *It's bad for your skin to be out in the sun so much*, she'd warned him, a retort that earned her an eye-roll and a snarky response about having a face for newspapers, not Instagram, anyway.

He was reluctantly fascinated by her, yes. He needed her for his work, yes. But he wasn't going to let himself be drawn in by her. A certain level of journalistic integrity was required for this kind of work, and sharing an umbrella when it wasn't even raining seemed a pretty clear break in protocol.

Besides, just because he was fascinated by her, just because she had certain qualities, didn't mean he had to like her. In fact, he was pretty sure he didn't. She was meddlesome and used to getting her own way, ready to steamroll anyone and everyone who didn't comply. Her vision for the future—and for people's happiness—seemed to be the only thing that mattered, no matter what anyone else thought.

"You know, you're a lot to handle sometimes," he offered, as he strolled alongside her, catching the supplemental shade of her umbrella every few seconds. Annie tittered a laugh and waved him off, an infuriatingly cute gesture. He frowned. He didn't want her to be cute.

"I have been told that before," Annie said, picking up her pace. She was surprisingly fast for a woman of her height. Blond curls bounced at her shoulders, almost hypnotizing him. "Usually by people who can't keep up."

"I can keep up."

"Sure. If you say so."

"I do say so."

But he was at least five or six steps behind her now. Apparently, all of those yoga classes and aerial aerobics exercises she promoted all day on Instagram were no joke. He could practically hear her smirk.

"Then prove it."

What a woman. He knew she was just trying to get under his skin, just trying to give back to him everything he was throwing at her, but *still*.

He huffed the directions to Barnett's Place. Once inside, the familiar scent of fresh-baked sourdough and brown paper bags welcomed him like an old friend. And some people—like Marie behind the bakery counter and David who restocked the shelves—literally greeted him as an old friend, which, he guessed, he was. All his life, George had been coming to this shop, and nothing much had changed over the years. Annie didn't need to know that this place was like a second home, though, so he covertly waved to his friends in the green aprons as he let her explore the aisles at her leisure, following behind as she wandered and filled a squeaky-wheeled buggy with her goods.

"You know what I still don't get?"

"Most things, I'd imagine."

He let the barb slip past him, mostly because he couldn't help but respect anyone who could get out a good burn so quickly. Even if it was at his expense. "Why are you doing this? This whole matchmaking thing. It doesn't make any sense."

Of course, it did make sense if Annie really was a spoiled, selfish little rich girl who saw everyone in the world as her human-sized puppets. But still, he couldn't help but ask the question. He was a journalist, after all. If there was a deeper truth to Annie Martin, he wanted to find it.

Her heels clicked against the tiles—green and white, flecked with gray and reflecting the buzzing lights overhead—with every step, and he watched her carefully as she selected notebooks, pens, ink markers, Wite-Out, sticky notes, loose-leaf... Everything a kindergarten teacher or a first-year law student might need, but nothing a social media star did.

The wheels in his head spun rapidly, practically burning up in their quest to understand her. She couldn't be as altruistic as she painted herself. He knew better than to trust anyone who made those claims for themselves. Annie merely shrugged.

"Can't I just want to do something nice for my friend?"

"Sure, you *can*, but do you think a lot of people would spend an unconscionable amount of money on what I assume is an intricate red-string conspiracy diagram in their quest to do something nice for their friends?"

An impolite scoff echoed down the empty sundries aisle, cutting through the sounds of the acoustic Rick Astley playing over the loudspeakers. "I'm not making a conspiracy diagram. Don't be ridiculous."

"You are *literally* holding red string right now."

Annie blinked down and confirmed that, yes, she *did* have a ball of crimson twine in her hand, red and guilty as a criminal holding a still-beating heart. A second later, her cheeks almost matched that color. "I was thinking of getting a cat. I hear they like to play with string."

"Look, all I'm saying is that I know a story when I see one. Not a news story, but a story you're not telling anyone. Maybe not even yourself. There's more to this than you're admitting."

"There's nothing going on."

"Sure."

"I'm trying to help my friend. I found matches for her sisters, and now it's her turn. This is how I could repay them for everything they've done for me."

"And what have they done for you?"

"I thought we talked about the whole interrogation thing."

"Sure, but you can't blame a guy for trying."

Actually, she *could* blame a guy for trying, and he could see that she was close to doing so, too. George was pushing her too far, he could see that now in the knotting of her shoulders and the white-knuckle grip on her shopping cart as they approached the first checkout counter.

A shot of guilt stabbed through his chest, but that painful sensation was paired with an instinctual confirmation. He was onto something. No question about it. The smiling, enigmatic international woman of mystery wouldn't be showing such obvious signs of distress if he wasn't. She was too poised for that.

Shifting his attention, George squeezed himself between the cart and the candy-decked wall-aisle so he could help unload her wares onto the short conveyor belt. Partly out of the intense, burning desire to have something to do besides puzzle her out, and partly because his friend was standing behind the counter.

Short and pale and straight out of an unflattering caricature drawing, Marshall Barnett sat up upon a wooden stool, ringing up customers as he always did. What he lacked in height and beauty and eyesight, he made up for with the biggest, warmest heart of anyone George had ever known.

If there was any truly good person on the Planet Earth, George believed it was him.

"Hi, Mr. Barnett."

The man's dark, slightly cloudy eyes lit up at the sound of his voice. A childhood accident had left the man blind, but he knew his most devoted customer's voice by heart. His big, toothy grin spread as he reached for the first item on the belt. "Georgie! How are you? How have you been? My, this isn't your normal order, is it?"

"Oh, no, these are for me," Annie said, drawing Mr. Barnett's attention in her direction. She was soft and smiling, just as she was any time she wasn't speaking to George. In spite of himself, the green ache of jealousy settled in his stomach at that realization. "My name's Annie. I just moved into the neighborhood."

"Annie, eh? Pleasure to meet you. I'm Mr. Barnett. Always nice to meet one of George's girlfriends. He doesn't have too many of them, you know. I thought I'd be dead and buried before he brought another girl in here. The boy's a loner, through and through—"

"She's my friend," George said, pointedly, as she dropped a particularly heavy pack of staples to the belt, finally emptying the cart. "We're *friends*."

"If you say so, my boy."

As the rest of the transaction continued, Annie pulled back from her usual, cheery persona. Of course, she didn't let on to Mr. Barnett or let it seep into her voice, but her movements grew decidedly small and hesitant. Her eyes distant.

Alarm bells ran out in the back of George's mind. Oh, no. What had he done?

When they walked into the bright sun and out onto the curb outside of the grocery store, Annie wouldn't let him take any of the grocery bags. Despite their weight and just how many there were, she slung them all along her arms, stumbling under the strain and refusing every offer of help. Together, they walked back towards her house along the tree-lined sidewalks.

"Friends, huh?"

Oh. She'd heard that. It had been an honest mistake, really. A slip-up. Or maybe a slip of deep down, repressed wishful thinking. He shrugged. Maybe letting her think that they were friends would make her soften up around him. Lower her guard.

"Yeah," he said, the half-truth straining his voice. "Friends."

For a long, bitter moment, she examined him from the corner of her eye, making no pretense as to what, exactly, she was doing. This wasn't a shy inquisition, but a reading. Apparently, she didn't find what she was looking for. Angry, resentful disappointment lit a blazing fire in her eyes. He worried that it would come out and consume him next.

"I can't believe this. You don't get to manipulate me into giving you what you want. Lying about being my friend, putting on this act, isn't going to get me to cough up my life story for you, okay?"

He blinked, his pace alongside hers faltering. She'd called him out on it.

"Listen, I don't know what's going on with you or why you're doing this, but I do know that if we're going to work together, then we need to trust each other," he said, carefully. "You don't need to like me, and I don't need to like you, but we do have to at least try to be honest. Okay?"

"I *am* being honest. And if you don't know how to take *no* for an answer when you ask me a question, then maybe you aren't the kind of guy worthy of my trust, how about that?"

He struggled to keep up with her quick pace, but it didn't matter. Their pace had brought them back to her house in record time. "I'm just trying to understand you."

Stopping at her front gate, she turned on her heel to face him. "Understand this: I am exactly who I say I am. Don't look for any hidden depths. Don't search for anything that's not there. What you see is what you get. Everyone else seems to get that. Why can't you?"

"Because I don't want to believe that this is all you are."

"Ouch."

Annie reeled back just as George realized what he'd said. Without another word, she started for her front door, shoving through the front gate and leaving him out on the sidewalk to call weakly after her.

"I didn't mean it like that—"

"You're a writer, George. You know better than anyone how to say *exactly* how you feel."

Chapter Seven

Annie

Alright. New day. New sunrise. New winds blowing. Everything was starting afresh and Annie needed to start fresh with it. No more thinking about George Barnett and his stupid, beautiful, piercing eyes or his landmine of incessant questions or the half-dozen calls and texts from him she'd ignored the last few days or the way he'd called her his friend or the way he'd basically owned up to not believing that they were friends—or could be friends—at all.

No, today was the kind of day she could handle. A busy one.

Long before her brother and Harper had set a date for their wedding, Luke had promised to be the honorary auctioneer and the final lot at a charity event supporting the local firehouse—a bachelor and bachelorette auction—and, now that he was on his honeymoon and unavailable, Annie had stepped in to help the cause.

She loved events like this one. Having fun while raising money for a good cause. In her opinion, there was no better way to spend a Saturday, no better way to spread a little sunshine in this world. Back in Los Angeles, she'd spent lots of time volunteering with charities and hosting fundraisers, and, here in Hillsboro, she and her brother were no different. She even used her internet clout to highlight the causes, which made her entire career feel a little less useless in the grand scheme of things. George's words about her profession dug into her skin, and she found herself nearly ecstatic to be here in the firehouse, waiting for the festivities to start.

Besides, who didn't love supporting a group of selfless firefighters? Especially when they happened to be muscle-y, handsome, practically perfect examples of the profession?

The county hadn't seen a wildfire for some time, but everyone knew that Northern California was a ticking clock with an alarm, but no hands. You knew that someday, your number would be up, you just didn't know when that day would come. The last one seemed singed into the community's collective memory. Everyone wanted to give and give generously to the people who might protect them from the next big one.

The moment Annie strolled up to the firehouse, where the auction and the subsequent garden party—held in Fireman's Memorial Park just across the street—would be taking place, she drank in the sight of the small squadron of volunteers and regulars alike. All clothed in tight, gray T-shirts and their uniform pants and suspenders, they looked more like calendar models than real, true firefighters. Yeah...it would probably be fairly easy to forget about George Barnett in a place like this.

At least, that's what she'd thought. Now, as she stood behind one of the fire engines with Chief Bloom—a tall, slender woman with a close-cropped shock of white-blond hair crowning her rugged, lovely face—and waited for her turn to be called up and start the auction, the firefighters were, unfortunately, out of sight and out of mind, meaning she found her thoughts drifting back to George.

Who did he think he was, trying to figure her out like some Rubik's Cube? Like he implied, they *weren't* friends and they weren't going to become so. Usually, Annie couldn't stand the idea of someone not liking her, but in this case she had to make an exception. He wasn't content with friendship—he wanted to know her, to ferret out her secrets so he could expose them to the world. That, she couldn't allow. No, they were unlikely allies and business partners at best. She needed something from him. He needed something from her. And once their business was concluded, they would both go back to their separate, unincorporated lives.

That meant her personal life, her private thoughts and feelings and motivations, weren't any of his damn business.

Apparently, her distraction didn't go unnoticed. Chief Bloom gave her a slight nudge as the Board of Directors—on the other side of the great fire engine—gave a speech to their waiting audience.

"Are you alright, kid? Nervous?"

"Oh," Annie said, rattling off the first thing that came to mind, blunt and blasé and only halfway joking. "Just thinking about the social implications of a bachelor and bachelorette auction in today's climate. Isn't it a little bit dated?"

Chief Bloom chuckled. "Yes. Absolutely. But you'd be shocked what a little old lady will pay for an hour-long dinner with a fire-fighter, and dated or not, I've got to keep the lights on in here. No matter how good my brownies are, a bake sale never quite brings in the same amount of cash."

Annie let out a small chuckle of her own, but she knew it wasn't even halfway convincing. Her usual one-woman floorshow of a persona was slipping, and it was all George Barnett's fault. She wondered what sort of write-up he would give an event like this. Then she wondered whether he might be here today, but quickly dismissed the idea. The article in his office about the miniature horse farm aside, bachelor auctions didn't seem to be worthy and serious enough for his brand of reporting.

"You still look troubled. Do I need to get out my spreadsheet? Show you some numbers on the impact of a slightly sexist practice?"

"No. No, I'm fine."

Fine was an overstatement, but it would have to do for now. At least she could comfort herself that George Barnett was proving to be an excellent diversion, and if slyly dancing around answering any *real* questions about her life was what it took to get her mind off her empty house and her empty, empty life, then so be it.

The beginnings of the auction went well enough. The assembled crowd of party-goers lingered in the firehouse garage as Annie was helped up to the small step in front of the fire engine's door, where they promptly moved a podium and a gavel in front of her. Chief Bloom had been right. The wallets of Hillsboro opened up the second that she started introducing the bachelors and bachelor-ettes—all resplendent in their tight, gray T-shirts and firefighters' pants—and the bidding rose so fast she could barely keep up. *Miss Anika Barnes (34, loves ice-skating and apple picking), Mr. Logan Young (31, loves craft beer and poetry readings), Mr. Andrew Jones (40, avid jogger and CrossFit expert), Miss Stacey Holmes (29, former military and loves dogs!)...* They went and went and went and the donation barometer—a water tank marked with lines that Chief Bloom filled with the engine's hose every time they reached a milestone—rose so quickly that Annie barely had time to acknowledge George's presence directly at the center of the crowd.

He stood there in a checkered dress shirt and too-tight jeans, with a slightly askew tie around his neck and a notepad in hand, looking more like a dark curly-haired peak Robert Redford than anyone had a right to. Not once did he ever take those magnetic eyes off her, and not once did she ever raise hers to meet his gaze.

But then, it was her turn to go up on the auction block. And she couldn't escape the heat of his stare. With every teasingly self-deprecating word she spoke, with every passing second of her smile, the heat intensified, smoldering beneath her skin until she was *sure* everyone could see the blush splattering the skin beneath the collar of her floral-print party dress. He was too handsome. It wasn't fair for him to stand there, arms folded across that broad chest of his, smirking through his stubble. He had to know the effect he had on her.

Annie swallowed hard, trying to snap herself out of it. *What is the matter with you? You once gave a full thank-you speech to a room of celebrities who had gotten too drunk to remember to donate one red cent to the cause they were there to honor.*

"And, ladies and gentlemen, unfortunately, we have saved the least for the last. Sadly, our previous auctioneer and final lot in this auction, Mr. Luke Martin, is no longer a bachelor and therefore was disqualified. In his place, I'd like to introduce myself. Annie Martin. Mid-twenties, but it's quite rude to ask for a lady's age. I like mornings and rainstorms and board games and movie nights. Let's start the bidding at fifty dollars. Do I hear fifty?"

Please...someone bid on me. I couldn't live with myself if not a soul bid on me.

Paddles went up. Several of them, in fact. A rush of surprise rushed through Annie's blood. Maybe it was for the best that she was already blushing. Maybe people wouldn't notice how shocked she was that anyone wanted to bid on her.

"Uh, sixty? Do I hear sixty?"

Seventy-five. Ninety-Five. One-twenty. Sweet old women and rugged men in flannel button-downs raised their paddles over and over again until, at last, things were slowing down around three-hundred and twenty-two dollars.

Annie prepared herself to close the bid at three-hundred and twenty-two dollars. The sweet old lady in the back, who stood with her perpetually Snapchatting granddaughter, would be the ones to take her to dinner, where they would all drink a little too much wine and giggle a little too much.

It sounded like heaven, as far as Annie was concerned, and she was beyond grateful that the man in the center of the room hadn't made any of the commotion she'd feared from him.

Clearing her throat, she opened her mouth to give the final *going once, going twice...*

But then, George Barnett had to go and do what he always did. He had to go and ruin everything. Right there, in the middle of the crowd and in front of everyone, he threw his notebook in the air like a betting paddle and crowed as loud as he could:

"Four hundred dollars!"

Titters of shock and confusion and delight rippled through the crowd. Great, everyone in Hillsboro would know about this by tomorrow. Fantastic. Simply wonderful. Trying to keep her composure, Annie tightened her grip on her smile and regained control over the situation. George couldn't have her. Plain and simple. She wouldn't allow it.

"Sir, you don't have a paddle."

"No, but I have four hundred dollars." Then, he dug in his pockets, where he retrieved a handful of coins. "No, make that four hundred dollars and . . . sixty-two cents."

"If you don't have a paddle, then, I'm afraid—"

But George wasn't listening to her anymore. Turning that devilish smile away from her and towards the crowd, he enlisted their help. "Come on, folks. What do you think? Should she let me have it?"

The little old woman who'd actually won the auction was the first one to wave her hands and cheer this turn of events on, and soon after, the rest of the crowd joined her. Annie's blood ran cold.

She didn't want to go on a date with him. On a date, they couldn't have the barrier of their "work" between them; she couldn't use it as a shield. On a date, even a fake one like this, she would probably *have* to talk to him about her life, herself, even though the thought of sharing any of her true self with him—with anyone—was enough to send her running as fast as she could go in the opposite direction.

No one liked the real Annie Martin. They only liked the performance. And going on a date with George Barnett would ruin all of that. She was sure.

But with every cheer and every clap, she knew that she couldn't refuse. At least not publicly.

"Well . . ." She settled a beam on her face, even though she didn't expect anyone to believe that fake smile for a minute. "If the people have spoken. Going once...Going twice...Sold. To the generous gentleman in the ridiculous wannabe *All the President's Men* get-up. Thank you all for coming! Enjoy the party!"

Annie wasn't the kind of woman who stormed. She floated. She glided. On the rare occasion, she even favored a prance. But today? She didn't just storm out of the firehouse. She thundered, walking past well-wishers and chatterers straight out of the building and across the street to the park where the after-party was to be held.

She had half a mind to go home directly, but she couldn't just up and leave the event entirely. Maybe she was in a foul mood and maybe she wanted to turn around and sock George right in the jaw, but she was not going to abandon an obligation. She always kept her word, especially when it came to charity.

Only a few steps across the street, though, and she heard George's familiar footfall and breathing behind her. She couldn't help but snap at him.

"What did you do that for?"

"*Local reporter does good for the bravest firefighters in the country* sounds like a pretty good headline to me. Besides, I can expense it to the paper. Probably."

Annie rolled her eyes as she crossed the street and entered the park, which had been outfitted for an afternoon garden party, complete with a generous wine-pouring station and canapés carried on trays by the volunteer firefighters. "I really didn't think it was possible to be as dumb as you look, but here you are, proving it every time we speak."

"And I really didn't think it was possible to be as nice as everyone says you are, and here *you* are, proving me right every time you open your mouth in my direction. Besides, the real question here is why were you trying to keep me from doing it?"

Oh, he knew *exactly* why she didn't want to go on a date with him, and the fact that he could stand there and pretend as though he didn't was just galling.

"Did you want my undivided attention for an hour so you can insult me some more?"

"Did you want to deprive the firehouse of funds just because you can't bear to be around me?"

In her march to get them to a quiet corner of the party where they could argue in relative privacy, she stopped and wheeled around to face him, her heart racing the entire time. *Rats.* She hated being so short, hated having to look up at him like this. Beside her, there was a small, low row of stones delineating a flower garden. She stepped up on them, getting a handful of extra inches so she could square off with him properly.

Now, they were eye to eye, and she could see the vibrant array of colors that actually made up what she'd long thought of as boring, brown eyes. Greens and honeys and deep ochres combined, catching the light of the fire burning in his gaze.

Great. Now, she was angry at him for messing in her business *and* for being so good-looking. Impossible.

"Why are you trying to get under my skin?"

"Why are you trying to micromanage me?"

"You're impossible."

"And you need to be cut down to size, brought back down to earth, princess."

Before she could protest, a pair of strong, warm, and impossibly sexy arms wrapped around her waist and swung her back down to the soft grass. Too soon, he let her go, and she was left with the conflicting feelings of wanting to shove him as far away as possible *and* wanting him to draw her back into his embrace.

"Back down to earth? Oh, very funny. Very clever. And don't call me princess."

George sighed, pointedly refusing to meet her gaze. All around them, folks from the auction started to pour into the after-party, so he lowered his voice. "Look. I was just trying to do my bit for the community. And…and I wanted to apologize, okay?"

"Yeah, when does that start?"

His jaw opened and closed. He blinked furiously at her, as if he'd never had anyone refuse one of his clearly transparent apologies before. "You are…you are a frustrating woman, you know that? Difficult, even."

"I'd rather be a difficult woman than a cruel, unfeeling man who pulls stunts like this without caring who he's hurting. You'll pick me up at eight tomorrow and you'll wear a *decent* outfit, alright? And you'll bring me the names, background checks, and recent photographs of at least three candidates for Rose Anderson, is that understood?"

He smiled as the realization dawned that, yes, she would in fact be going out with him. She wanted nothing more than to punch that smirk off his face. "Yes, ma'am."

"Good. Now, move out of my way before I show you just how *difficult* I can be."

Chapter Eight

George

George spent most of Sunday at the office and decided to get changed for his date there. He'd always kept a small collection of clothes there, just in case he ever needed to run to an event or a press conference or meet with a source at the last minute. Today, he had thought it was probably best to crawl into work, get a few hours of research done, and change there so he could avoid seeing Annie in their (now-shared) neighborhood. He got the sense that she needed a little cooling off before they met up again.

He hadn't meant to buy her at the auction. Really, he hadn't. It was just that one minute, he was standing there, watching the bids climb higher and higher and she looked so beautiful and alive as she laughed at a joke some guy in the front row said and he imagined what it would be like if she were laughing with him and the next thing he knew, he'd become the Fire Department's most generous benefactor.

Figuring out justifications for why he'd done it became easy after the fact. He was just trying to get an "in" with her, just trying to win her back to his side after their disastrous last encounter. A one-on-one "date," such that it was, would be a good chance for journalistic research and insight.

Was any of that true? Or did he just get transfixed by the way laughter made the silver flecks in her eyes pop like snowflakes?

He didn't know. And frankly, he'd never been particularly inclined to turn his journalistic gaze inward. Oh, no. That was for *other* people and *their* flaws.

George couldn't remember the last time he'd been on an honest-to-goodness date, couldn't remember when he'd actually asked a girl out, made plans to see her, and followed through on those plans. And been excited about it. His usual working schedule was too irregular for even brief affairs. The idea of dating someone regularly…that was impossible.

So, truth be told, when he changed out of his usual work outfit into something a little sharper for his date with Annie Martin, he couldn't help but feel a tingle of worry in the pit of his stomach as he inspected himself in the mirror. What if he looked ridiculous in this "fancy" get-up, complete with an old jacket he'd gotten at a thrift store years ago? What if he was too rusty? What if he made a fool out of himself tonight?

Sure, it wasn't a real date. It was a means to a journalistic end, nothing more. Maybe with a glass of wine or two and some violin music floating through the air, she'd feel more inclined to open up to him.

It was work. Not a real date. But still…

He knew that Annie didn't like him. That hardly took great journalistic instincts to figure out. In fact, if it wasn't for his help with her ridiculous Rose project, she wouldn't be speaking to him at all. But…what if, at the end of the night, she actively hated him?

That shouldn't bother you, he reminded himself. The problem was that no matter how many times he reminded himself of that fact, it still bothered him.

"What in the hell do you think you're doing?"

George paused in his self-inspection, spinning on his heel to find Mynette sitting on his couch, eating a box of takeout nachos as though she were watching a football game instead of him.

This wasn't in and of itself entirely unusual. Mynette skulked around this office like appearing in the silent shadows, instead of secretarial work, was her job. What *was* unusual was that it had taken George this long to notice her. Apparently, he'd been too lost in his thoughts for her presence to even register in his peripheral vision.

Oh, no. He was in deep with Annie Martin, wasn't he?

Returning to straighten his lapels, he acted as nonchalant as it was humanly possible to be. He and Mynette had both been at the paper about as long as each other, and he'd always enjoyed the sibling dynamic they shared, but she didn't need to know about this date, especially given how much effort he was putting into it. "I'm...uh...Nothing."

Setting her nachos aside, Mynette sniffed the air. Her eyebrows knitted together in confusion. "Is that cologne? Are you wearing an *ironed shirt?*"

"I have a date tonight," he confessed.

"I know. Everyone's already heard. I just wanted to hear you own up to it."

George scoffed. "You know, I'll never get used to small-town gossip. Have we considered turning our paper into a tabloid?"

"There'd be no money in it. Everyone around here gets gossip for free." She raised one eyebrow. "So."

"So, what?"

"So, what the hell are you doing, going on a date with Annie Martin?"

"It's not a date. Not a real date. It's—"

Mynette scowled. He should have known better than to try and get around her. "I know what it is and I also know that the two of you have been prancing around town all week. I know you danced at her brother's wedding and *furthermore*, I know that you are wearing a clean, pressed shirt which I've never seen you do in your entire life. Spill. This isn't about some story, is it? You like her."

"I don't like her," he said, too fast.

How was he supposed to convince anyone else of that fact when he couldn't even convince himself? How was he supposed to go on this "date" and act detached and professional when he was bouncing on the balls of his feet like some kid about to go to prom for the first time?

"The shirt says otherwise."

"Will you stop harping on about the shirt?"

"Only when it stops meaning something," Mynette quipped, pleased with herself.

George left the relative safety of the mirror, suddenly sick of his own reflection. He had two choices here. He could confess that, yes, there was something…interesting, intriguing even, about Annie Martin, that maybe he was starting to think that the *more to her* he'd been looking for wasn't some deep, dark secret, but a singular, fascinating person who was hiding for some unfathomable reason.

Or...he could protect himself. Protect his own reputation. And he could do the exact opposite of telling the truth.

He hated himself for it, but he chose the latter as he dug through his drawers for a spare pocket-pad and a pen.

"It *is* about a story, alright? Just not this matchmaking thing she said we're doing. I...I think there's a story there, with Annie Martin and her brother. I don't know what it is, but I know I have to find it."

Mynette's posture changed. She sat up, rod-straight, and appraised him. "You're using her, then. Working with her so you can use what you find. Not exactly ethical."

The edges of George's mind tugged. There was a reason he had decided to go after Luke Martin in the first place, a reason he hadn't given up the story after two years. Yes, he cared about justice and uncovering secrets and everything a good journalist went into the profession for, but there was more to it than just that.

"I need a break. A big one. I can't keep writing puff pieces about small-town life anymore, not if I want to keep doing this."

"You don't *just* write puff pieces about small-town life," Mynette protested, pointing to a few of the bigger stories hanging up on his wall, the pieces that earned him this desk and the begrudging respect of his editor. It was all good. That work had made him proud. It just wasn't enough.

"Yeah, but the hard-hitting stuff I've done hasn't been picked up anywhere big."

Mynette chewed her bottom lip. "Alright. Just...be careful. Don't go so deep undercover that you forget who you are and what you're really doing. Don't fall in love with her or anything."

"Don't worry. There's no chance of that."

"Sure," she replied, a laugh hiding in the twin centers of her dimpled cheeks. "Whatever you say, George."

Reaching into his pocket, George withdrew the receipt from his auction purchase and handed it to her on his way out of the door.

"By the way, I need to expense this."

"*What?*"

He'd decided to walk around the block a few times. Despite being chronically late by nature—something of an oversleeping journalist's curse—when it came to dating, George would usually take great, great pains to be exactly on time. First impressions were important and all that. But tonight, even after he'd left the office behind and the noise in his head had slightly quieted, that nervous strain of jitters hadn't quite left him.

Yeah. A good walk would get rid of those. Right?

He went around her block—careful to cross on the opposite side of the street, so she wouldn't catch him if she happened to look out the window at just the wrong moment—once, twice, and even though the sun was disappearing over the horizon, his nerves didn't follow suit.

Don't fall in love with her. Please. As if he had a romantic bone in his body.

Sure, Annie Martin was beautiful. And headstrong. And surprisingly funny. And being around her, despite what she said, made him feel a little less like a cynical and embittered person, which was something he couldn't say for anyone else he knew. Save perhaps Marshall Barnett.

Did she have kissable lips? Sure. Did he sometimes let his eyes wander down to them when she was talking? Naturally. Did he wonder what it would be like if this was a real date instead of a fake one that she only agreed to in order to save face with a local charity? You bet.

But falling in love with her?

Obviously not. And he wasn't ever going to be doing something as absurd as that. George wasn't an emotional man; logic, not love, was his guide in everything. At least, that's what he told himself.

During his second loop around the block, he staggered to a stop when he realized that the small blocks here meant that they were only one-house deep, and when he'd made the loop halfway, he was staring right at the back of Annie's house. A small garage and a set of twin garbage cans beckoned him.

Investigative work. He could just tip over those bins and have a quick rifle through them, couldn't he? Just peruse and see if there was anything of interest to Luke Martin or his sister. Plenty of honorable journalists had gone dumpster-diving before. He wouldn't be the first.

The call of a story whispered in his ear, siren-beautiful and just as alluring. He stopped himself short, though. That truly would be a betrayal of her trust. She'd never look at him the same way, much less speak to him again, if she found him going through her stuff.

But it was in this hesitation at the back of her house that Annie Martin found him when she called from her second-story alcove window.

"Hey!"

George balked at the sudden shout, and stepped back so he could see her. From this angle, it was impossible to see much of her look for this evening, but in the glow of the room behind her, she practically sparkled.

She knocked the air right out from him.

"Uh...Hello?" he said, trying to act natural.

"What are you doing? You're four minutes late," she reminded him, neglecting to mention that she was, also, late.

He should have had an answer for that, but he came up shockingly empty. It wasn't like he could confess to almost rifling through her garbage cans for information. "I was just...I just thought I would—" Dumbly, he pointed towards the twilight sky without taking his eyes off her. She was always beautiful, sure, but there was something about this otherworldly glow of her right now, leaning out of a window high above to tease him, that tongue-tied him even more than he otherwise might have been. "I thought I saw a shooting star."

She rewarded him with a laugh and a raised, curious eyebrow. "And you were going to chase after it?"

"No. Because clearly, it landed right here."

Embarrassment threatened to drown him. Why had he said that? And if he was going to use some romantic junk on her, why did it have to be such *bad* romantic junk? Couldn't he have come up with anything better than that? Annie, mercifully, didn't seem interested in dissecting his bad work. Instead, she rolled her eyes and waved him back towards the house.

"Just come to the front gate."

Moments later, George rang the aging bell, and was greeted not only by the excited yowling of Monster, who jumped at his heels and preened for pets, but by Annie herself.

Well…kind of Annie herself. The person staring back at him from the other side of the door was, without question, Annie Martin. The smirk hiding in her left dimple. Those glittering, inquisitive eyes. He'd recognize them anywhere.

But as much as she was Annie Martin, she didn't much look like her. The Annie he knew was perpetually decked-out in the highest of high fashion. She was a walking lookbook who never had a single thread, hair, or stitch out of place. She was high glamor in human form. Perfection.

And tonight? Tonight, she wore a pair of slightly dirty boots, high-waisted jeans with a bottom-knotted flannel shirt, and her hair in twin, ringleted ponytails that framed the red-lipped smile on her beautiful face. The shirt was a half size too big. The belt was a little bit askew.

He wasn't one of those pounce-and-grab, ultra-masculine men, but the moment he saw her like that, perfectly imperfect but smiling as though this was the way she'd always wanted to look, he couldn't help but want to pin her against the wall and kiss that pretty red lipstick right off her.

The force of the want shocked him, as she stood there, a strange expression on her face.

"You look—Um, you look—"

Annie rolled her eyes and gave a sarcastic, defeated twirl.

"Come on, lay it on me. I look like I'm making fun of the townsfolk. I look like a cheap Pollyanna knock-off."

"Beautiful," he said, before he could think better of it. "I was going to say beautiful. It just didn't seem good enough."

Annie shook her head and reached for her purse, which she slung over one shoulder before going about the work of locking Monster up in the house behind her.

"I'm not a girl who can be flattered."

"Somehow, I did use my investigative skills to determine that. But would an apology work? Or a truce?"

"Depends on what you mean."

She closed the door behind her and leaned against it, inspecting him with an incisive, cutting gaze. He knew that they weren't going to get anywhere if they didn't bury whatever weird hatchet lay between them.

Sure, he didn't exactly know where he wanted to go from here, emotionally speaking, but he knew that he didn't want to be stuck in that *you're a cruel, unfeeling man* territory forever. Maybe it was true, but for some reason, he couldn't stand the thought of her believing it of him.

"I'm sorry for pushing you the other day. And I'd like for tonight to be normal. Just two normal people, going out on a normal date. A truce. I won't interrogate you, and you—"

She raised a half-joking eyebrow at him. "Won't treat you like the enemy?"

"I'm up for it if you are."

With that, he offered her his arm, hoping on hope that she would actually take it, not because he had bought her time at the charity auction, but because she actually wanted to.

George couldn't remember the last time he'd actually cared if someone liked him or not. But here he was, his heart hammering in his chest, hoping that for one night, Annie Martin could at least try. Her teasing smile dissolved into something real, and she slipped her arm in his.

"So, where are you taking me?"

"Somewhere I bet you've never been."

Chapter Nine

Annie

A truce. Annie probably should have known better than to agree to something like that, but when he smiled at her under those long eyelashes, making her feel like she was the only woman in the world, her knees shook. Just like her resolve.

He was, despite this temporary détente, the enemy. At the end of their time together, he'd write an article about her brother, and every small, vulnerable moment she spent with him was a risk. Luke was the most important thing in her life, the entirety of her family, and protecting him was—and had always been—her first priority.

But...she was so lonely. And maybe one night of escape, one night where they weren't forced together by some deal they'd made, one night where she could pretend that someone out there could actually like the her beneath the fancy clothes and makeup...

Besides, as much as she liked to make other people happy... maybe there was something to be said for making herself happy, too. Maybe it wasn't such a bad thing.

*

The Bronze Boot was a mess of contradictions, a technicolor expressionist painting of light and sound. Part old-school honky-tonk, part rustically high-end drinking hole, the wooden paneling and dark, double-paned stained-glass windows were illuminated by neon signs of flowering cactus plants and moving beer logos.

It looked like it hadn't been renovated or redecorated in half a century. It was a far cry from the usual places Annie frequented back in L.A., and that's exactly why she loved it immediately. Not because she didn't love the city where she'd grown up, the place where she'd created herself, but because this was something vibrant and strange, with the jagged edges of authenticity that a place like L.A. was very good at sanding down.

Annie strolled straight in, clinging to the slim documents folder that George had given her on the walk over—that Eris Majors seemed a promising and handsome choice—and headed for the colorful, glinting lights of the bar. It took George, who'd been holding the saloon doors of the joint open for her, almost like a gentleman, a moment before he could stagger behind her.

"This place is fantastic," she muttered.

"You..." He almost choked on the word. "You like it?"

Just like him to be painfully small-minded. The only thing that kept her from rolling her eyes was her internal promise to really connect with him tonight, to try and be here with him in this moment. She couldn't very well do that if she was all eye-rolls and quiet derision. "What, did you expect me to run out of the door screaming?"

"No, you're just always surprising me, that's all." His voice was soft and slow, almost crooning over the voice of the jukebox in the corner. When they made their way up to the bar, he ordered them a pair of local beers and assessed her as they waited for them. She didn't pay him much mind. Whipping out her phone, she took several pictures of fading beer-label coasters and a nearby cake stand that included a few leftover bake sale items from the fundraiser. The pictures would make it onto her professional feed sometime, but she wouldn't mention who she was with when she took them. George leaned in closer beside her, and she became acutely aware of his warm breath on her neck when he spoke, his wide, broad chest pressing near to hers. "What do you like about it?"

Her brain tried to remind her that he was the enemy, that he was fishing for some morsel of a story that he could spin out into some fantastical myth about her and her brother. But if this really was a truce, then she couldn't very well hold back. Besides, when was the last time she got to tell anyone the truth about herself? When was the last time she'd let her mask slip? "I know what people think of me. What I encourage them to think. That I'm this sophisticate who loves fine wines and expensive clothes and all the kind of things men think that the frivolous women of the internet obsess over. And I do. I like nail polish that coordinates with my shoes and cute wine charms and cookies decorated to look like celebrities. But I also love adventure. I love strangeness. I love going places where the people are real."

"And Hillsboro is real?"

"Hillsboro is *very* real. In fact, I think the Bronze Boot might be the realest place I've ever been."

"And what about you?" he asked, his eyes piercing in his reflection from the mirrored wall behind the bar. "Do you feel real?"

Why was he looking at her like that? Like she was some kind of puzzle he couldn't solve? And why did it awaken all of the slumbering butterflies in her belly? And why, against all odds, did she want to bottle that feeling so she could experience it forever? The beers arrived, and despite Annie rarely drinking the stuff—it wasn't her brand, after all; her fans wanted her drinking spiked seltzers and bottomless Prosecco—Annie guzzled a long, hoppy swallow before leaning in slightly. Close enough to smell George's musky, earthen cologne. A scent so warm and inviting that, if she'd been a little more tipsy, she might have wanted to nuzzle into his neck to smell more closely.

"You want to know a secret, George?"

"Desperately," he said, his gaze intense and his smile infectious.

"If I ever felt real, I don't even think I'd recognize myself."

"What does that—"

"It means that I want to have fun tonight," she said quickly, before she could word-vomit anything else hideously embarrassing. Was it possible the beer had gone to her head that quickly? Or did she—horror of horrors—actually trust George Barnett? Maybe a little bit? "Will you let me?"

"Yeah. I think I'd like to see that."

If this was what first dates were supposed to feel like—bashfully smiley and confusingly intense and warm and tingly and giggly and honest—then it was no surprise that Annie hadn't really been on many. It was almost too much. Too much feeling for her little body and her tightly bound heart to contain.

It didn't help matters that she knew she was supposed to wake up tomorrow and dislike this guy again. That, once he walked her home and all of this was over, they'd be nothing but partners again. Partners using each other for a means to an end.

Just as she was about to drown that particular thought in another swig of beer, the sounds of the jukebox slowly declined and a piercing microphone screech took its place, drawing her attention towards the small stage in the corner of the room. The bartender, who'd only a moment ago been slinging drinks and making minimal friendly conversation, now stood in a small center spotlight, adjusting the microphone to raucous applause from the crowd below.

"Ladies and gentlemen, cowboys and cowgirls, let's have a warm, Bronze Boot welcome for Richie, the Singing Cowboy!"

Just at that moment, Richard Abalos—her real estate guy—strutted onstage, in a pair of slightly too-tight acid-washed jeans and leather chaps, a worn fringed vest, flannel undershirt... The *whole* cowboy get-up.

Oh, and he was carrying a guitar and wearing one of those harmonica contraptions around his neck. Annie vaguely remembered him saying something about the Bronze Boot, but now she was *here*, actually witnessing the spectacle with her own two eyes. It was perfection.

Annie couldn't help it. The electricity of the cheering crowd infected her too, and she let out a *whoop* of excitement. On the stool beside her, she could feel George turn and stare at her, but she didn't care. For the first time in a long time, she didn't care how she looked. She was having too much fun for that. Up on stage, with his polished belt buckle and his glittering smile, Mr. Abalos—sorry, Richie the Singing Cowboy—beamed down at them all.

"Alright, alright, alright, good evening and *buenos noches* to all of the lovely ladies out there. I see some familiar faces, and some new ones.

Welcome, *bienvenidos*. Like he said, I am Richie, the Singing Cowboy, though if you're in the market for a new house, please take my card because I also do real estate. Now, who is ready to have a good time?"

The crowd erupted again, lifting their drinks as they whooped and hollered their approval. Without any further ado, Richie went into his first song, a classic song about spurs and leaving lost loves that almost reminded Annie of some black-and-white movie she'd once watched...or maybe one of her brother's video games? She wasn't sure. All she knew for certain was that her toes were soon tapping and she couldn't keep her eyes from wandering over the practically bouncing guy at her side.

He was...he was enjoying this. He liked the kitschy cowboy and his dated music. Liked the bar and its neon and mismatched décor. Maybe...maybe he even liked being with her?

Leaning over to him, she tried to speak over the din of music. "This totally doesn't seem like your scene."

"It isn't," George said, shrugging. "Not usually, anyway. Doesn't mean I can't enjoy it now that I'm here, though."

For a moment, she was content with that answer. It didn't matter why he'd brought her here; all that mattered was this small part of him he was now revealing to her. The part that knew how to have fun, how to enjoy himself. Who knew good music and a good time when he found it. But when that moment passed, she knew she couldn't stand the mystery any longer.

"Why'd we come here if it isn't your scene, then?"

"Because I wanted to see how you'd handle it."

That made more sense than anything she'd previously hypoth-esized. "Ah, so this was another journalistic test. A good opener for your story?" She dropped her voice into a mockery of his low, gravelly one. "*Annie Martin is sitting across from me in a Honky-Tonk, listening to a real estate man sing about love. She drinks from a sweaty beer. And I have to wonder... what secrets is she hiding?*"

George barked out a laugh. "Well, what secrets *are* you hiding?"

"Off the record?"

"Of course."

This is fun. I'm having a good time with you. You're making me feel things I've never felt before, things I know I shouldn't feel for anyone like you, much less you in specific. I want to close the space between you and kiss those infuriating fast lips of yours. I want to be myself around you, even when I'm not quite sure who she is.

But the one secret she couldn't tell him, because it wasn't true? *I trust you.* That's why, when she finally opened her mouth, she didn't kiss him. Or throw herself into his arms. Or even tell him that she was having a good time. She just said, with her brightest smile:

"I'm a Libra."

About half an hour later, they'd fallen into companionable joking territory, laughing, drinking and engaging with the performance on stage as Richie sang and danced his way through half of America's Old West Songbook. Annie wanted to drink in every moment, every slightly scandalous joke that the cowboy whipped out between songs and the patterns the electric lights painted across George's handsome face as he clapped along to the harmonica solo during "I Wanna Be a Cowboy's Sweetheart." For once, no one was looking at her. No one expected anything of her. She could just *be*.

And she was surprised to find that just being at George's side was a nearly perfect place to be. She almost felt like she belonged there.

Finally, when the music stopped for a moment so Cowboy Richie could take a long drink from a nearby glass of water, the crowd lowered to a hush, but began rustling. Annie realized that they must have been regulars, readying themselves either for a longer break or some kind of tradition at this point in Richie's act. The man clapped his hands together over his guitar, almost in gratitude.

"Ladies and gentlemen, now we have come to the interactive portion of the evening. The floor is clear. Our hearts are open. And now," he played one bold, defiant strum on his instrument, a demand and a challenge, "it's time to dance."

With a lightning strike of jealousy, Annie watched as the couples and groups of friends made their way laughing to the cleared dance floor. She'd always loved those movies where the two main characters swept out into a crowd to the sound of music, dancing and spinning until the world dissolved around them and there was nothing else but the two of them. Nothing else but the stars in each other's eyes. Annie knew she would never have anything like that, nothing so special, but she couldn't help but feel a little bit envious of the people who *did* have it.

Beginning with a rhythmic whistle on his harmonica, Richie began a honky-tonk rendition of "Come On Eileen" by Dexy's Midnight Runners. Boisterous and loud and spectacularly romantic. The floor came alive with the music; the air around Annie moved with the sound, with its pulsating rhythms and stops. Then, a hand reached out in front of her.

"Do you want to dance?"

She glanced up at George, who now stood in front of her with a cocksure grin and an outstretched hand. Her fight or flight instincts kicked in. It was only a dance, she realized that. But considering all of the silly romantic notions she had about moments like this one, she knew that agreeing to dance with George Barnett in particular wasn't quite the same as agreeing to dance with anyone else. This was one of her favorite songs. This crowd was vibrant and happy; her heart was beating in time with the rhythm of this room. He was smiling down at her as though she was the most important being in the entire universe. All of that combined was enough to sweep a girl up into some fairy-tale fantasy.

"Oh, no, I don't—"

"Come on," he said, a small smile lifting his stubbled jawline. "I promise I'm better at this than at waltzing."

"I—"

Her protest died in her throat. She *knew* that this was a bad idea. But God, did she want it anyway. Annie Martin was a certified Good Girl who did Good Things and made Good Decisions. But for the first time in a long time, she wanted nothing more than to indulge in the sweet forbidden fruit of a bad one.

"You said you wanted to have fun. What better place to start?"

"It's just that I—"

I don't know how to dance to music like this and I really try not to make a fool of myself whenever I possibly can and I don't want these feelings that I'm feeling for you to grow any bigger because if they do then I won't be able to shove them in my dresser drawer and lock them away forever like I do with the rest of the things in my life I try to forget. I want, I want, I want. But I know, I know, I know I can't.

But George reached out and touched her hand, a touch so gentle, so unlike the thundering brute of a man he always tried to pretend he was, that part of her wanted to cry. Their eyes met. And she knew she was a goner.

"Trust me. Please."

Oh, no. She'd been wrong. She hadn't been a goner when their eyes met. She was *really* lost—or really found, she wasn't sure which—when she slipped her hands in his, and they let their bodies join the bouncing crowd.

She didn't know how to dance to this music. She didn't know how to move her feet in these ridiculous cowboy boots she'd bought for herself when she moved to Hillsboro. She didn't know if anyone was looking at her and judging her or if they were going to snap pictures and sell them to that gossipy YouTube channel tomorrow.

All she knew was that she was dancing with George Barnett. His hands were at her waist, and they were both sing-screaming the words to "Come On Eileen" in slightly ridiculous cowboy accents, and her heart was in her throat, and she was sublimely, supremely, unabashedly happy.

Happier than she could ever remember being before.

Eventually, when The Singing Cowboy's set was over and the beers had been drunk, they made their slightly stumbly way back towards Annie's house, pausing only momentarily for a very necessary ice cream pit stop.

Annie had gone for classic chocolate; George had surprised her when he'd gone for a scoop of lavender. The man was truly full of surprises. Tonight had shown her that.

Tonight had shown her a lot of things, actually. Like how easy it was to get swept away by cowboy music, a few sips of beer, and a handsome and infuriating man egging you on. As they made their way back to her new little house, Annie shook her halfway eaten ice cream cone accusingly in George's direction.

"I can't believe you got me to do that!"

"You're a fantastic dancer," he said, with a smile that made her breath move a little bit faster.

"I was on top of a chair! If anyone took a picture, it's going to be on TMZ in less than an hour."

"And that would be so bad?"

Annie chomped off a bite of her ice cream cone to punctuate her point. "You know how I feel about so-called journalists."

His smile turned into a smirk, but it was no less devastating. "Yes, you find them incredibly helpful to your research and for getting out of the house every once in a while."

Honestly. The arrogance. As they continued down the streets of Hillsboro, lit by golden streetlamps dotted here and there, Annie knew that tomorrow she'd have blisters and a sore throat, but for now, she was going to enjoy this warm, cozy feeling that wrapped itself around her, insulating her from the consequences of this evening, every time George looked at her.

"Well, at least you're right about that. Thanks for the beers and the company. Even if you did make me embarrass myself."

"It's not possible for Annie Martin to embarrass herself. You have to know that."

He was baiting her, she was almost positive of that. It became even *more* apparent when he hopped up on her front step, playfully blocking her way into her own house. It was all too easy to give into the urge to roll her eyes.

"Okay, what are you doing now?"

"I think you owe me a secret," he smirked. "One better than your star sign."

Trust me, he'd said earlier tonight. And she had. She'd let him twirl her around the dance floor, allowed him to coax belly laughs and songs from her. She'd trusted him with this night.

But she still wasn't sure she trusted him with her secrets. A compromise was in order. If he wanted her trust, then he had to give her some back in kind. Relationships, in her experience, only worked when everyone involved was giving and taking.

She wasn't going to be the only one in this relationship—in whatever *this* going on between them was or turned out to be—giving up something.

"Oh, that. Well. Why don't we trade? You tell me a secret, and then I'll tell you one."

"Okay. That sounds fair," George said, with a smirk but not a trace of irony in his voice. He did seem interested in fairness; the articles on his wall proved that. She'd expected resistance from him or at least another dose of his infuriating attempts at arrogant humor, but she should have known better. "Anything in particular you're wondering about?"

Yes. And she knew she shouldn't ask it. The night had been great, far surpassing her expectations. Asking this question would probably ruin it. But she couldn't help herself. "Why are you so determined to expose my brother? When you don't really know if he's done anything wrong?"

George's smirk faltered slightly. "Man, you get right to the point, don't you?"

Annie shrugged.

"Because I love Hillsboro. And I've seen so many people's lives torn apart by rich folks who think they can just do anything they want. I am just trying to protect the people that I love, you know? I haven't spoken to my family in years. Long story, but..." He shrugged. "Hillsboro is the only family I've got. I would do anything to make sure they're safe."

Something stirred within Annie's heart. She knew that feeling, knew it in the marrow of her bones. Everything she did, she did to protect her family, too. Her brother and her found family, the Andersons.

"But what about you?" George said, after a moment. "What are you hiding? Why are you fighting so hard to keep me from telling this story?"

"Besides the fact that my brother's done nothing wrong?"

George nodded with a slight roll of his eyes, clearly not believing her. "Yeah. Sure. Besides that."

"Because my brother's all that I have. My only friend for most of my life. Our parents were... They weren't great. Weren't really parents. Luke dropped out of high school and took his first job just to make sure I had a uniform for school. For most of our lives, it's just been us. And I would do anything to protect him, just like you'd do anything for Hillsboro."

She tried to ignore the feeling dominating her body, the one that told her she and George were more alike than she'd realized, that they were kindred spirits somehow.

"And what about—"

Before George could finish her question, Annie raised a cautioning finger. "No way. It's my turn to get a secret from you."

As she walked up the front steps to her house to meet him, George mulled that over. "Okay. My secret? I meant it, tonight when I said that you looked like a shooting star."

Annie rolled her eyes. Reaching beneath the honeycomb planter May had given her last year for Christmas, she retrieved her key. "Flatterer."

"You don't believe me?"

"On the subject of Annie Martin, I don't trust anyone except for Annie Martin, and even she doesn't have all the facts."

Yeah. That was just opaque and mystifying enough that maybe he wouldn't ask her any more questions.

"Alright. Your last turn. Make it a good one, princess," George said, a teasing note in his voice.

This time, when he tossed that nickname her way, she didn't mind it.

This would have been the perfect time for her to clarify her earlier remark. To tell him that she'd never believe any nice thing that ever came out of his mouth, that she didn't believe even the best thoughts she occasionally thought about herself.

She could have said . . . *everyone in this world thinks I'm this great, confident, untouchable princess who knows herself and has everything figured out, but the truth is . . . I'm more lost than anyone. And I'm so insecure that every time I think I might know which way to step so that I might find my way again, I second-guess and step backwards, because I don't trust myself to be right about anything. I want to make people happy because I don't want anyone to ever feel as badly as I've felt. Because I want people to like me. Because I don't know if I have anything else to offer.*

She could have said that. Every word of it would have been the truth. But when she opened her mouth to answer him, she caught a flicker of silver in his deep eyes, and another truth came out.

He was still a reporter, after all. The story he was writing about her family was still very much on the table. As much as she wanted to trust him, as much as she already did, she had to remember that.

"I had a nice time tonight. This was the best date I've ever been on."

"That's a terrible secret!"

"Not to me, it's not." Another truth. Telling him she liked him—that he wasn't entirely her enemy—was as big a risk as she'd ever taken with her heart. Especially when she wasn't sure how long it would last. Slipping her key into the lock, she glanced back at him, daring him to say anything else. "Goodnight, George."

"Goodnight, Annie. See you tomorrow."

It wasn't a goodnight kiss at the door. But when Annie closed it behind her and leaned against it, her heart was hammering as though she'd just gotten one.

Chapter Ten

George

Feelings. Normal people had them. Most people indulged them every once in a while. George had pretty much shoved his in a drawer a long time ago and now tried to think as little of them as possible. Feelings were risky in a business like his. They complicated everything. One minute, you were laughing and having a good time, genuinely enjoying the company of someone you just met, and the next, you realize that they're in the center of some great conspiracy or crime.

One of his first lessons as a journalist had been just that. *Some of the best people you'll ever meet are also some of the worst.* No one ever is who they appear to be on the surface. No one is simple, unflawed.

But when George woke up the morning after their "date" fully ready to initiate the first of their Operation: Blooming Rose (as they'd decided to call it) meet cutes, he couldn't escape one singular, ridiculous, shameful feeling.

Excitement.

Last night had been a roller-coaster of feeling and sensation, things that he usually didn't allow himself to indulge in. For a handful of hours, they both set aside their ulterior motives and lowered most of their defenses and what had he discovered?

He liked Annie Martin. He liked her more than he should. And now, he was excited to see her again.

So excited, in fact, that when he brought his breakfast selections to the checkout counter at Barnett's, he was whistling that same ridiculous song they'd been dancing to last night. For some reason, he hadn't been able to get it out of his head. It lingered, like the scent of her perfume.

None of this went unnoticed by Marshall Barnett, who rang him up at the grocery counter with a mischievous smirk.

"Good morning, boy. I guess the rumors are true, then."

"Just here for my breakfast, Mr. Barnett."

The man ran George's bakery bag under his nose before handing it over to him. "And a lemon poppy seed muffin. You only eat those when you're in a really good mood."

As if he would let seeing Annie again dictate his stomach. Of all the ridiculous things Mr. Barnett had ever said to him from that side of the counter, this was truly the most ridiculous.

"Where'd you get an idea like that? My moods do not dictate my breakfast."

"You learn a lot about people sitting behind this counter all day, son. I'd reckon I'm a better detective than you."

"Alright," George said with a laugh, counting out his change to pay for the meager meal. "Lay it on me, old man."

Mr. Barnett beamed as though he'd been waiting for this moment his entire life. A minute ago, George had been so sure that the old man was telling tall tales, trying to get a reaction out of him, but his confident smile suddenly made George question everything. *Had* he let his feelings for Annie pick his breakfast? Was he really that suggestible? "You bought a lemon poppy seed the day after the Yankees won the pennant. You bought a lemon poppy seed the day after that movie about those reporters won the Oscar. And you bought a lemon poppy seed this morning, the day after you went on a date with a certain young lady named Annie Martin." Mr. Barnett paused and waited for George to respond, which he elected not to do. The man's smile only grew. "Do I strike true, counselor?"

"It wasn't a date," George mumbled.

"Maybe you can lie to yourself, but the lemon poppy seed doesn't. Do you want an extra one, for the road? Or for a certain special someone?"

I really should protest. I should explain to him that it wasn't a date and that it never would be a date and that the hummingbird in my chest is only visiting. I can't feel anything too deeply for Annie Martin because she's still my subject.

Arguing, though, would be pointless. The old man clearly knew him better than he knew himself.

"Oh, just give it to me."

Later that afternoon, George found himself on the grounds of the Anderson Flower Farm, a place he recognized from a few events in high school and the rare photo spread in the local newspaper, but one he never thought he'd be spying on.

Annie had gone away after their "date" with his small, manila folder of three potential choices, and she hadn't wasted any time getting to work on setting them up with Rose. Through the morning, George watched in slight awe as, between bites of lemon poppy seed muffin, Annie did research and made phone calls before deciding on the perfect plan. This time, Annie wanted the meet cute to happen on Rose's home turf. *It'll relax her; she'll be more comfortable if she's in her own space.* It would be the perfect setting for an accidentally-on-purpose meeting between her and the man Annie had picked out for her.

That's how he ended up here, hiding at the base of one of the trees lining the long driveway leading to the Anderson house, with a walkie-talkie in one hand and his telescopic lens in the other. The communication device was totally unnecessary given that they both had, you know, cell phones, and he didn't even know where she had managed to buy them, but Annie was nothing if not thorough. She worried that, despite never having trouble with reception before, the cells would cut out right at some key, opportune moment, leaving them both unable to talk; she'd insisted that walkie-talkies were best. What started as a one-woman matchmaking service was now turning into a full-blown spy operation.

She was up at the top of the hill, stationed in the bedroom window of Harper Anderson, who had abandoned the space for her honeymoon and her new home with her new husband. When George had asked if Harper knew that her bedroom was being occupied, Annie merely brushed him off and said that Harper would be thanking her once they found her sister a love of her own.

George had met the fast-talking, sassy Harper Anderson a few times. He was almost entirely, 100 percent certain this wasn't true, but he didn't have it in him to argue.

As he took his position in the shadow of his tree, the walkie-talkie crackled to life in his hand. Annie's modulated voice came through it. "Do you have eyes on the target, Turtle?"

George narrowed his eyes. She'd "given" him a code name, but he'd assumed she was joking. "Are you really going to call me that?"

"It's fitting, isn't it? They're reclusive and hard-shelled and slow as molasses. I mean, come on, it took you ages to walk down that hill. Over."

"I'm not inclined to walk fast for people who compare me to a turtle."

"Turtles are also very, very cute. Over."

"You think I'm cute?" George thought back to last night. The way she'd looked at him when they were dancing. Was it possible that she was flirting with him? "Err, over."

Her bubbly laugh came through the line. "Not really. I just said that to soften the blow. Now, seriously. Do you have eyes on the target? Over."

That definitely wasn't the feeling of his chest deflating. Following the path down to the end of the hill, George saw a black pickup truck making its way up the hill. Bingo. He knew that ride anywhere. It belonged to Eris Majors, number three on his list of potentials.

His father's company usually made deliveries to the Anderson household, and a well-placed phone call from George suggested that maybe Eris do the delivering today. At the same time, Annie had convinced Rose to receive it.

The perfect crime, if only it would work. Which George wasn't entirely convinced was an inevitability.

"Yes, I have eyes on the target. The target is heading up the hill now. I'm not saying 'over' again."

"Fine. Great. Move in closer."

George eyed the tree lording over him. The only way he would be able to get closer to the road without being seen would be by climbing the tree and reaching out on one of its upper branches. "Closer?"

"Yes, closer. He'll stop a few yards away from you. That's where the Andersons always get their deliveries, right there on that little landing area. I can't hear from all the way up here. You're going to have to tell me how it's going. Please. I have a really good feeling about this one."

He could fall and break his arm. He could fall and break his *neck*. Generally risk-averse, George didn't like to put himself in situations where paralysis was a possibility. But still, he clipped the walkie-talkie to his shirt, gripped twin knots in the tree, and made his way up, grumbling until he found a suitable branch upon which to perch.

"I feel ridiculous," he muttered into the walkie-talkie.

"Well, your butt looks great, if it's any consolation."

George's pulse thrummed. "*What?*"

"I'm sorry, I think there must have been some static on the line. Now, quiet. They're coming."

Sure enough, Eris's truck crawled to a stop just where Annie said it would, and Rose wandered down the hill to meet him, giving a wave and a surprised grin at the sight of him. Their conversation floated up to him, just above the noise of the truck's engine.

Oh, Eris! How are you? I feel like I haven't seen you in forever!

Rose, hi. I didn't realize... I didn't realize you were going to be here.

Well, I do live here.

Right, but you're... I didn't... I usually don't make these deliveries.

And I usually don't collect them. Maybe it's fate.

"Okay, it seems... Good. Yeah, seems good."

"Yeah, but what are they saying?"

Your flowers are looking so beautiful. I was actually thinking that I might, you know, start putting some arrangements in my restaurant. Do you still do that sort of thing?

Yeah, all the time. I'd love to—

A low, dangerous growl hit George's ears and sent an immediate river of chill-bumps down his neck. Carefully, he glanced down at the base of the tree, where an oversized white beast stared up at him, its teeth bared.

The animal looked wild, feral. One bite of its massive, toothy jaw and George would, no doubt, lose at least half of a limb. He'd always liked dogs—small dogs, sweet dogs, like the one Annie had—but this wasn't a dog; this was a creature, one that seemed singularly focused on him. A thrill of terror ran up and down George's spine.

"What is happening?" Annie hissed through the machine in his hands, dragging his eyes away from the imminent death currently growling at him from ground level.

"Um, she is saying that she'd be happy to do some flower arrangements for his restaurant."

The growling got louder. Rose and her new beau—who genuinely did seem to be hitting it off, which George guessed made him a better matchmaker than Annie now—were so invested in their conversation that they didn't even notice. Annie, though, missed nothing.

"What's that?"

"I think it's their dog."

"Oh, Stella? She's harmless. What are they saying now? I can see her shoulders shaking like she's giggling."

And she *was* giggling. As Eris got back in his truck and began to drive off, Rose walked down the hill to wave him goodbye, all while the dog got more and more intense, standing up on its hind legs so it could press its dinner plate paws into the bark of the tree.

That's when George realized that the greatest danger here wasn't actually the knife-sharp teeth of the white monster about to pounce...but the animal barking and alerting Rose, who was walking closer with every second, to his presence.

His heart thundered in his ears and he leaned slightly towards it, whispering as loud as he thought he could get away with.

"Shh. Pup, *please*. I'm begging you."

Not only would the dog *not* be swayed, but the sudden shift seemed to catch its attention and its full ire, resulting in a full-on bark-fest. Yowling and gnashing of teeth.

And it doesn't matter how—certainly not as far as George's pride was concerned—but the next thing he knew, he was lying on the ground, trying not to get eaten as he fought his way to his feet and the snapping-jawed creature bounded for him.

"Stella! What are you—"

It wasn't like Rose could ignore him then, not when he'd basically fallen at her feet. Her eyes widened as he stood, rubbing the back of his neck sheepishly.

"Uh, hi, Rose."

"Stella, go!"

Easy as that, the animal obeyed, eyeing him cautiously and running off towards one of the far reaches of the property, probably to terrorize a small village of helpless rabbits or something, if George had to wager a guess. Rose narrowed her eyes at him. Seemed she hadn't forgotten their last encounter, when he was at Annie's side for her last two terrible matchmaking attempts.

"What are *you* doing here?"

"I was..." George's throat tightened as he scraped his mind for a lie. "I was spying on Annie Martin."

Rose blinked, her head giving a little shake of confusion. "Annie?"

At first, George wasn't sure why his first impulse had been to lie, to protect Annie and her schemes from her friend. Maybe he was just getting soft. Maybe he just didn't want to deal with an angry Annie. Or maybe there was something else, something he didn't want to admit to himself. Something that had been growing since last night, when she smiled at him like she actually saw him for the first time.

He didn't have time to go into that right now. No time for anything but getting himself out of this mess.

"Please...*please* don't tell her. I heard through the grapevine that she was going to be here today to visit you and I thought..." He shuffled his feet and tried to look repentant. "Well, I thought maybe I could get a lead on a story."

"So you're spying on her?" Rose asked, one suspicious eyebrow quirked. His pulse jumped. "Like you did that one time at her house?"

"I wouldn't call it *spying*—"

"I would. And so would Annie. You know, I'm not going to cover for you if you're being a creep."

George inspected the earth around his boots. Pine needles and stray flower petals did a dizzying dance, a colorful, early fall patchwork routine. He couldn't stand meeting Rose's eyes as she judged him.

He'd been given to understand that the Andersons had almost adopted Annie as a fourth sister, letting her into their lives and their circle as long ago as when the Martins first moved to town. Seeing Rose Anderson angry was a ground-shaking, gossip-stirring, rarest of rare events, but he could imagine that if the rumors were true and Annie *was* as important to the Andersons as she seemed to be, she could dole out endless righteous rage for any slight—real, imagined, or fake.

"Fine! I'm not being a creep. It's just that Annie is trying to set you up and she wanted me to help her—"

Rose's lips thinned into a thin line. "Say no more. That's Annie for you. Always meddling. Don't worry. Your secret is safe with me."

"Really?"

"Yeah. How else am I supposed to get her to stop matchmaking unless I play along for a little bit?"

It was as good a dismissal as any, so George started for the bottom of the hill, where he'd parked his car an hour ago, before this whole affair had started. Only a few steps into his escape, Rose called out to him again.

"George?"

"Yeah?"

He turned to face her, fully aware that this entire conversation was on silent display to Annie, who couldn't do a thing to stop it or to eavesdrop. Rose's eyebrows knit together in concern. She wrung out her hands.

"I know you're writing a story on Annie. I know that's why you're getting close. But please... be gentle with her. Annie may not look it, but she's fragile."

There it was. A reminder of everything that George had been trying not to think about since buying her at that stupid auction. She put on this act of the untouchable girl, both as flat as the image of her on a phone screen and also endlessly complicated. It was like she put on this act, this floor show of existence, so that no one would see who she was beneath it.

She repeatedly insisted that she had no hidden depths, yet everywhere George looked—whether that was deep in her eyes or here, in the concerned face of one of her best friends—he glimpsed suggestions of them, like if he could just break through the thin sheet of ice at her surface, he would plunge into deep league after deep league of Annie Martin.

And there was the problem, wasn't it? Well, one of the problems. On the one hand, from a journalistic point of view, he needed to bring light to that shadowy, concealed part of her. It was his job. It had been his mission since the Martin siblings had arrived here in town. But, despite all of his values and everything he believed in, there was a part of him that dreaded what he would find... and what exposing it would mean.

There they were again. Those inconvenient feelings. Nagging at him again.

George nodded once, trying to maintain something resembling a reassuring smile. "I'll try."

Chapter Eleven

Annie

Annie hadn't been sleeping well. Actually, she hadn't been doing much of anything well. Her house was so incredibly quiet. Even with Monster's little doggo snores, she found herself lying awake at night, staring at the ceiling and listening to the taunting *tick-tock-tick-tock* of the clock down the hall from her bedroom, a sound so reminiscent of a horror movie in its echoing that eventually she ripped the batteries out of the thing and threw it in a pile for donations.

When she and her brother had been growing up, their house had been quiet, too. Their parents were never around, always out somewhere else, which meant that coming home in the afternoons after school were nearly silent affairs. Silently doing their homework. Perhaps the ping of a microwave meal before rustling into bed. It was only once she and Luke moved out together, once he'd begun work on his company and she'd been finally free to do whatever it was she wanted with her life that she decided she'd never let the house be quiet again. In Los Angeles, they'd built part of their home as a working office, where investors and development teams alike could come and meet with Luke, their conversations and arguments filling the hallways with ruckus. She'd host parties and evenings and concerts and events of all descriptions; she injected her life with enough noisy emptiness that eventually, she forgot what it was like to live in the quiet.

The quiet reminded her how alone she was. She hated every passing second of it.

It didn't help that there was something else keeping her awake too. The house echoed her thoughts of George Barnett, her memories of him, and made each one louder and more intense with every returning refrain.

The combination of these two factors—her dying need to escape the silence of her house and the realization that if she spent any more time than was strictly necessary with George Barnett, then she might find herself in a situation she had no hopes of recovering from—led her to offering her help to Rose in her shop that fall afternoon.

Anderson's Flower Market was just that, a small shop on the town's main square, where casual and professional buyers alike could swing by for florals from the nearby Anderson farm in bulk, or they could choose from one of the beautiful arrangements Rose spent most of her days making.

Annie always thought the place should be called Roses by Rose, but unfortunately, none of them listened to any of the many, many rebranding pitches she'd made over the course of their friendship, so Anderson's Flower Market it remained.

Of course, Annie told herself that she wasn't just crashing the shop hours for her own sake, but for Rose's too. Besides the obvious assist of helping out with small chores around the place, since one of her sisters was out on an extended honeymoon and the other was off to parts unknown, exploring the world with her high school sweetheart, Annie took it upon herself to ensure that Rose wasn't too alone, either.

Oh, and there was the small matter of Eris Majors.

"So," Annie began, as she looped the branded Anderson's Flower Market apron around her body and reached for the broom she often used on volunteer days like this to brush up the greenery cuttings Rose left on the floor. "Any big news in your life?"

Annie had never been one for pleasantries, but Rose, who drank a cup of coffee behind her combined marble worktop/checkout counter choked on the liquid, and paused over a large sheet of brown butcher paper upon which she was doodling flower arrangement ideas accompanied by words like "Spooky??" and "Feel the fall."

"I beg your pardon?"

"Anything new in your life? We haven't gotten to talk very much lately."

Sometimes, it occurred to Annie that people underestimated Rose. As the sweeter, quieter, gentler of the three Anderson sisters—and, frankly, when she spent so much time next to Annie herself, who was basically a slightly prettier version of a hurricane in human form—she developed a reputation as just that. Demure and retiring, the kind of girl who wouldn't ever think to say a cross word or refuse to take someone's cleverly laid bait.

But that reputation was just a shield. A scrim used to conceal the clever mind behind the sweet smiles. Just when Annie thought she'd managed to drop the perfect hint that Rose should deliver the details of her romantic life, Rose just lifted one eyebrow, continued with her pencil work, and airily replied:

"Yeah, not since you and George Barnett started getting close."

"Who told you that?"

"Nobody had to tell me. You two have been palling around all over town. You danced at your brother's wedding. I saw the two of you getting cozy in the town square last week. You're working on that article together. I mean, for goodness' sake, Annie, he *bought you at an auction.*"

She whispered that last part like they were characters in a Jane Austen novel and that was a particularly telling piece of the tale. Still, she wondered if there was something else, something Rose wasn't telling her.

What *had* George said to Rose when he'd fallen out of that tree on the Andersons' farm? Annie had watched the entire exchange, but with the walkie-talkies not engaged, she hadn't heard a word of it. That not knowing had been nettling her since yesterday, contributing to her restless sleeplessness, but since their talk hadn't ended in Rose running him off the property at the sparky end of a deer prod, Annie had assumed it was nothing.

Now...she wasn't so sure.

She shrugged and tried to play it cool as she tried to focus her energies and attentions on the stray flora at her feet.

"He was just trying to get under my skin."

Rose smirked. "I wish someone would try to get under my skin that way."

"That can be arranged. But I thought you didn't want your love life to be arranged."

It was Rose's turn to shrug. Her doodling carried her attention away, but every time Annie glanced up from her menial labor, Rose's eyes were far-off and distant, the same dreamy, satisfied, confident look she always got when she talked about love.

"I've always believed that love would find me. And even if it doesn't, I'm still going to be happy. Having or not having some man isn't going to change that. Men are like ice cream. Nice to have, but not necessary for your overall health and happiness."

"So, you're telling me that there isn't one guy in this entire town who might be a little step up from ice cream? A little better than nice?"

Please tell me that Eris Majors is better than ice cream. Please tell me someone *could be. I need a little hope here, Rose. Anything to help me believe that I can make love happen for you.*

"I've known them all since I was a kid. *None* of them are better than ice cream and some of them are even worse."

"And why is that, exactly?"

At this point, Annie fully gave up on the prospect of gathering up the dozens of little green bits from the hardwood flooring. She was desperate to find Rose love. Rose deserved it. But Annie wasn't going to get anywhere if Rose was going to be so stubborn.

"Because you can't just fall for somebody because they're there and they're convenient. You have to fall for somebody because they see you. And because in this big and lonely world they make you feel less alone."

"You're the kindest, most big-hearted person I've ever met, Rose. I doubt that there's no one in this town who could make you feel all of that."

For some reason, Annie's mind flashed to George. With his big, toothy grin and his spitfire wit and his shabby secondhand sweaters.

She shook her head, wishing she could clear it as easily as her broom could clear this shop.

"If he's here, he's been very good at hiding," Rose said, simply. Unhelpfully. At last, she set down her pencil. "Is that why you came here today? To question me about my love life? Because you know, two can play that game. What's really going on with you and George Barnett?"

"You said it. We're working together on this possible story for his newspaper. That's all. Nothing more," Annie said, repeating the same lie she'd been telling everyone who would listen since they'd started this little arrangement of theirs.

"I don't know. I heard about the two of you together at the Bronze Boot. Sounded like he saw you. Like he made you feel a little less alone."

Rose was good. Too good. So good that Annie wondered if she even knew she was angling for gossip or if she genuinely, actually, completely cared about Annie finding that special someone.

She hoped it wasn't the latter. If Rose Anderson was waiting for Annie to fall in love and for someone to fall in love with her, she was going to be waiting a very, very long time.

"I don't really go in for that stuff."

"You just lectured me about finding love!"

"Yeah, it's good for *you*. And for Harper and Luke and May and Tom and whatever guy is lucky enough to sweep you off your feet. But I'm just not…" *I'm just not good enough. I'm not* enough *enough.* No, that was no good. Annie couldn't say that, not out loud. It was too dour and gray. She repainted the truth with a more colorful varnish. "I'm the matchmaking type, you know? Not the match-made type."

"If you say so," Rose conceded, clearly not wanting any more of an argument than she'd already gotten. Mercifully, she returned to her drawings and her pencils. "But I think George Barnett likes you."

I think George Barnett likes you. Annie wanted to parrot the words back at her in a mocking tone, but truth be told, Annie had the same suspicion from the moment she came to the window and found him looking up at her as though she was a fallen star. But something like that wasn't possible for her. It wouldn't ever be possible. Giving in to hope for things like love and romance only led to the most painful kind of heartbreak.

Annie wouldn't let herself get sucked into it, no matter how her enduringly moony-eyed romantic of a friend swooned over the possibilities.

"You sound awfully confident for someone who couldn't be more wrong."

"He does!"

"He's using me for a story. He wants to get close to my brother. And he wants my matchmaking expertise for this—" A light bulb illuminated in the front of Annie's mind, flooding her with clarity. That was it. Matchmaking. Annie didn't have to pretend she wasn't finding the perfect love for Rose; she just had to make it *seem* like that was true. She just had to be smarter about this than she had been before. Keeping her vibe as casual as she could possibly keep it when she was practically overflowing with excitement, she approached Rose's desk like a lion tamer approaching a wild beast. "Hey. Can I ask you a huge favor?"

"...What?"

It wasn't an agreement or anything even close to it, but it *was* a tacit surrender on the whole subject of George Barnett's feelings for her. That was good enough as far as Annie was concerned.

"So, George and I are working together on this story about finding love in a small town. You know, the agony and emotional isolation of small-town life and romance. All that click-bait-y jazz. So, we were thinking about doing this speed-dating night."

"Let me guess. You need me to go to make the numbers even."

Bingo. Annie laid it on thick this time, really piling up the taunting as she spoke. She'd had plenty of experience using this *well I guess you're just chicken if you don't want to do this* tactic over the years of trying to get her brother to show his face at public events, so she knew how to play it.

"I mean, if you're *so sure* that love isn't going to happen with anyone here in town, then what's the harm? You'll go, you'll have a few drinks, and then you'll be back home all snug in bed with your copy of *Flower* magazine before ten."

Despite anticipating one of the moments-long stare-downs she usually had when she pulled this trick on her brother, Annie only watched as Rose considered the proposal, then brightened with her usual soft, pink blush of excitement.

"You know what? Sure. I'll help you out. But I have one condition."

"What is it?"

Rose's small smile turned into a taunting, self-satisfied grin. Leaning across her desk, she pointed her pencil squarely at Annie's heart, as if it were some kind of magic wand that she could use to reawaken it. "Admit that George Barnett likes you. Even a little bit."

When Annie hesitated, Rose scoffed.

"Come on! You have to admit it! He must like you."

"Believe me," Annie said, a little more bitterly than she'd wanted to. "He doesn't."

Because no one can. Not really.

Chapter Twelve

George

Annie assured him that this farce was going to be the way to Rose Anderson's heart, but George just couldn't see it. Speed dating? Really? What was this, the eighties? Had everyone's phones collectively died? Had every dating app in the world suddenly gone dark at once?

And, more importantly, what wily scheme would she concoct next? If this didn't work, what other dated romcom gimmicks would she rope him into? Would they have to find Rose a romantic pen pal, one who was also her enemy in real life? Would they have to send Rose to the top of the Empire State Building to find her true love? Would they have to compose a Disney-style musical number and accompanying flash mob?

He didn't know. All he knew was that one night he was drinking alone on his couch, reading a Dorothy Thompson biography while *Broadcast News* played in the background, and the next he found himself thoroughly entangled in Annie Martin's life. And he wasn't entirely sure—much to his own shock—that he hated it.

Le Chat Bleu, one of the hip wine bars in the center of Hillsboro, was the kind of rustic, shabby-chic gem that people came to

Northern California to find. With worn leather seating and tables made from used wine barrels, the entire place was illuminated with soft overhead lighting and what appeared to be roughly thousands of candles. Usually closed on a Wednesday night, Annie had hired the venue—which they'd given her for the generous price of *free* as long as she supplied her own food and booze and made sure to clean up once they were done... that was small-town hospitality for you—and when George arrived to help her set up—something he offered before she'd even asked, yet another shocking development considering he *rarely* did extra work unless it was for a story—he'd found her setting out even more candles and staining the dark-washed wood surfaces with blood red rose petals from a tote bag she carried at her side.

The candlelight caught every imperfection and every feature of her delicate face. But the glow he saw in her came from somewhere deeper, somewhere within her.

That wasn't sentimentality, he assured himself. That was just fact.

For a moment he stood in the doorway, watching her move through the space as she hummed some sappy love song under her breath. He could almost place the tune, but the name escaped him. Possibly because he was too busy drinking in the way her hips swayed as she walked, the way her fingers caressed the flower petals as she sprinkled them like fairy dust all around her.

It was when the song reached its chorus, and the lyrics were all about stars and moonlight and forever, that George snapped out of it.

"So this seems like a good idea to you?"

Annie didn't balk at his presence. Her lips *did* slip into a small smile, though. "Yeah, why wouldn't it?"

"Because it's objectively a terrible idea."

Entering the wine bar fully, George let the door close behind him so he could help her with her task. Picking up a discarded lighter nearby, he began the slow and steady work of illuminating the candles she hadn't gotten to yet.

"If that's how you use the word objectively in your stories, then I think you may need to get a refund from whatever fake college you got your journalism degree from."

"I went to Stanford."

"Well, it's not Northwestern, is it?" She smirked before continuing. "Now, why do you think that?"

"Why do I think I went to Stanford?"

"No, why do you think this is *objectively*," she threw up sarcastic air quotations around that word, "a bad idea?"

"Because you can't control all the variables."

"I controlled all the variables I needed to control. I set up this night. I invited you, me, Rose, and Eris. With only the four of us, it won't be much for speed dating, so we'll just get to sit back and watch as the sparks fly between the two of them. It's the perfect plan."

Hm. What was that old saying about the best-laid plans? For a moment, George paused in his candle lighting to think about the woman in front of him. She wasn't stupid. She had to know that a million things could go wrong tonight. That her scheme could easily fail in any number of ways. And while she was optimistic about everything—well, optimistic about everything but him, it seemed—she wasn't the kind of person to blindly storm forward without considering all of the consequences.

He narrowed his eyes slightly as he tried to square all of this information with the woman currently re-applying her lipstick in the reflection of a polished silver candlestick.

"Do all of your plans go perfectly according to plan?"

"Usually."

An alarm bell went off in the back of George's mind at that answer. He knew its familiar ring all too well. *Liar.* "Is that so?"

"Yes. It's *so.*"

"Interesting."

Retiring her lipstick to the bottom of her purse, Annie cleared her throat. "Why...why would you say it like that?"

George, still pretending to be useful, continued with the candles even as he could feel her still, abrupt attention from all the way across the room.

"Who have you match-made before? Like, who were your first subjects?"

"Harper Anderson and my brother."

"I don't even know them and I know that's not true. He worked on her farm for ages trying to get into her good graces. Everyone knows that. Them falling in love was inevitable and definitely not your doing."

He wasn't trying to accuse her of lying. But he couldn't stand here and let his curiosity go unanswered. There was something else here, something more than she was admitting, maybe even to herself. He needed to find it.

"May Anderson and Tom Riley."

"Come on. Everyone and their brother knew that you were trying to set both of them up with rebounds from L.A."

Turning on him, Annie sent her skirts flying like a villain's cape in a sci-fi movie. She tensed her jaw and set upon him, maneuvering across the room straight towards him. Of course, she tried to couch everything in a joking, lighter-than-air tone to hide the fact that he'd really struck a nerve, but by now, he could see almost straight through that act.

"What are you getting at? I didn't invite you here to nitpick my past successes."

"Well, considering your first two selections for Rose Anderson ended up drenched in punch and fountain water, I'm just saying that it might be time to consider that they haven't *been* successes. Did you ever think of that?"

"Are you saying—"

"I'm saying you might be a bad matchmaker."

The clicking of her heels abruptly halted. George's heartbeat stopped with it. Yeah, he'd wanted to strike a nerve, but he didn't want to spark World War III here. And if the set of her shoulders was any indication, she was already drawing up battle plans.

"And you think you could do better?" Annie scoffed. "Please. You don't understand anything about the human heart."

"I understand how to take a girl on a pretty good date," he reminded her with a smirk, tossing her own words from their Bronze Boot night back in her face.

Annie brushed away invisible dust from the pleats of her skirt before turning to the tables she was supposed to be busy setting. "I never should have told you that."

"Why, because it was true?"

"No, because it's humiliating,"

She's just trying to protect herself, George told himself in an attempt to quiet the *ping* of hurt. *Besides, it shouldn't matter if she likes you or not.* "It's humiliating to like me?"

Annie looked up from the napkins she'd been hastily folding into intricate pope's hat designs. "No...I...I didn't...Listen, I didn't say that."

"Ah, so the princess really *does* like me," he teased.

"I didn't say that either. Stop putting words in my mouth."

Oh, there are many, many more things I would rather be doing with your mouth.

George straightened. The thought was so intense and so bold that he couldn't help it. The force of his own desire for her shocked him down to his core. Maybe it *did* matter to him if she liked him or not.

When he didn't respond to her, Annie tossed her hair over one shoulder and gave him a dismissive wave of her hand.

"You know what? I don't have to listen to this. In fact, it might even be better if you're not here tonight because then Rose and Eris will feel awkward with me as the third wheel and ask me to leave so they can drink wine and stare into each other's eyes all night."

Once again, alarm bells went off in the back of George's mind. There was something going on here that she wasn't explaining. There was a truth hiding just beneath her beautiful, optimistic surface. No one could be this naive. No one could be as smart and worldly-wise as Annie proved herself to be *and* believe that this contrived scheme would actually work the way she'd planned it.

He'd been watching as she flitted from task to task, from justification to explanation, and now he watched as she turned her attention to the perfectly acceptable flower arrangements dotting each of the wine barrel tables.

She was panicking, he realized. He was getting far too close to the truth for her comfort.

He also realized that they'd had this argument before. He'd pushed her too hard and searched too clinically for the truth before, a search that she'd rightfully demanded he apologize for. If he was a smart man, or a better one, he would have stopped there and just hoped on hope that one day, eventually, she would trust him enough to tell him what he wanted to know on her own.

But he couldn't just leave it be. He needed to know.

"You don't really think that's going to happen, do you?"

"Well. It certainly *could* happen."

"It also certainly *could* happen that the invading aliens from *Independence Day* could descend upon all of us right now and without Will Smith to save us, we'd be goners. But I'd say the probability was low."

"Are you going to help me with the flowers or not?"

"I'm just saying that you're a smart, clever, funny, organized, determined, resourceful woman and you're spending all of your time taking Instagram pictures of green smoothies and failing spectacularly at finding love for your friends which, by your own admission, is the one thing you want to do above everything else in this world. I am clearly missing something, but I don't know what it is."

"You know, I don't understand why everyone thinks that creating pretty things and enjoying them is such an empty pursuit," she said, her fingers trailing along the petals of the floral bouquet in her hands. The pinks and yellows of the arrangement brought out brilliant silvers in her eyes. "I actually *like* taking pictures of sunsets and yoga mats and pink water bottles. Just because men don't like it doesn't mean it isn't valuable."

"Point taken. I'm sorry," he said, and he meant it. "But the matchmaking. It's a waste of your time and your talents. You just aren't very good at it."

"I'll have you know I also got people in L.A. together."

"Really?"

"Yeah." Annie had now been rearranging the flowers in her hand for a full two minutes, and she continued to fuss over it instead of meeting his gaze. "Like... Just... so many people."

"Who?"

"You don't know them," she said, with an air of finality.

"I might. What are their names?"

"... Brad and Jennifer. And, uh, David and Neil."

George suppressed a laugh, but only barely. "Those are the names of two celebrity power couples, one of which hasn't been together since at least 2005."

"How did you know that?"

"I read the tabloid magazines when you're in them. Sometimes I even pay attention to the parts that you aren't."

"Why would you do that?"

He shrugged. "Sometimes it's nice to keep up with the Kardashians."

"No, I mean, why would you read magazines when I'm in them?"

When she glanced up at him then and their eyes met, George's heart hesitated in its normal beating. Annie was looking at him with such trust, as if she really expected him to come out and say something ridiculous like, *because I like you and I want to know more about you.*

Which was true. But he could never say that. Not out loud. Not even to himself.

His mind flashed back to Rose and their conversation on the flower farm just the other day. *Be gentle with her. Annie may not look it, but she's fragile.* George still wasn't any closer to figuring out what that meant, but one thing was absolutely certain.

He *was* going to write a story about Luke Martin. And it would be devastating and appropriately damning and everything that a good exposé ought to be.

Even now, he didn't know how to be gentle with her. How to acknowledge her fragility the way that Rose wanted him to. He was poking and prodding and taunting her over and over again, trying to provoke the truth from her lips. If Annie was starting to feel anything for him, or if she suspected that he was feeling something for her, then that would eventually break her heart. He needed to let her down gently. He needed to remind her that this couldn't last.

"I am still going to do a story on your brother. And you are a big part of that story. Aren't you?"

"Right. The story. Of course." Annie blinked and stepped away from the bar, heading over to straighten an already perfectly straight flower arrangement on a nearby table. Hurt stung her voice, but she kept her head high and her shoulders back, just as she always did. George knew she needed this, but now that it was done, he couldn't help but feel a little sick about the whole thing. "Well. I hope you're getting plenty of what you came here for."

"Hey, now—"

When the front door of the bar slammed open and a cowbell over the thing cut off the end of George's protest, he was almost glad for it. He didn't know what he was going to say anyway.

But then, he looked up and actually saw *who* had interrupted them, and any trace of gratitude slipped away. Rose had indeed come tonight, just like Annie had promised.

And just like George had promised, things hadn't gone to Annie's perfectly laid plans. Because when Rose entered, she didn't do it alone. She did it as the head of a twenty-person parade, all of whom excitedly slipped in behind her.

Beside him, George heard Annie mutter, "Oh, you've got to be kidding me."

Rose, for her part, beamed as she made her way through the now crowded wine bar towards them. "Hi, Annie! Oh, good to see you, George. I really hope you don't mind. I told a few friends about your article for the *Hillsboro Gazette* and lots of people wanted to help contribute! And we wanted to make sure the speed-dating numbers lined up!"

Chapter Thirteen

Annie

It was fine. Really. It was fine. Annie had faced worst disasters in her amateur party-planning career. There was the time they'd had to move an entire masquerade ball to a basement because of a nearby tornado warning or that time she'd had to secretly whisk an aging celebrity away to the hospital in disguise because she thought she'd had a cardiac episode and didn't want anyone to know. (She was fine; she just wasn't used to dubstep music and confused the loud pulsing noises coming from the speakers with an erratic heartbeat.)

Hosting an extra twenty people at what was meant to be a party for, at most, four people, wasn't impossible, and for the most part, Annie thought she'd managed to pull it off without much of a hitch.

Thankfully, with the way the numbers shook out, Annie was able to participate mostly as an observer and occasional drink-fetcher, keeping time as the speed daters ran through partners and conversational topics. From the outskirts, she watched as person after person poured their hearts out to George about their dating struggles—apparently Rose had really convinced them all about their lie about working together so they could write a story about romance in small towns—and tried not to think about her own struggles. Oh, not with getting a date for herself, but for Rose.

As the night moved on, and as the wine bottles continued to stack up, a handful of people started to drift off. Bright and early wake-up calls the next morning. Babysitters waiting. The usual stuff.

Annie was more than happy to accommodate, of course. No one needed to stay here; she waved them all off with a smile and well wishes . . . until she realized she was going to have to join in the fun to even out the numbers.

And guess who just so happened to have an open seat across from him?

That's right. George Barnett. The one person she didn't want to talk to right now. Well aware that the attention of the entire room was upon her, Annie smiled down at him as though everything was perfectly fine.

"George," she said, brightly. "Do you want to come out of the rotation so the numbers are even?"

He had the gall to smirk at her, as if he knew exactly what she was after. "And miss all of the fun? I don't think so. Come on. You haven't been properly wooed all evening."

She should have known that he wasn't going to be merciful, especially given the little power play he'd forced her to endure earlier this evening. This time, though, he wasn't alone in trying to bend her will. Rose was right there, a few tables down from him, half a glass of wine deep and very, very happy to make Annie do whatever it was that made her the least comfortable.

"I agree. I think you should join in, Annie. Live a little."

Peer pressure. Annie was really good at giving it out. She was even better at spotting it when others were doing it to her. Because of that, she knew how powerful a weapon it was, knew that she wasn't going to be able to just wave her hands and make this go away. No, unlike what all of the after-school specials had taught her, she was going to have to give in to this peer pressure.

That didn't mean she had to like it. Pressing the button on her timer, she invited the group to commence with their time before taking a seat across from the infuriating, eighth wonder of the jerk world.

This was the bachelorette auction and the fireman's garden party all over again. She had to play nice in public when what she really wanted to do was storm away in the other direction and not speak to him, maybe ever again.

Did the thought of not talking to him, even in theory, kind of break her heart a little? Absolutely. But wasn't heartbreak already inevitable in this dance that they were doing together? Like he'd said...he was going to do a story on her family. He was, if her experience with journalists was anything to speak of, trying to ruin her family.

Their story was doomed before they'd even started writing it. And that fact, clawing and nagging persistently in the back of her mind, made her want to hate him more and more every time he opened his mouth, despite the fact that her traitorous heart seemed to be feeling more and more for him instead.

"Hi, my name is George Barnett," he said, extending his hand as she took her seat, a hand she didn't take and had no intentions of doing so. He practically chirped his greeting. "I'm a journalist here in Hillsboro and I'm—"

"Oh, I know who you are."

"Yes, but you said you needed to introduce yourself to everyone, even the people who you already know, and tell them one fact about yourself. You aren't going to break your own rules, are you?"

If he'd pulled that line on anyone else, she might have laughed. But as it was, she wasn't exactly in a laughing mood right about now.

"My name is Annie Martin. I'm a social media marketer and philanthropist, and I split my time between here and Los Angeles and I just couldn't give up my matcha lattes."

Apparently pleased with the fact that she was saying anything at all instead of just ignoring him for five minutes straight, George reached for one of the cutesy conversation starters Annie had drawn up this morning. "And now we pick a card."

The thrill of panic shot up Annie's spine. She'd created the conversation cards when she'd thought that this entire thing would just be between Rose and Eris, when they were all supposed to be suggestive and romantic. The last thing she wanted was George asking her if she thought beaches or mountains were more conducive to romance or whether she thought Italian food or steak was better for a first date.

She didn't want to think about running away to the mountains with him or whether he'd still want to kiss her if she had garlic pasta breath. She didn't want to be thinking about him romantically at all, especially not when he'd just made it very clear that his interest in her started and ended at the story he was writing about Luke.

"We don't have to talk."

"Of course we do."

"Because of your story?" Annie snapped, revealing more hurt than she'd intended to.

"Because it's speed dating," George said, his eyes softer, more apologetic than they had been before. His fingers hovered over the cards. "And that's what you do at speed dating."

"Fine." She rolled her eyes. "Read it."

Greedily, he snapped up a card and inspected it with a wistful expression on his face, reading it once for himself then deigning to repeat it out loud.

"If you have a hobby, like, say, matchmaking or meddling extensively in people's lives, what exactly caused you to go down that particular life path?"

"The card doesn't say that. Give it to me."

He pulled the pink paper out of her reach before she could snatch it, drawing up his face in a scandalized expression. "You don't trust your speed-dating partner? Now, that doesn't sound like the foundation of a happy relationship."

"No. And I'm sure you're glad that I don't. What does the card really say?"

She obviously couldn't see her own expression, but whatever look she fixed squarely on him must have been terrifying enough that he sobered up slightly and actually read the text on the card out loud.

Only...when he spoke the real words out loud, she immediately wished, with everything that was in her, that he hadn't.

"Would you be willing to tell me the story of your first kiss?"

Kiss. The word struck her squarely in the chest with the violence of a half-dozen speeding cars. Then, the full question truly sunk in. She'd written it as a fun and flirty conversation starter for someone else, *not* for George and certainly not for her.

Her first kiss hadn't been lovely or romantic. It had been terrible. A memory not worth thinking about.

"No. Next question."

"It says, alternatively, would you be willing to tell me the story of your *best* kiss?"

The card most certainly did not say that. She knew because she'd written every last one of them and even in her most deranged matchmaking state, she couldn't have written a question so invasive.

For a brief moment, she indulged in memories of kisses gone by and tried to think of a single one that stood out from the rest of the crowd—in a positive way, that is. She could think of plenty that would earn a place on the "worst kisses of all time" list, but not many that she even would have considered decent, much less *the best*.

Instead of word-vomiting all of that in George's direction, though, she flipped the question back around to him. To her surprise, he didn't balk or try to weasel out of the truth when she did.

"What's yours?"

"They were the same. Jeni Zhao, tenth grade. You never forget your first love. Or your first heartbreak. I thought she was going for a kiss but she was just reaching past me to grab a soda so I kissed her ear instead. Got called 'lobelover' for the rest of the year. Now, what about you? What's your best kiss?"

His truth was disarming. Told so bluntly—full of humor and heart and even a little bit of melancholy—that she couldn't help but stare at her hands and stumble out a meager truth of her own.

"I don't think I've ever had one."

"Everyone's had a best kiss."

She shrugged and tried to hurry them along to the next topic. This was going to be the longest five minutes of her life.

"Not me. Do I get to ask a question now?"

Reaching out for the card, she tried to force the change. But a warm, big, strong hand reached out and covered her own, stopping her in her tracks and drawing her eyes straight to him.

This wasn't like before, when he was digging beneath the surface of her for some cold, callous purpose. This was softer, a little more desperate, even. Like he really couldn't believe what he was hearing. Every word was low and deliberate, electric and magnetic. She found herself leaning further and further across the table and into him with each passing breath.

"You mean to tell me that you, Annie Martin, queen of all she surveys and beauty icon of her generation, hasn't ever been kissed so sweetly that she could cry? Never had someone run their hand up your cheek and look into your eyes like you're the only person in the universe who understands them, and then kiss you like they want you to feel the way that they love you for that?"

Annie tried not to think of her heart as a metaphorical thing, as a piece of herself that could get ripped or torn or stomped on. That made life a little bit easier. But in that moment, she knew, no matter how much she wished it wasn't true, that her heart was squarely in his hands.

It hurt more than she was willing to admit, being here, wanting to kiss him and knowing that she was nothing more than a piece in a story he wanted to tell. This moment should have been romantic. It should have been the culmination of every stolen glance in his direction, every laugh that warmed her from the inside out, every brush of her fingertips against his skin. It should have been the fulfillment of the promise their dancing at the Bronze Boot made for them. That they were more than just two people who accidentally collided in this vast universe, like two electrons that accidentally bump into each other in their random paths around an atom.

This moment should have been a symphony. It should have been a Criterion classic. It should have been opera.

Instead, it was nothing but disappointment. And bitter, dashed hope.

Her heart may have been in his hands, yes, but with every moment he spent looking at her, asking her why she hadn't yet been kissed the way she wanted him to kiss her now, he tightened his grip.

"Was that how Jeni Zhao kissed?"

"Annie," he muttered, the word almost stern, a sharp rebuke trying to get her to return to the point.

She adjusted the pearl necklace hanging at the base of her throat. All of a sudden, the thing felt too tight. Choking. "No. I've never been kissed like that."

"Why not?"

Because you never asked me. And you never will. All of the insecurities Annie had ever felt about herself festered in this moment, digging beneath her skin and invading her, right down to the very core of her being. The way he stared at her, it was like she was completely on display for him. As if he was going to guess at her every secret and hidden doubt if she so much as blinked wrong.

"I guess... I'm just not good enough to be kissed like that. No big deal."

George's voice was low, intense. Truthful. "It is a big deal. It's a very big deal."

The hairs on the back of Annie's neck stood on end. This was torture. She wanted it to end, and quickly. "Why do you even care how I've been kissed? Another anecdote for your story? I don't think readers are going to have any interest—"

"No, because I'm a man who's inclined toward justice and what's right. And no one ever kissing you the way you deserve to be kissed... there's no justice in that at all."

Their eyes met across the table. The flickering candlelight caught every feature of that face she found so beautiful, everything she would never be able to have. It was all so very close, and yet... love felt further away than it had ever been before.

He didn't just have her heart in his hands. He was stealing it. And she had no hope of ever getting it back.

She needed to get out. Now. She couldn't do this, not for another minute. Not for another second. Forget what the timer said. Shoving away from the table, Annie plastered her old, reliable, and thoroughly plastic smile upon her face, clapped her hands, and addressed the mingling crowd.

"Alright, everyone! Have we gone completely around the circle? Oh, good! Well, I hope we've made a few love connections tonight or at least found lots of new friends here in town! Unfortunately, the venue needs us out now, licensing laws, you know. So thank you all so much for coming! Good night!"

Get away from here. Go, go, go. Without staying behind for pleasantries and goodbyes, Annie made a beeline for the bar, where she'd stashed all of the clean-up materials. Maybe if she looked busy, no one would try to talk to her. Maybe she could survive this.

Of course, George was not so easily swayed. As bemused townsfolk exited the bar, some exchanging numbers, he made for the bar, something like regret written into the shadow-drawn lines of his painfully handsome face.

"Annie—"

Smile, Annie. Smile and pretend everything is fine. That's what you're good at, isn't it? Yes, it was what she was good at. So why, all of a sudden, did she want to cry? "It's okay, George. Rose is going to help me clean up." Annie looked down at the crate in her hands, trying to avoid her own reflection in the plastic spray-bottle of surface cleaner. "You should go back to your office. See how that story of yours is coming."

Part of her hoped he would stay anyway, that he would fight for her and tell her that the story wasn't the real reason he was there, that he really did feel something for her and that he would forget about the whole thing if only she would kiss him right now, right this minute.

But when she looked up again...George was gone.

Chapter Fourteen

George

For the next few days after the speed-dating incident, George did exactly what Annie asked him to do. He practically locked himself in his office and returned to his story and his Annie-less life.

Strange how there was so much less color in it without her. How the fall weather seemed sharper, crueler, when he was walking alone instead of at her side.

He'd never realized how gray and muted his office was. Monochrome newsprint hung up onto graying concrete and brick walls. Dulled silver finishes and a well-worn silver laptop. He never thought he would miss Annie's bold, floral prints and the brilliantly colored sunglasses and nail polishes that finished off her wardrobe, but there he was.

For a few fleeting, weak moments, he even considered going down to the Anderson Flower Market, Rose's shop, just across the street to purchase some flowers and liven the place up, but the risk of running into Annie there was just too high. He couldn't impose on her now, not when he knew she was still recovering from their last encounter.

Annie never had a problem telling people when she wanted to see them. When George was welcome back into her life, she would no doubt let him know. For now, he would just have to make himself content with throwing himself back into his work, his coffee, his takeout meals.

And his research. The research was the most important thing.

As he stared down at stacks of school and business records he'd been able to amass from AppeX Industries and the Martin family, he searched for any hint of connective tissue that might link them and some kind of grand conspiracy, some kind of deep and hidden secret that he could uncover.

Families with this much power, with this much money...no matter how good they seemed to be on the outside, they *had* to have something to hide. They always did.

Still, the longer and the harder he looked at the sheets, the blurrier the numbers and letters became. The less connected everything became. This hadn't ever happened before on a story, not once. Something about this one was different. Something was broken in this story, or with his desire to finish it. He just couldn't put his finger on what part, exactly, needed fixing.

Somewhere between a copy of a paper Annie had submitted to a state literacy fair in tenth grade and a mostly redacted and rescinded police report regarding a "domestic incident" at Luke Martin's first apartment in Los Angeles, his office door slammed open, revealing Mynette, standing there as though she was an angry principal barging in on an illegal Dungeons and Dragons club operating during school hours.

Apparently, the entire office had decided to collectively give up on knocking.

"What's wrong with you?"

"What do you mean, what's wrong with me?"

Oh, God, it wasn't really that obvious, was it? The last thing he needed was everyone in the office micromanaging his, admittedly, staggered productivity.

"Man, I have to edit all of your work and you've been sending me more spelling errors than a kindergartener trying to write *Faust*. You're never that messy. What is wrong with you?"

Of course. They weren't concerned about the fact that he'd rolled in here half-awake and fallen asleep at his desk twice. They weren't concerned about him. They were concerned about his punctuation. George returned to his paperwork, shuffling around timelines and pieces of the puzzle in the hope that something, anything, would soon click.

He'd been invested in the story of Luke Martin and his place in Hillsboro for almost two years. He couldn't afford to confess that there wasn't anything there. He had to find something. He knew there was something there.

"I'm just focusing on this Martin family thing," he muttered.

"Not very much, apparently. I haven't seen your lady-shaped shadow around here in a while."

"I don't need to be around her all of the time. It's healthy to have a little journalistic distance," he said, despite the fact that his heart thrummed painfully at the thought. He knew a little distance was good for both of them, but still . . . he missed her. Horror of horrors, he actually missed Annie Martin, the woman he used to think was a stuck-up, spoiled, arrogant little princess.

"Not when you want to marry her and have lots of babies, it isn't."

"Mynette!"

The woman in question held up her hands in a mockery of surrender, even as her eyes hardened slightly. "Just saying. Not that she's good enough for you, anyway."

Mynette stared at a spot on the concrete floors, while George tried to come to terms with two things at the exact same time. One: everyone thought he was in love with Annie Martin, a love that apparently kept him from doing his job. And two: Mynette very much resented that.

"You *really* don't like her, do you?"

"I *really* think she's had everything handed to her on a silver platter. Some people just have it so easy in this life while the rest of us have to swim through so much garbage to get even a sliver of something worthwhile."

George's heartstrings thrummed again, but not for the same reasons. The first time, it had been because he missed Annie. This time, it was because he felt guilty for it. He swallowed hard, trying to bottle up the sudden conflict rising up in him and threatening to overtake everything. Since he and Annie had started hanging out together, he'd become so wrapped up in her that he'd forgotten why he'd taken on this assignment in the first place, why it was so important to him.

This wasn't just about taking down some rich family for kicks or for the sake of his career, though he didn't mind the level of prestige and success that it would bring him. No, it was about fairness. It was about making sure that no one was playing with a stacked deck.

"Well, that's why we do what we do, right?" he said, his voice thick. "To bring back some kind of justice. To level the playing field."

"I guess so." Mynette's shoulders slackened and she pressed the full weight of herself against the doorframe, as if she'd lost all of her will to fight. George knew the feeling. "What do you think they're hiding?"

"I don't know. It's just that in my experience, anything that looks perfect really isn't."

"And you think your experience is universal?" she asked.

Over the years, George had always wondered why Mynette hadn't gone into journalism herself. She always knew the exact right—and, at the same time, the exact *wrong*—questions to ask. Suddenly, under her stare, he felt like a butterfly pinned up on a wall, trapped beneath the magnifying glass of a calculating scientist.

He knew why he was doing this with the Martins and their company and their sudden dominance over the city of Hillsboro. He knew that he did this job to protect the little guy, to defeat the giants who would otherwise threaten fairness and justice. And he knew that if there was something wrong with the way that the Martins and their family did business or conducted their lives, then he would use every resource at his disposal to expose them.

All of that was true. But, at the same time, something else was true. He fiddled with the pen in his hands, an ancient fountain pen created by some company in France that his father had given to him on the day he'd started high school. Why had he kept the thing after all this time? He fiddled with the shiny, blue stone cap, focusing on his own reflection in the polished surface.

"I don't know. Maybe…"

Finding an ending to that sentence that didn't make him sound like a weak, fanciful coward proved more difficult than he'd expected. When George found that he couldn't finish for a long moment, Mynette prodded him again.

"Maybe what?"

"Maybe I'm hoping it isn't. Maybe I'm hoping that I'm wrong. That we're wrong. About the Martins and their company and... well, everything."

If there was nothing there, he wouldn't get the prestige he craved and he would have wasted two years of his life chasing a ghost story. But at least he wouldn't have to one day look Annie Martin in the eye and tell her he thought that she and her brother were crooks who'd taken advantage of a broken system. At least he'd always get to think of her the way he did now—as a beautiful, wonderful, heart-stopping mystery of a woman.

Mynette clucked her tongue as she stepped into the room, pulling the door closed behind her. The action was so calculated and deliberate that it drew all of George's attention. "You'd better not hope that."

"Why?"

"Because I have it on good authority that our esteemed boss and editor has been talking to some pretty big names about picking up this story and taking it national."

It was a bombshell piece of news. Bigger than any he'd ever reported on. His heart roared in his ears as everything he'd ever wanted, everything he'd ever dreamed of getting, was suddenly dangled just out of his reach. He wanted to be a nationally recognized journalist, a newshound who exposed wrongdoing and brought evil that festered in the darkness out into the light. It had been his driving force for so long.

If what he thought Mynette was saying was true, then this story could be his chance to get all of that.

He'd thought that was the case all along, but now ... now it was real. Tangible. So close that he could almost hear the distant echoes of his Pulitzer speech.

"Are you sure?" he asked, his voice a low mutter. He didn't want to speak any louder for fear that his voice would crack with excitement.

"Yeah. It's just a possibility at the moment, but it's definitely something in the works. You could finally get the big-time recognition you've always wanted. Finally do all that good you want your work to do."

"Wow."

George leaned back in his chair, his mind racing. This was the big break he'd been dreaming about. This was how he would get everything he'd ever wanted—the desk in a New York City office or a Washington bureau. The awards. The accolades.

The problem with all of those images? Annie Martin wasn't in a single one of them. A sickening, metallic taste filled his mouth.

"You're not getting cold feet, are you?" Mynette asked, after another moment of interminable silence.

"No. No, not at all. I'm just..." George drank in a slow, deep breath. It shouldn't matter to him what happened to Annie. Her proximity to him shouldn't affect him in the slightest. He tried to shake it off as best he could and present a strong front to Mynette. "Just processing what all of that would mean."

"I think it means that whatever you're doing here needs to be put on hold until you go back to Annie Martin and get a real angle on this story. This could be big, and I think she's going to be your in to finding whatever it is that the Martins are hiding."

There she went again, strong with the journalistic instincts. She'd always said she liked being behind the secretarial desk, that she liked the safety and security of it, but George had to wonder why she wasn't sitting behind *his* desk instead.

Not that it mattered, anyway. Annie had made it clear that they were through for now; he wasn't going to push her again. He didn't want to become some stalker-creep who hid in her bushes and waited for a chance to stumble back into her life. Besides, she already thought he was just in this for the journalistic doors she could open for him. It wouldn't do him any good to show back up at her house and start asking questions again. She'd see straight through him, just like she always did.

"I don't think she wants me around right now."

"When has that ever stopped you before?"

"She's not just the subject of a story. She's—"

Thankfully, Mynette cut him off before he could say something truly stupid, like that she was someone he actually cared about. He wasn't the kind of guy who had room in his heart to care about people. He cared about ideals and principles and the harrowing act of dragging a cosmically imbalanced universe back into equilibrium.

"Please don't tell me she's more than that."

George readjusted his reply, bearing in mind the fact that he had a reputation to uphold and journalistic standards to meet. "She's just not someone I want to stalk. I don't want to go through her garbage cans. I don't want to investigate her personal life."

"But you *do* want a Pulitzer. You *do* want the truth. You do want to use your brains and your skill to actually make the world a better place for people. Don't you?"

Don't you? It was a challenge, not a question. Even worse, she wasn't done.

"You've never let your personal feelings get in the way of a story before, George. Don't let them now."

"I won't," George vowed. "I promise."

But an hour later, when he was once again sitting alone in his office, staring down at a stack of papers that were no closer to getting him anywhere—not closer to Annie, not closer to the truth—he glanced up at his wall of stories. The ones he'd poured his heart and soul into. The ones he'd lost friends and loved ones over. He stared at the series he'd done exposing the Winslow Family.

His heart ripped at the seams, but he knew what he needed to do. If he'd given his all to the Winslow story, then he needed to give his all to the Martin story, too.

Quickly, before he could change his mind, George dialed the number for a contact he had in Los Angeles, a guy named—apparently from birth—Eagle. Ex-military and resourceful, the man could find anything. George usually only went to him in the most dire of circumstances. If the Martin family had nothing to hide, then Eagle would be the man to prove it.

"You're go for Eagle," the gruff voice on the other end of the line said, after picking up on the first ring.

"I have a job for you. Usual pay scale. Usual fact-finding mission. I need you to look into the Martin family. The brother runs AppeX

Industries. The sister is Annie Martin; she's one of those online celebrity types."

For a handful of heartbeats, there was nothing on the end of the line. Then, George got his reply.

"Consider it done."

With that, the phone clicked, ending the call and leaving George with one last, lingering hope that all of this would turn out alright. All he could do was pray that the man didn't find anything.

Chapter Fifteen

Annie

Annie hadn't been spending a lot of time at home. In fact, she would characterize her days as *endeavoring to spend as much time as possible away from home.* She woke up as early as she could to take Monster on a long walk, then she went out to a café or a local restaurant for breakfast. Breakfast was followed by a shower and heading straight to Rose's to see what she could help out with around the shop. Annie would try to pop by May's shop to see how the new shopkeeper—a cute girl named Elena who was so shy, she jumped every time Annie talked even a little bit too loud—was doing with all of her responsibilities.

For a while, she considered just dropping everything and going back to Los Angeles. The ghosts and whispers of doubt crept up on her in her darker moments. *What are you still doing here in Hillsboro anyway? You could be living a big, glamorous life in the Hills. No one here in this backwater cares about you. You think any of them would mind if you just up and disappeared one day? Come on... Leave all of this behind. Go back. Go back.*

Under that logic, the temptation to run away was strong. Why *was* she staying here? No one would care if she left. Her brother was now settled and wouldn't care about her or need her anymore. Maybe returning to Los Angeles and getting on with her own life would be exactly what she needed.

But every time she even considered it a little too hard, she rejected the idea completely. Maybe no one cared about her. Maybe they were all just being polite and acting nice to her out of a sense of small-town decorum. *She* still cared about them. She still cared about finding Rose someone to love, about making her friend happy. And, despite it all, she still cared about keeping George away from her brother's story.

There was something else, too. Something she didn't want to look at too closely. Leaving Hillsboro would also mean leaving George behind entirely. She wasn't willing to do that. Not just yet, anyway.

It was a conflict from the depths of her heart she hadn't yet resolved. She wanted to hate him and to defend her family against him. She actually *did* hate him for, on the one hand, reminding her that she was just a story to him and on the other hand, talking to her about how she deserved to be kissed as though she were really the princess he mocked her for being.

She also didn't want to leave him. She wanted to hear him laugh again. To see the tips of his ears turn red when he blushed. To get under his skin and watch him squirm as they played their usual games of wit.

Annie was at war with herself. And she was spending as much time as she could trying *not* to fight that war. Or, honestly, even thinking about it.

Which was why she was over-the-moon excited when, one morning on her walk with Monster, her FaceTime screen illuminated with an incoming call from her brother's phone. Immediately a wash of release flooded her entire being. She'd missed Luke more than she could say. He'd always been a guiding, steadying presence in her life. She hadn't wanted to bother him with anything while he was on his honeymoon, but now that *he'd* called *her*...

He would know what to do about George. He would know exactly how to fix everything. He always did.

Swiping the screen to life, Annie blinked furiously as her screen was flooded with sunshine. She stopped on a nearby bench, out of the way of the other walkers and joggers, so she could fully take in the picture of her brother, sitting on a picturesque beach, covered in frothy, white sunscreen.

Well, at least he wasn't going to get sunburned.

"Luke? What are you doing? Aren't you supposed to be on your honeymoon? You shouldn't be calling me," she teased.

But before Luke could even open his mouth to respond, another figure entered the frame of the phone screen. Monster yipped happily in Annie's lap when she realized it was a slightly tipsy, slightly pink-cheeked Harper, wearing a sunhat and oversized sunglasses.

"I'm here too! Don't worry! We've been having plenty of honeymoon time. We just wanted to check in and see how things are going back home."

"We're homesick," Luke confessed, something to which his wife took obvious offense.

"Don't say that! We're not homesick. We're just..." Harper adjusted herself in the lounge chair she and her new husband were sharing, tipping up her chin defiantly. Annie swallowed back a laugh. Harper would be way too proud to admit, on her first trip out of the country, that she actually missed home and all of the people in it. "We're just eagerly awaiting news. I mean, I love Hillsboro, but we don't have enough places that will serve you unlimited fruit juice and maraschino cherries in pineapples, you know?"

The image on Annie's phone screen pixelated as Harper waved a giant pineapple cocktail right into the camera lens. This time, Annie allowed herself to laugh. At least, for the moment, she wasn't twisted up in knots, thinking about George Barnett and her stupid feelings for him. Holding Monster close to her chest with her free arm, she waited for Harper to settle back down into her lounge chair before replying.

"Well, what do you want to know?"

No matter how pixelated the image of island paradise, Annie couldn't miss the look Luke and Harper shared, one that Harper broke by pulling her sunhat low over her eyes, tipping her head back, and slipping down lower and lower until it looked as if she was going to sleep.

Annie knew better. Harper might have been giving them the illusion of privacy, but it was very clear that she'd be listening in to everything. For a man on his honeymoon and freshly married to the love of his life, Luke's expression turned severely dour. Too serious.

"It's just that I've heard some rumors, Annie. Some rumors that are making me nervous."

Great. Annie should have known that the infamous Hillsboro rumor mill wouldn't have been stopped by multiple oceans. Tossing her head, she tried to give the appearance of a woman with nothing to hide, even while the clawing, aching need to confess everything to her brother scratched at the back of her throat. Yes, she'd wanted to tell him everything, to beg him to tell her what to do about her feelings and George Barnett and this story that he was wanting to write about them and the very real possibility that he might destroy the fragile peace of their lives.

But when she'd seen Luke and Harper sitting there, all snuggled and sun-kissed, so happy in their closeness, she knew she couldn't be the one to ruin that. No, she'd just have to handle everything back home on her own. Besides, she couldn't let her brother pick up after her messes for the rest of her life, could she? No. She had to learn to stand on her own two feet. She had to learn to handle her own heart.

And, maybe more importantly, she had to learn how to protect her family the way her family had protected her. Luke had spent his entire life looking after her. Maybe, with this journalist and his story so close at hand, it was her turn to look after him.

"What kind of rumors? You know how gossip is in a small town like this, big brother. I wouldn't worry about it if I were you."

"I'm not worried about the rumor. I'm worried about you. I heard you're hanging out with some reporter from the *Hillsboro Gazette*?"

A lump developed in Annie's throat, but she washed it away with an exasperated huff, the same one she delivered any time anyone tried to insinuate that she and George were involved in anything less than a professional way.

If only she could scoff at her own feelings and conflicts as easily.

"We haven't been hanging out. We've been working on a story," Annie said, even though the words sounded hollow even to her own ears.

Luke didn't believe it for a second. His eyes narrowed slightly, which she could only see because he'd slipped his sunglasses up on top of his baseball cap.

"What kind of story?"

"It's about finding love in a small town and how hard that can be." Annie paused for a moment, and tried to fill in some details to lend an air of truth to her story. "We even held this speed-dating event. You can ask Rose all about it."

Still, Luke's skepticism deepened every line of his face.

"Is this the reporter who has been begging me to do an interview with him?"

"Yes, but he's not so bad."

That was... the understatement of the century. And maybe not even a correct or entirely truthful one. He *was* pretty bad. He was using her to get to a story, all while dangling the warmth of friendship and love right in front of her nose like delicious bait.

He was also wonderful. And funny. And engaging. And handsome.

Her brother didn't need to know that last part.

Luke held his hands up in surrender. "You know I trust your judgment in everything. But if you're lonely—"

"I'm not lonely!"

Lie. It was the most brutal, blatant lie of all and they both knew it. After all, that's why she hadn't gone back to Los Angeles full-time. That's why she was spending all of her time checking in on the shops and worrying about Rose's love life and going on long walks even when she had to wear a sweater over her exercise gear.

She hated that she was the cause of the worry in her brother's eyes, hated being this burden whose emotions were getting in the way of him having a happy honeymoon. A seasickness settled in her stomach, one that had nothing to do with the rollicking crash of waves in the background of Luke's side of the conversation.

"If you're lonely, then just please remember that you have plenty of people in Hillsboro who love and care about you. Plenty of people you can turn to if you need someone to talk to. You don't have to latch on to some guy just because you think he'll listen to you."

"I don't want to bother them," Annie said, quietly, and it was the truth.

That was something a lot of people didn't know about her. If she thought she could improve someone *else's* life, then she had no problem being a bother. She had no problem fussing over Rose if it meant her falling head-over-heels with the man of her dreams. But when *she* needed something…she wasn't the kind of person who would crawl to someone's door for help.

A burden. All her life, she'd been fighting against being one. She wasn't about to start now.

"You're part of their family, Annie," Luke said, gently. "They love you."

"I'm okay being on my own. I promise." This time, when she smiled, it was because she really meant it. "I'm just helping George and the *Gazette* with this story about small-town romance. That's all. I promise. Once we're finished with that, I'll probably never even see him again."

Luke's eyes once again winced in that concerned way of theirs, awakening the beginnings of a few crow's feet wrinkles at either of his temples. Another thread of guilt made its way through Annie's heart. She must have contributed to most of those wrinkles.

"You're my sister. I care about you more than anything. Please take care of yourself. I couldn't handle it if someone hurt you."

"Don't worry. I'll be alright."

No matter how many times she said that, either to herself or out loud, she wasn't sure she believed it. Apparently, neither did Luke, whose face betrayed a distinct unhappiness with her. Usually, Annie relished these moments; they were some of the few times in her life when she really, genuinely felt like someone loved her and cared about her. When Luke didn't look convinced, Annie tried to recover the moment with a joke. "Unbelievable. Getting lectured about life and love by my brother. Look, you get one little wife and all of a sudden you're the emotional expert?"

"I just want you to be happy. Go see Rose. Have family dinner with the Andersons. Just...please don't let yourself be alone. And don't fall into the arms of some stranger because you think he's your only option."

Annie hesitated. Was *that* what she was doing here? Was she just projecting her wants and needs and fears and hopes onto George?

"I won't. I mean, I will. I mean, I will go see Rose and I won't fall into George's arms."

"Good. And eat a slice of Millie's pie for me. There may be drinks in pineapples here, but they don't know anything about pie."

With a few more pleasantries and farewells, Annie was once again left alone on the bench. Alone in this town. Alone, alone, alone.

Her hand, wrapped around her cell phone, was shaking more than she could ever remember it shaking before.

She didn't want to be alone again. She didn't want the dull background noise of loneliness to consume her life. She needed a cause. A goal. A someone.

With trembling fingers, she searched her phone contacts and found the name she was looking for. The name of the only person she wanted to talk to right now. She'd been using the matchmaking and her shop-assistant-ing and her charity consulting and her dog walking as a laundry list of distractions, but right now, she needed more than a distraction.

She needed George Barnett.

Chapter Sixteen

George

She'd asked him to meet her at her brother's house. He didn't know why or for what purpose. Maybe she'd somehow caught wind that he'd hired a slightly shady private investigator to look into her past and was going to feed him to her adorably mangy mutt somewhere in the back woods of her property. Maybe she'd realized she wanted to be kissed like she deserved after all and had decided she wanted it to be with him.

The reasoning or the motivations didn't matter, though. He didn't even think about not going. When he heard a slight tremble in her voice, a warble he'd never heard from her before, he knew he didn't have any other choice. Story be damned, he wanted to be there for her. Something in him needed to know that she was all right.

It was strange, coming to a house he'd inspected the floor plans and Google Earth images of, a house he'd spied on from a distance but never set foot in himself. The ranch-style house was cut into the side of the hill, a crown set atop a sea of silver maple trees, each turning slightly golden in the early fall breeze. Despite the chilled evening settling in over the horizon, the house lights were off, but the porch lights—thousands of tiny stars strung up along the trellis overhanging the wrap-around terrace—beckoned him onward and upward.

He tried not to think about the fact that this house had no gate, no security, none of the hallmark signs of someone who had something to hide.

When he finally arrived up at the house, he saw his hostess sitting at a table beneath the star-filled sky of the terrace, bathed in their artificial glow. She was dressed more casually than he'd ever seen her, in an oversized T-shirt marked with a fading *Star Trek* logo and loose-fitting athleisure pants. George wondered if she secretly liked space adventures or if she'd raided her brother's wardrobe, but he could tell this wasn't the time to ask. Annie wasn't wearing any shoes. No makeup, either. Her hair fell limply against her shoulders in loose, soft, untreated ringlets. The table beside her practically overflowed with charcuterie and snacks, a bottle of wine, and twin glasses.

It looked like a date, but something in the air told him it wasn't. Maybe it was the chill that spread goosebumps all along his neck or maybe it was the wistful, distant way she surveyed the Mayacamas Mountains in the distance. Maybe it was the fact that she didn't break that stare even when his boots creaked one of the terrace floorboards beneath his feet. He tried to come up with better ideas than *date* or *murder* but when he came up empty, he spoke, hoping that maybe that would pull her from her reverie.

"This is not quite the spread I was envisioning, princess."

Annie smiled, but didn't stop looking at the view. Strange. If he didn't know any better, he would think she was staring at it as if she'd never see it again. "What were you envisioning, out of curiosity?"

"I don't know. Something distinctly more true crime documentary. I feel like I just stumbled into a Hallmark movie."

It was beautiful. Even if he didn't quite know what was going on here, he couldn't deny that. Annie had a flair for the dramatic, for visual statements, and even without any makeup and in oversized clothes that looked more comfortable than gorgeous, she couldn't help but embrace that part of herself. She shrugged as a bit of gallows humor poured from her lips.

"I felt like if my life is going to end tonight, I might as well go out beautifully."

"What's that supposed to mean?"

For the first time, Annie turned in his direction and sized him up. This wasn't like any of their previous encounters before, where she would judge him like a steak in a cooking competition—on style, presentation, and creativity. This was something deeper, something infinitely more disconcerting. For once, she wasn't looking at his clothes. She was looking at *him*.

"Did you bring your notebook?" she asked, picking up a glass of wine and bringing it to her lips.

"I always bring my notebook. Why?"

She gestured to the seat across from her. George approached, but stopped almost as quickly when she spoke again. "Because this is your interview. Your no holds barred, no questions off the record interview with Annie Martin. You can't have my brother, but I'm willing to uphold my end of the bargain. Any question you want answered, anything you want to know. I'm here."

He searched her face for any signs that she was joking, that this was some kind of prank she was pulling on him, that any minute now the staff of the *Hillsboro Gazette* would come out from the bushes so they could laugh in his face about this.

He didn't find anything. Nothing but quiet resignation. And a little touch of bravery in the way she wrinkled her forehead. That made everything even *more* confusing.

"You can't be serious. You've been dodging me and every one of my questions for weeks."

"I changed my mind."

"Why?"

That question hung in the air like heavy storm clouds as she ran her finger along the rim of her wine glass, letting a quiet hum emanate from the contact. It sounded, to George, a little bit like the warning strings of a horror movie's score. Annie's slight, mysterious smile, though, told him that there was nothing to worry about.

"I think you need to ask your questions before I can answer that one."

"You're talking in riddles."

"Nope. Just waiting for you to start the interview."

Part of him wanted to pick her up, shake her, and demand to know who she was and where she'd hidden the real Annie. George tried to run through the last few days to figure out what the hell she was getting at here. In the end, he could only come up with one explanation that made sense.

"Are you mad at me? Are you trying to push me away?"

"No," she rushed out, but then corrected herself. "I mean. Yes. My brother is the most important person in my entire life. He always has been. And if talking to you can save him a lot of headache and grief, then I'm going to do it. So...go on. Ask."

In her level gaze, George didn't find any hints of hesitation or regret. In fact, she was challenging him. Demanding that he do the job he'd been trying to do for so long. A little voice in the back of his mind demanded to know why he was looking a gift horse in the mouth, why he wasn't over the moon with joy about the prospect of sucking Annie dry of information so he could finally expose her brother and whatever shady business dealings they probably were engaged in.

But, as he looked at her, sitting there and struggling with the bottle opener currently lodged in a bottle of Barn Door wine, he knew exactly why. He didn't want to find anything. He didn't want to have to expose her, didn't want to know that she was all the things he'd been afraid she was.

But when she looked at him, unspoken words filled the silent air between them. *George, it's okay. Just ask.*

Slowly, he sunk down into the chair she'd offered him and removed his recorder and notebook from the pocket of his jacket. He placed them both on the table.

"Do you mind if I record this?"

"Nope. Go ahead," she said, her voice slow and flat. Once she'd triumphed over the cork, she offered up the bottle in her hand. "Wine?"

"I think I need a glass, yes. Thank you."

A moment later, the wine flowed into both of their glasses, and Annie picked hers up, holding it forward in a truce.

"Cheers. To the truth."

"To the truth," George repeated, but the words were weak, hollow, uncertain.

They both drank, probably a little more than anyone should in a single gulp. At least George knew that her calm, cool facade was just that—a facade. As he turned to his notebook and opened it to a fresh page, she curled her legs up into her chair, hugging them to her chest. For a moment, he stared at the blank page before him, trying to think back to the hundreds of times he envisioned this interview, trying to think back to a time before he felt anything but warmed-over distaste for Annie Martin.

"It's weird, sitting across from you as a journalist," he muttered, after the moment of silence stretched too long for comfort.

"That's what it's been this entire time, hasn't it?"

Her voice cut with an edge of hurt. He deserved that.

"It was supposed to be that easy. But it wasn't. And it definitely isn't now." Thankfully, she didn't ask him to explain what he meant. "You mentioned…on our date to the Bronze Boot, that your brother looked out for you. That you had kind of a rough upbringing. That's not in any of his corporate biographies," George said, remembering all of the slightly bland versions of his origin story—boy tech wizard makes good—he'd read over the years of research he'd been doing into him.

"We're private people. We don't really like airing out our child-hood inadequacies for the public."

"You weren't inadequate. Your parents were."

The words were too personal, too sincere for an interview like this, but George couldn't help but say them. He couldn't just sit here and let her think that something about her was broken or wrong. He just couldn't.

"That's not how it feels. When a parent makes it clear that they don't care about you…that is the definition of a scar you can't stop picking at. You asked me why I've been on this string of bad matchmaking. *That's* why. Because I can't be alone. Because the second I start to feel lonely, I worry that I'm going to feel that way for the rest of my life. And because I never want anyone to feel as lonely as I felt back then."

He watched as the arms looped around her knees tightened. The skin where she gripped her arms turned white from the effort. She stared out at the horizon again.

"But you know, constantly needing other people is really taxing and you get worried that the more you need people, the less they're going to like you. That the longer you're around, the more attuned they'll become to your flaws. That the more they see you, the less they'll like what they see."

George's jaw twitched, he wanted so badly to reach out and take her hand in his. *I have liked you more and more with every passing second, Annie Martin. In fact, I'm afraid that if I don't stop soon, I might start actually loving you.*

It was a ridiculous thought to have. But they were far past journalistic distance and professionalism. He knew that whatever else she disclosed now, he'd be forever torn between the secret and the woman who shared it with him. A heavy weight grew in the pit of his stomach as she shrugged and tossed her head and offered her weak smiles, all of the things she did when she tried to pretend that all of the hurt she was feeling didn't bother her.

"So, matchmaking is kind of perfect. It distracts me from being lonely and it makes me, maybe, a little bit more important to people. Maybe if I do enough nice and good and meaningful things, then they won't care that I'm annoying and that my face isn't symmetrical and that I talk too much and that I'm just not lovable."

Not lovable. He wanted to erase everyone who'd ever made her feel that way from her memory.

"But even with all of that, where my brother was concerned, I always thought I needed to let him live his own life. That I was the ultimate burden keeping him from doing everything he ever wanted. So, when I turned eighteen, I decided that I was going to be a big, strong woman and stand on my own two feet and so I answered this advertisement for a modeling gig in Los Angeles. I thought, *perfect.* I'm pretty enough and I could, you know, earn some money to stop being such a leech on my brother. So...so, when the photographer asked me to take my clothes off—"

George's heart stopped. His mouth went dry. His world plunged into darkness. This hadn't been the story he was expecting.

"I didn't hesitate. I posed and I preened and I pretended like it was all very cool, very normal for me. That's why I don't like being called Annabelle, by the way. The photographer always called me that. When I was little, I used to think it was such a regal, important name. Like a queen. But now, I really do prefer just being Annie. Anyway, eventually the photographer put two and two together, realized who I was, and who my brother was, and the threats started. You can imagine that Luke did everything to make sure I was protected and safe and that the pictures were destroyed."

She went on then, detailing the ways they'd had the photographs scrubbed and every mention of her fledgling "modeling career" erased from the internet using internet privacy laws, etc., etc., but George barely heard a word of it. Instead, he focused on the sickening bile rising up in his throat and the familiar taste of it that coated his tongue.

Guilt.

All this time, he'd been searching for justice, searching for just the right person to tear down so he could feel like the conquering hero again. He'd thought he'd found that in Annie and in Luke—the golden siblings who'd had everything handed to them, who'd probably fought and bribed and stolen their way to the top. But he'd been wrong. So very, very wrong.

"So . . . that's my story. I can give you the numbers of people who can do the fact-checking and who would tell you everything you want to know about the gritty details, such as they are. But *that* is why I'm here. Because the only story my brother has is me. There aren't any shady business dealings. He hasn't acquired his empire through cruel force. Everyone in his company gets paid very well and none of them ever have to crunch or sprint or whatever it is they call eighty-hour work weeks in tech. He just has me. Stupid, problematic Annabelle."

Pain shot through him. She spoke like her very existence was a curse. Like she was a broken thing beyond repair. How many other lies did she believe about herself?

"He's lucky to have you, Annie."

"Come on. I thought you were a man who believed in the truth."

Now, for the first time, he felt like he really, truly saw her. He'd always thought she was hiding behind her bubbly, take-no-prisoners-when-it-comes-to-friendship persona. But he'd imagined she'd been hiding a ruthless, sharp-elbowed witch somewhere deep within her, not a sad, broken girl who pretended to be happy and friendly all the time so no one would suspect how deeply lonely she was.

He wanted to pull her into his arms and hold her there, crushing her to his chest until she knew exactly how much she was admired. Until she knew that she wasn't—and could never be—alone. He wanted to, but he failed. His voice, too, failed him.

She didn't seem to have the same problem. After letting a long, slow, low breath out, she squared her shoulders and turned slightly towards him. At least that hadn't changed. She still knew exactly how to make him feel like the only person on the planet.

"Can I ask *you* a question now? It's something that's been bothering me since the first day I walked into your office."

"Yeah. Sure," he said, relieved to have his slack jaw finally working again. "What is it?"

"On your wall, you have all of these fantastic stories and letters and pieces of journalism about Very Important Things." She adopted a self-aggrandizing tone, just sharp enough that he could practically hear the capital letters as she spoke. "Local disasters and take-downs, the kind of really meaty stuff that a guy like you really seems to go for."

George didn't like the way that phrase hit his ear. "A guy like me?"

"I mean, you know who you are. You want to save the world. You think you're being Superman by being Clark Kent, like every keystroke is going to be the salvation of all humanity."

Okay. He had promised her honesty. He couldn't deny, in any good faith, that she absolutely saw through him.

"Go on."

"So why does a guy like that, a guy whose proudest moments in life are when he shoves injustices from the dark and into the light, have a framed picture of a puff piece he wrote about a miniature horse farm?"

It took him a moment before he actually realized what in the world she was talking about. *Oh, right.* The story about the Odie Hills Farm. His breath left his lungs. Of everything in the world she could have asked him after she'd just spilled her most precious secret, she asked him about the ponies?

"*That's* the question you wanted to ask me?"

"Was I supposed to ask something else?"

"I thought you were going to ask something way more serious than that."

It was the biggest relief he possibly could have asked for, the perfect balm to the aching moment they'd just shared. Laughter danced on the edge of the clouds of breath that passed from their lips and into the cold night air. Annie shrugged.

"Nope. That's what I want to know. What's the deal with the ponies?"

George shifted in his seat. "So, the Odie Hills Miniature Horse Farm used to be incredibly popular. It was the place where the rich and famous went to buy their little darling children the cutest little animals money could buy. But what happens when the little darling children grow up? What happens to the miniature horses then?"

Annie shook her head, leaning forward to pour herself a glass of wine without taking her eyes off his face. After what she'd just told him, he didn't expect to be able to smile for a good and long time.

But thinking about that story, thinking about sharing it with Annie, of all people, was perfect. He couldn't help but smile.

"Mrs. Newman, the woman who ran the place, asked herself that question one day and realized she didn't like the answer. Or the answer she came up with just wasn't good enough anymore. So, she quit the business and stopped selling the ponies altogether."

"What did she do instead?" Annie asked, her own lips turning up in a smile.

"She opened it up as an animal therapy farm. Anyone who wants to visit and wants to love the animals is welcome there. She takes donations sometimes, but…she gave up her entire life, her entire business, because she wanted to do right by more people. Because she wanted to do something good. I put that story up because I always wanted to remember that."

"Remember what?"

She asked it with an ease that told him she wasn't trying to make him feel bad. But he felt bad all the same. He'd been pursuing her for so long now, trying to convince her to trust him just so he could one day expose her secrets to the world.

He'd lost sight of what was really important.

"That doing good in this world still matters," he muttered, almost a confession.

"And why would you need reminding of something like that?"

"Why are you so interested?"

It was a dodge, a way to avoid telling her the complete truth. But she didn't seem to mind. Dragging a square of cheese through the quince paste on the charcuterie board before her, she drew dizzying patterns as she spoke.

"Because I want to understand you. I just put a lot of trust in you and I need to know that I didn't just make the biggest mistake of my life."

George leaned forward, pulled in by the uncertainty in her eyes. She'd trusted him. Now, it was time that he trusted her.

So, with his lips so close to hers he could almost taste the air between them, he asked her something he'd never asked any other woman ever before.

"Have you ever been to the Hillsboro Museum?"

Annie blinked, but he was already on his feet, reaching for her hand and tugging her up to meet him.

"Uh, no—"

"Good. Because I want to show you something."

Chapter Seventeen

Annie

Annie didn't have the first clue where he was taking her, but after she'd trusted him enough to confess her deepest, worst secrets, she figured she could trust him with the rest of her evening.

The raised-wood building just at the edge of town was vaguely familiar to her; she must have passed it a thousand times without ever bothering to go inside. A plaque glinting in the light of the streetlamps informed her that this was the Hillsboro Town Museum, established in 1941. The windows were dark, the curtains covered, and when Annie stepped out of the car, she got the distinct impression that the place was, you know, closed.

"I don't think we're supposed to be in here after dark."

"Is this the first time you've broken the law?" George asked, snorting as he rounded the car and headed straight for the front door.

"I think you can guess that it is."

After all, he probably knew more about her and Luke than she did. He'd been poring over their records for so long. Chuckling, George ducked his head and fished out a ring of keys from his pocket. They jangled in the quiet evening, but their sound brought Annie at least a small measure of peace.

"Well, don't worry. Your record will remain clean. I'm friends with Mrs. Riley, Tom's grandmother? She does volunteer hours here on the weekends and she thought it would be easier if I just had a key when I needed one for research purposes."

"You really are such a nerd, you know that?"

The words were out of her mouth before she could take them back. She wasn't supposed to be laughing and joking with him like nothing was wrong. She was supposed to be steeling herself for the worst, for the moment when he looked at her and decided she wasn't good enough for his friendship or attention anymore.

Still, old habits died hard. And no matter how much she tried to convince herself that, sooner or later, this would all slip through her fingers and she'd be alone again, she couldn't stop herself from wanting to tease him, to see his smile, to laugh with him.

"I do know that. Believe it or not, you're not the first person to have told me that."

"Smart aleck."

They made their way up the steps and George slipped the key into the first of the three locks safeguarding the door of the museum.

"Smart aleck? Is that the kind of language they use in L.A. now? Has cursing gone out of fashion?"

Annie fiddled with the hem of the T-shirt she'd borrowed from her brother's collection. "I don't curse for the same reason I don't break into places. I like my image to be proper and appropriate and, you know, good."

She didn't always *feel* good, but still, she tried her best to be it.

The final lock clicked and George stood to his full height, where he looked down at her and smiled. Completely and totally sincere.

"You are good, Annie. You're better than most of the people I know."

Don't say that. You can't even begin to know that is true, she wanted to say, but the words lodged like a cough in her throat. He actually did know. He knew better than anyone who she was and what she'd done and what she was trying so desperately to hide. And he still liked her.

He still liked her. The thought made her traitorous heart soar.

Nudging her shoulder, he pointed her inside, where the automatic lights had flickered to life. "Come on. I want to show you something."

The museum certainly wasn't like any of the ones Annie frequented in Los Angeles. Those places were perfectly austere squares of space where art and artifacts could be pristinely showcased. The museums she knew were sterile places where all of the personality of a building could be filed away. But the Hillsboro Town Museum wasn't like that at all. In fact, it was full of character, as if the small, wood-frame building itself was part of the exhibition. Annie began to wander the rows of dioramas and glass-box cases, letting her fingertips brush along the cool surface of threadbare velvet ropes keeping the public from touching the pieces on display. They weren't particularly impressive pieces—for example, in one corner, stood a creepy diorama filled with homemade dolls with glassy eyes depicted in a schoolhouse, and Annie was sure the thing would give her nightmares—but still, there was a humble charm to them. She loved the idea of people in this small town coming together to document and celebrate their own history, to record it so that future generations could remember where they came from.

Everything, she remembered, was important to someone. And what a beautiful, precious thing.

She could only hope that *everything* included her.

"I've never been in here before. Not even in the daytime," she said, pausing in front of a framed deed to the town square's land.

"It's a great little place. Used to be the schoolhouse before the big county public school got built, so the original structure is almost a hundred and fifty years old. You know, the first teacher's name was Baroness Deremeadow. She wasn't royalty. She was actually a mail-order bride who changed her name because she thought that she'd get a better husband. Turns out, he ordered her, but died and left her all his money when he did, and she built this. Fun fact—"

Annie spun on him and raised one of her eyebrows. This over-talking thing wasn't George's usual gimmick. "Are you stalling?"

"Yes," he admitted without prodding. She breathed a laugh, turning to see that he was now standing beside her, so close that they both shared in the same glow of a penlight illuminating a framed pencil drawing of the Hillsboro valley from the early 1800s. She nudged him, her heart feeling a little lighter now that he was so near.

"Come on. I thought we promised to tell each other the truth."

"You're right. You're always right. Okay. So." George clapped his hands and walked further down to the end of their aisle, leading her past cases and cabinets filled with trinkets and icons of the past. "About twenty years after Baroness Deremeadow showed up here in town, a man by the name of Ezekiel Winslow came in and bought almost all of the available land in town. This is his statue."

Stepping right past one of the velvet ropes, George placed both of his hands atop a glass box atop a pedestal, which held the bronze head—and only the head—of a statue of an old man with spectacles and whiskers.

"Where's the rest of it?"

Smirking, he held out one of his hands to stop her. "I'm getting there. Don't rush me."

Taking the liberty of sitting on the school bench behind her, Annie looked up and watched as George pointed to a large map of the area pinned up on the wall behind Ezekiel Winslow's bodiless head, using it to highlight his points as he spoke.

"So, for the next hundred years or so, the Winslow family acquired wealth. And property. And power. And they used all three to make Hillsboro their own little play land. They underpaid their workers and bribed their kids' ways through the school system and bought whatever they couldn't get on their own. Normal rich people stuff."

Annie couldn't help but think that was a dig at her, that it was his reasoning for chasing down her and her brother for all these years. But she didn't say anything about it or ask any follow-up questions, because before she knew it, she was watching George's sad face in the reflection of the glass covering the map of Hillsboro. He sighed, then continued with his story:

"And then one day, a stupid kid in college who thought he might have a head for journalism started paying attention. And he found out that the then patriarch of the family was planning to start a brush fire. One that would probably destroy Hillsboro and definitely make them a lot of insurance money. On top of that, they could have renegotiated rent prices and land leases and made more money on one little fire than they would have in their entire lives."

A familiar scratch tugged at the back of Annie's mind. She'd read that story in his office. The Winslow Family was the one he'd taken down in the *Hillsboro Gazette*.

"That was you. I read that story. How did you—"

"I told you a fib when you met Marshall Barnett at the grocery store. We aren't related, but I did get my last name from him. My dad's last name was Winslow. I changed it when they kicked me out and cut me off. Marshall Barnett was the closest thing I had to a real dad back then, the only person who really looked out for me, so . . . if I had to pick a new last name, that seemed as good as any."

All at once, with those few little words, her entire perception and understanding of him clicked into sharp focus. That was why he'd been chasing this story about her and her brother. That's why he was dedicated to the truth, constantly searching for and exposing it wherever he could find it.

One day, he'd chosen the fate of thousands of people over his own family. He'd chosen to do the right thing. No wonder that, for all of this time, he'd been willing to choose what he thought was a good story over her.

"What happened next?"

George shrugged. "After, most of them sold their lands and fled town. Ole' Ezekiel here is the head of a statue that came down once the last of them left."

"But you stayed."

"I stayed. Or, I came back after Stanford."

"Why?"

"Because I love the bagels at Barnett Grocery Store," he quipped.

Annie shot him a look, a serious, throat-choking look. She needed to completely understand him. She needed to know what he was going to do with her secret. If she was going to end up a bodiless statue in some small-town museum. "George."

"Because my family still had connections with every paper in the country, the series about them didn't get picked up in the media. Any time I applied for a job with my real name, I got rejected before I could even get a phone interview. But Hillsboro still respected me. They still cared. And I've been working all this time, just hoping that I could, one day, write something important enough, something big enough to get me where I want to be."

"Saving the world."

A self-deprecating—and terribly, heartbreakingly handsome—smile crossed his face. "As much as you can save the world with a thousand words in newsprint."

Her eyes traced the shape of his lips, and all she wanted was to kiss him, something her brain berated her for. How could she possibly want to kiss the man who had basically just told her he was going to sell her story to the highest bidder? How could she still feel something for this principled, handsome, infuriating, betrayer of a man?

"Well, the story of an Instagram star's nude photos and her tech whiz brother paying to cover it up for the sake of their careers? Seems like you'll have that *New York Times* byline by the end of the week," she said, sadly.

But, to her surprise, when she looked up to see the triumph in his eyes, instead, she was met with confusion. Righteous indignation. Leaving behind the statue of his ancestor, he closed the space between them so he could stare down at her as he spoke.

"Annie, I didn't expose my parents because I wanted a big byline. And I don't want a big byline because I'm some arrogant jerk who wants attention. I told the world about my family because I believe in justice. And I want the big byline so I can get it. So enough people will actually listen to the truth to force some change in this world."

A lump appeared in Annie's throat. She hadn't cried all night and she didn't want to start now. But there it was, that familiar heat behind her eyes, that itch that could only be cured by tears. Was he saying what she thought he was saying?

Two fingers touched the bottom of her chin, tilting her face up so she was once again looking him squarely in the face. There was no escaping that honesty in his eyes. And if there was one thing she knew about George, it was that he believed in the truth above everything else.

"It wouldn't be justice, telling the world about what happened to you for some sick joke of a news story. It would be a tragedy."

Annie's vision went watery. She blinked, trying to clear it, but then, the tears went and went and went, cleansing all of the burning, painful tension she'd been holding in her heart from the moment those pictures were taken. It was the relief of years of terror, of looking around every corner in fear that someone would find out her secret and tell it to the world. "You're...you're not going to run the story?"

"No. I'll still do my due diligence on your brother and his companies, but I haven't found anything in two years. I don't think I'll find it now. But will you answer me one more question?" he asked, offering her a wry smile.

"Anything."

Right now, with relief and joy coursing through her veins, she would do more than anything for him. She would do everything for him. It wasn't just because he was keeping her secret, but because, in this moment, she realized what a good man he was. He wasn't just some newshound looking for a big story that would put him on the map. He actually believed in goodness. In truth. In justice. In all of the things she used to roll her eyes at him for talking about.

George bent down to join her on the bench. She was so aware of his proximity, of his closeness, that she instinctively leaned into the warmth radiating from his slender, handsome frame. "Your brother had a police report filed and then scrubbed. What was it?"

This was the one part of the story that could actually hurt her brother personally. But when Annie reached out and brushed her fingertips along the top of George's hand, sending shocks of electricity through her entire body, she couldn't help but trust him. Completely.

It was maybe the first time in her life that she'd done that.

"The man who had my photographs wasn't as . . . professional . . . as I think my brother would have liked for him to have been in one of their meetings. So, Luke almost broke his jaw."

George practically choked on his shock.

"Talk about unprofessional," he said, once he'd recovered.

"I think Luke would have preferred the term *hostile negotiations.* I'm just jealous I didn't get to punch him myself."

"Yeah. I'd like a piece of him, too."

They were so close now. Their fingers intertwined and their foreheads so close that they almost touched. Annie swallowed back a wave of want, fresh and intense and focused entirely on his lips.

"George?"

"Yes?"

"Thank you." *For keeping my secret. For believing in what's right. For being good and honest and trusting me the same way that I trusted you. For being so good and for being the kind of person I never thought I could find for myself. The kind of person I never thought would give me a second look.* All of that was too wordy. Besides, sometimes it was best just to keep it simple. "For everything."

"I'm only trying to do what's right. It's all I can do."

You could kiss me, she thought, but suppressed the urge before she could say it out loud. She did want to kiss George, more than words could express, but she didn't want it to be like this. When she finally did kiss him, she didn't want him to think it was out of gratitude or some misplaced sense of debt.

When she and George Barnett kissed for the first time, it would be the best, most pure, most perfect meeting of souls in history. She could wait one more night.

"Come on. We don't want to get caught in here when the creepy statues start coming to life."

Annie pretended to pout. "I never get to do anything fun."

George laughed as he reached up to switch off the overhead lights. "We'll see about that."

She didn't have the first clue what, specifically, he was talking about, but still, she agreed with him. They would see about it. Because she now had her heart set on George Barnett, and she couldn't help but begin devising a plan to make that dream a reality.

Chapter Eighteen

George

When George woke up the morning after, he couldn't quite force himself to sit still. Getting to sleep the night before had been difficult enough, and once he was fully awake, his every nerve ending was electrified like live wires, pushing him to walk a little faster, think a little less coherently, and breathe a little heavier than before.

Was this what it was like, when you were about to ask someone out on a real date? He'd never done it before, and the sensation was overwhelming. It dominated his every moment, his every impulse. Everything in him called out to Annie, wanting to be near her so he could finally say those words aloud.

After last night, there was nothing between them. Nothing to keep them apart. No veil of journalistic modesty to keep him from kissing her like he wanted. Finally, *finally*, he could admit to her... and to himself... the real depths of his feelings for her.

But a man couldn't just walk up to a woman's house, knock on the door, and confess that he was falling deeply in love with her. No. He'd promised her an adventure, something fun. And he was going to give it to her.

Which was how he ended up leading her away from her house that afternoon, a blindfold covering her eyes and a smile on his face. It was impossible, now, to avoid thinking about how soft and touchable her skin was beneath his hands as he guided her down her front porch steps. He wanted more, wanted to hold her closer, wanted to press himself against her until he knew what her every curve felt like.

Promising himself that there would be time for all of that later, he swallowed those desires and tried to focus on the task at hand: getting her into his car so they could make their way out of town.

"What is all this about?" Annie asked, once she'd said goodbye and told Monster she would be back in fifteen minutes.

He'd asked her why she'd told the dog they would be back in fifteen minutes, but she assured him it was just because dogs couldn't tell time. Ridiculous woman. How was it possible that something so silly could make him like her even more than he already did?

Though she'd been surprised at his sudden arrival and protested that she'd had surprise plans for them today, too—plans that they couldn't do now that he'd made the first move—she hadn't resisted when George had asked her to put on the blindfold, but now, he could hear a slight hesitation in her voice. He shook his head as his thumb brushed against her cheek.

"I'm very sorry, but I'm afraid that would quite ruin the surprise."

"Is this about Rose and her boyfriend? Because if you're bringing me to their surprise shotgun wedding, then I would really like to be dressed cuter than this."

"No, it's not about that. Come on. In with you now."

As he helped her into the car, his hand brushed her waist, sending bolts of lightning through his entire body. He couldn't help but wonder what it would be like, holding her there while they kissed. It would be easy to kiss her now, to dip down, cup her cheek, and press his lips to hers in a soft, gentle embrace. But again, he restrained himself. Their first kiss wouldn't be like this. In a car. Randomly. Parked in front of her house.

He'd said it once before and he'd meant it. She deserved to be kissed properly. Perfectly. And he was going to do his best to give her that.

"Okay," Annie finally said when they'd hit the road. "Where are we going?"

"It's a surprise."

"I hate surprises."

George let out a barking laugh at that. Her? Hating surprises? He couldn't imagine anything so ridiculous. "You force surprises onto everyone you know, me included."

"They're fun to do to other people. I hate having them done to me. I like to be in control."

He knew the feeling. But for once, Annie Martin wasn't going to get her way.

"Don't worry. It won't be too much longer now."

For the rest of the ride, the two of them chatted about this and that—about Rose and Eris, about how Annie would have used a blindfold with a higher thread count if she was going to kidnap someone this way, about what they were going to do if the *Hillsboro Gazette* ever called them in to explain their progress on the imaginary news story they were supposed to be co-writing—and George tried his best to keep his eyes on the old dirt road leading them to their destination. For the first time in his life, he found it almost impossible to keep his eyes safely ahead and not at the passenger seat beside him, where Annie sat, drenched in amber sunshine, more beautiful than ever.

And it wasn't because she had suddenly become any more gorgeous overnight. He couldn't even attribute it to the new Korean skincare routine she'd tried last night and waxed philosophical about for the last ten minutes. It was because, for the first time since they'd met, he felt like he knew the real Annie Martin, the one that people didn't get to see very often.

Better than that, she knew the real him, too.

What a fantastically small thing—to be seen, really seen, by someone, and not have that person run screaming in the other direction. But, like most small and beautiful things in this world, it was so rare. George wanted to hold on to that feeling, of being known, for as long as he possibly could.

But soon, despite his best attempts at capturing the moment in his hands and bottling it up forever, he found himself at the familiar metal gates and fence he'd been driving them towards. Carefully, he parked on the side of the road—where several other cars were already parked—and made his way around to help Annie out of the car.

When he finally had her in position just right, he wanted nothing more than to dip his lips down and capture hers. He wanted to cup her face and cradle her chin and hold on to her with everything he had.

But they were on a deadline. And he knew that Annie Martin didn't like to be any more than fashionably late. With a flourish, he pulled the bandana from over her eyes, and waved his arms towards the gates, where wrought-iron painted in chipping gilt-gold read:

THE ODIE HILLS MINIATURE HORSE FARM.

"Ta-da!"

Annie's jaw dropped, like a boulder to the bottom of a stream. For a brief moment, panic gripped the back of George's neck. *Oh, no.* He'd never before considered the fact that she might hate this.

"What are we doing here?" she asked, her blue eyes wide as dinner plates.

"Well, you said you never got to do anything fun." He leaned against the gate and pointed up towards the white and silver balloons tied to the iron grating. "How about a little fun, Miss Annie Martin?"

The words were part invitation, part challenge, and he should never have doubted her. Her face broke into a cheek-splitting smile, and she ran forward, gripping his hand with one of her own and pushing the gates open with the other one.

Quickly, the two of them tore down the dirt path leading past the wide pastures and towards the farmhouse and the stable. For some reason, Annie was leading them, despite the fact that she'd never before been here, but George didn't mind as long as she kept holding his hand.

Soon, the familiar green farmhouse, with its red barn doors and yellow finishes—a gaudy thing straight out of a children's storybook—reeled into view, and Annie skidded to a stop, her soft brown kid boots blending in with all the dirt she kicked up. Ah, yes. So, now she clearly saw why he'd brought her.

The barn wasn't in its normal, colorful state, with animals and children running wild and happy all around. Today, it was decorated with floral decorations and balloons, streamers and hanging-candles, and a banner—decorated by helpful children, no doubt—proclaimed that today, Sugar Cube and Smokey were going to get married.

Yes, today was the honorary wedding between two miniature horses. George had been invited to this fundraiser/party months ago, but he hadn't thought he would go. But last night, when he and Annie had talked about this old place, he'd texted his host and asked if they could still RSVP.

It only made sense. He and Annie had met at a wedding. Their first date should be at one, too. Even if neither of them were brave enough to call it that.

Annie gasped and turned on him, delight brightening those blue eyes of hers and adding an extra sheen to her smile, one that you couldn't buy in any tooth-whitening kit. An unfamiliar rush of emotion flooded his chest. He was so glad to see her like this, so happy to have erased the sadness that had permeated her last night.

"Is this...? Is this what I think it is?"

He shrugged and tried to pretend that he hadn't put an incredible amount of thought into this. Tried to pretend it didn't matter to him that she was happy with this adventure he'd brought her on. "Your favorite thing is matchmaking. When I heard there was a miniature horse wedding and I was invited, I knew I couldn't, in good faith, take anyone else as my date."

After a moment, Annie sauntered over to him, and slipped her arm through his, just like a proper wedding date would. Her smile was painfully genuine and so beautiful it almost erased all of the memories of the tears she'd shed last night.

"Look at you," she mused as they made their way forward towards the wedding party.

"What?"

"You are a secret romantic after all. I knew there was something good deep down in there somewhere."

This would have been the perfect moment to tell her exactly what he was feeling, that now that she wasn't the subject of his story anymore, he was totally free to open his heart to her. He'd seen parts of her he never thought he would and, to his great surprise, he hadn't hated what he'd found and wanted to expose her to the world. Instead, he was starting to fall in love with her, and he wanted to wrap her in his arms and protect her from everything out there.

"I just like the miniature horses, that's all," he muttered.

"Whatever you say, George." She patted his arm with her free hand, sending bolts of electricity in her wake. "Whatever you say."

The difficult thing about a wedding for miniature horses was, as George found out, actually catching the little suckers. Given their little legs, he'd thought that they would be easy to wrangle and walk down the aisle towards their cutesy internet-worthy nuptials. This was, after all, supposed to be a fundraiser for the farm's outreach programs, for buses that would take foster children and inner-city kids out to the farm to experience the animals, and he'd assumed that the hardest part would be getting people to open their wallets.

But no. The miniature horses were deceptively quick. And he learned that the hard way. It started out so innocently, with him and

Annie checking in for the wedding and Mrs. Newman approaching him with a smile.

"George, do you think you could help me with something?"

"Yeah, of course. Whatever you need. What's up?"

Mrs. Newman, a tall, heavyset woman in her sixties with a kind smile and rough hands, had traded in her usual flannel-and-jeans combination for a slightly more formal black T-shirt, jeans, and blazer ensemble. She glanced at George with slightly nervous eyes, ducking her head as if she was ashamed of what she was about to say.

"My legs just aren't what they used to be and Sugar Cube has run off with her lead and harness. Do you think you could—"

George smiled. Mrs. Newman was one of those people who would drop everything to help another person. Even if he wanted to sweep Annie off of her feet today, he could take a few minutes out of that plan to help her. "No problem."

Famous last words. Ten minutes later, he was sweating, breathing heavily, and cursing his good nature for agreeing to do something this stupid. Before he'd started this fool's errand, he'd taken off his jacket and his top shirt and slender tie—he'd gone the extra mile to dress for this wedding...and to impress Annie—and as he watched Sugar Cube idle by the edge of her paddock, chewing grass as she waited for another round of their chase, he was glad for it. Just like he was glad that Mrs. Newman had agreed to help Annie get a drink and find their seats for the wedding. He didn't want her to see him like this, breathless and defeated by a tiny animal.

But, of course, nothing could ever go right for him. Because just as he was about to start off on another round of chase, a voice interrupted him. Beautiful as birdsong and twice as sweet.

And snarky. Very, very snarky.

"I didn't think it was possible to see a grown man get outrun by a tiny little horse."

From the corner of his eye, he caught sight of Annie leaning against the paddock fence, holding a glass of champagne as the wind blew her hair, giving her the appearance of a goddess who'd temporarily graced the earth with her presence. It wasn't fair that she looked so beautiful and he probably looked like he'd just gone a few rounds in a bullfight. George focused his attention.

"She's very tricky."

"Her legs are shorter than my dog's."

"Hardly. Besides, Monster is a sweet animal. Sugar Cube is very—"

But when he looked back up, Annie was no longer leaning against the paddock. She'd gone in between two of the lateral support beams and plucked Sugar Cube's harness off the ground, which she now held in the opposite hand to her champagne glass, casual and cool as ever.

Oh, how he loved her.

Annie raised one smug eyebrow. "You were saying?"

Reaching for his discarded clothes on the fence line, George beamed at her. He couldn't help it. "I was saying that we have to get this little lady down the aisle as soon as possible."

"And?" she asked, her voice taunting.

"...And that you're a much, much better miniature horse wrangler than I am, princess."

"There you go."

Maybe he shouldn't have given into her teasing so easily and maybe he should have tried to tease her back. But in that moment, nothing mattered but the fact that he'd won her smile.

Soon, they found themselves sitting in the front row of the packed miniature horse wedding, sitting so close that he could feel the warmth of her skin through his jacket. As the sun set over the farm, dropping behind the small animal wedding party and their dressed-up handlers, Mr. Barnett, who'd been a regular at the farm and had gotten ordained for the occasion, offered up a speech.

George was so wrapped up in Annie's closeness, in his desire to reach out and take her hand, that he'd barely heard any of Mr. Barnett's small homily. He heard things like *love is the completion of hope* and *it is the answer to the questions of life that we thought had no answer.* But he really didn't come back down to earth until a small sniffle shook the body next to his, the one he hadn't stopped thinking about since she'd cozied up next to him. He glanced out of the corner of his eye to see a twin pair of teardrops slipping down Annie's face.

"Are you crying?" he whispered, not accusatory, but still surprised. Annie stiffened and ran her hand over her cheeks, ridding herself of the evidence.

"No," she hissed. "I just have something in my eye. There's a lot of... a lot of pollen out here."

George didn't have the heart to tell her that it wasn't pollen season. Instead, he gently placed his hand over hers in a reassuring grasp, trying to silently communicate that it was okay. He'd never tell a soul that she cried during a miniature horse wedding. He'd never tell a soul that Annie Martin had a heart so big and so desperate for love that even this could make her emotional.

But he did plan on telling her how much he loved her for it.

About an hour later, the party was in full swing. The chairs for the ceremony on the barn floor had been cleared. A humble town band had taken up the northern corner of the open-air space, and the guests, with the wedding party retired to their stalls for the evening, danced and laughed as the cool night air blew through them. The temperature was steadily dropping, but no one could even feel the cold. There was too much warmth here for it to even be noticed.

But soon, when Annie stepped out for some fresh air and to get away from the dance partners swinging her around the floor, George saw his moment. Collecting one of the flower arrangements Mrs. Newman had told him he could have, he followed her into the starlit darkness of the evening, where Annie stood, gazing up at the constellations.

She glowed in the sunset. For a moment, George lost all ability to speak. His heart was too full for him to find the words.

But then, she dipped her head down and met his eyes. Her smile was all the encouragement he needed. Extending the small bouquet to her, he tried to keep his voice as even and steady and certain as his heart was.

"Here. I got these for you."

Annie took the bouquet and held them to her nose, breathing their perfume in deeply before pulling them away to inspect them.

"What are they? I'm sorry, I'm terrible with flowers."

"They're just wildflowers."

The word was little more than a breath on the chilled wind. There had been half a dozen different kind of flowers that he could have chosen from the wedding selection, but when he'd seen the bright, bold, wildflowers in this arrangement, he knew that these were the ones. He didn't have an extensive knowledge of flowers, but an article he'd written ages ago had given him a good knowledge of wildflowers. They were the perfect way to say how he was feeling now. How he felt every time he looked at her.

"They're beautiful," Annie said, taking a step closer to him.

"Do you know what they mean?"

The night air between them was filled with tension, it wrapped around them both, bringing them in closer and closer until the clouds of their breath melded into one. Annie dropped her eyes, slightly flirtatiously. His heart leapt. But he pressed forward.

"They represent joy and true love and promises."

"Oh. Less romantic than I was hoping," she joked, but he could see a small pain in her eyes. It was one he would do anything to correct.

"What if I told you that's how I feel whenever I look at you? Like, I've been standing in darkness and cold all my life, but suddenly, you arrive and you break the horizon, filling me with joy and—"

He was rambling now. A ramble that was only stopped when a small, soft, hesitant hand came to rest on his chest, just over his heart. Strange how her gentle touch finally made his heart slow down.

Annie looked up, searching his face. "Where is all of this coming from?"

"Annie... This isn't about a story for me. Not anymore. I'm here... I'm here for you." Her lips parted, but he didn't stop. He couldn't stop now. "You make me feel like the world is full of wildflowers. And I'm wondering…" He steeled himself for the worst, for her to look him in the eye and reject him. After all, she hadn't said anything encouraging yet. Hadn't smiled. Hadn't done anything to indicate that she might share his affections. But he couldn't hide anymore. Even if she didn't care for him, he needed her to know that she had bewitched him. "Well, I'm wondering if you maybe feel the same way about me."

And then, something strange happened. Annie laughed at him. She *laughed*. His heart shook and waited to shatter.

"George," she said, her voice almost scolding.

"What?"

Moving her hand from over his heart to his collar, she tugged it, pulling him closer, so close that he could see the sincerity, the warmth, the overwhelming *love* in her gaze. She shook her head slightly, brushing her nose against his as she went.

"You've got to be the worst investigative reporter in the world if you don't know how I feel."

George couldn't help the grin that spread across his face. She was right. It was there.

He reached up to stroke her cheek, relishing the sensation of her skin against his. He'd dreamed of this moment for so long. "I always find that it's best to do intense, thorough research before I come to any conclusions."

"I would hate to stand in the way of your journalistic process," she said, her smile almost brushing against his as she tilted her chin up to him. "Please…"

He knew what she was asking, and who was he to deny the wishes of a princess? Heart hammering in his chest, George brought his lips to hers, trying to put every feeling fighting for attention within him into the motion. Their bodies moved together in one wish, just to be closer to one another. Somewhere in the distance, the sun was setting. The chill of evening had come, but George and Annie were sparks and heat, lightning and electricity.

His hand came up to her cheek, cradling her with all of the gentleness of someone who never wanted to let go. And he didn't. He didn't want to let go. Not of Annie. Not of this moment. Not of the way her lips moved against his in a haze of want and warmth.

But it couldn't last forever. No matter how much he wished for it. Moments later, when they parted breathlessly, Annie gazed up at him with stardust in her perfect blue eyes. "So, that's what it feels like? To have the best kiss of your life."

"Yeah. That's it," he agreed, wondering how he'd ever before thought that any kiss he'd ever had was perfect when *this* was waiting in his future.

"I can't believe I went through my whole life never having that."

"Don't worry. You'll never have to go without again."

Without a second thought or hesitation, Annie took immediate advantage of that promise, kissing him like she never wanted to stop.

Chapter Nineteen

Annie

Annie could barely sit still. No amount of sunrise yoga or meditation or chewing gum from Gwyneth Paltrow's website that promised to fix fidgeting could stop her. Every muscle in her entire body seemed electrified from the inside out, almost as if the little particles that made her up were trying to leap out from her own skin.

She'd kissed George Barnett. She was starting to fall in love with George Barnett. She was possibly already very much in love with George Barnett.

How could one be expected to sit still and act normal after something so wonderful? For so long, she'd thought that love was a remote possibility, something she'd be able to watch at a distance, but never have for herself. But now, it was here. Right at her fingertips. All she had to do was open her heart and let it in.

It was a big step, a big leap to make after almost an entire lifetime of believing she would be alone forever.

Yesterday, when his lips had touched hers, she'd told him that she couldn't believe she'd gone through her entire life without kissing him. And that was true. The kissing was, well, it was beyond lovely. World-changing. It was nothing short of a tragedy that she'd wasted so much time of her life not being kissed by him. But even worse was the realization that she'd spent so much of her life not feeling this way. She felt so open, so free, so overwhelmingly happy, that a big part of her mourned for the years and years she'd spent unhappy.

Not that it mattered now. She never intended to feel that way ever again. Starting today, she wasn't just going to pretend she was happy all the time. She was actually going to *be* happy all the time.

That started tonight. Girls' night. A good, old-fashioned slumber party that would fill her home with human warmth, where they would all stay up late, talk about boys, and eat so much sugar that at least one of them passed out from the over-stimulation. Usually, Annie would use her brother's house or invite herself over to the Andersons' for a night like this, but not tonight. Tonight, she wanted to be in her own house, with her own things, surrounded by the people she liked best in the world.

Oh, and Mynette, the administrative assistant at the *Hillsboro Gazette*, the one who hadn't liked her very much. Annie thought now was as good a time as any to start making new friends, especially among the friends who were important to George.

When she'd called the offices and left a message inviting her, she hadn't been certain that she'd show up. But then, right on the nose of seven o'clock, a rapping, blunt knock on the front door assured her that she had. Rose never knocked, so she knew it had to be her newest guest. Annie threw open the door with a smile, thrill running through her at the sight of the woman on the other side of the doorway, all bundled up as if the mild California winter had arrived already, holding an overnight bag over one shoulder and a big pot in the other.

"Mynette! I'm so excited you came. Come in! You must be freezing."

"I brought soup. I don't really know what grown-ups eat at sleepovers. I haven't been to one since I was thirteen."

Her lips were set in a thin line, her eyes uncertain and shifting from left to right, as though she was afraid someone was going to jump out of the shadows and ambush her. Annie stepped aside, taking the pot when it was offered to her. Monster watched the whole exchange hesitantly from the couch arm in the living room, assessing the scenario. Not for the first time, Annie was grateful she'd gotten an adorable mutt from the shelter instead of a beast bred for protection like the Andersons' dog, Stella. She beamed at Mynette as the woman stepped inside and set her bag down in the entryway.

"Soup is perfect! It smells amazing. Did you make this?"

"It's my grandmother's recipe. Why did you invite me tonight?"

The question was abrupt and humorless, but still, Annie couldn't help but admire the woman who'd asked it. She knew what it was like, to try to wear armor to defend yourself in this big, complicated world. Leading her into the kitchen, where Annie retired the stew pot to the front burner to keep the soup inside warm, she tried to keep the tone light. Tried to subtly let Mynette know that this was a safe place to give the armor a rest.

"Can you keep a secret?"

"Yes."

Annie shrugged and leaned against the kitchen counter, trying not to wilt under the heat of Mynette's narrowed gaze. "I'm really, really bad at making friends. I usually ask the Anderson sisters over, but they're out of town and—"

"And I'm a placeholder?"

"No! Not at all!" She swallowed, hard. This was more difficult than she'd anticipated. But if she was really going to open her heart, if she was really going to try and take this happiness thing to its fullest, then she had to take her own advice. She had to take off the last of her armor. To tell the truth even when a joke would probably have gotten her out of doing so. "I just wanted to make some new friends. And you have always seemed so nice."

For a moment, Annie stared at a chipped spot in her kitchen tiles. Mynette cleared her throat.

"Well. Um. Thank you. For inviting me."

Relief washed over Annie, sweet and warm. Pulling her attention up to her new friend, she beamed a smile that she only hoped made Mynette feel as good as she felt right now. When she'd first met the *Hillsboro Gazette* assistant, she'd wanted to be her friend because she couldn't stand the idea of someone out there not liking her. But now . . . she just really wanted another friend. And she was glad that Mynette was willing to at least try it.

"No, thank *you* for coming."

Just at that moment, the front door swung open, knocking against the back wall and announcing the arrival of their latest guest. Not a second later, Rose shuffled inside, carrying a stack of white bakery boxes in her arms.

"Alright. I'm here and I brought four different kinds of pies from Millie's. Are we ordering pizza or tacos?"

Annie and Mynette shared a look. Soon, Mynette's lips tilted upwards in something close to a smirk. "Why not both?"

An hour later, they were all in their pajamas and sitting around the living room of Annie's little house, picking at boxes upon boxes of tacos and slices of three different kinds of pizza. They hadn't been able to decide on anything, but now that Annie had eaten her share of homemade soup *and* more carbs than she was comfortable admitting to, she was glad that their indecision had forced them to order just about everything.

One thing she wasn't glad about? Rose's offhand, dismissive comment about Eris moving to Petaluma. Annie's chest tightened at the thought.

"So, you're not going to see him again?" she practically screeched, caught so off guard by the news that she couldn't even pretend to be cool about the whole thing.

"No. I'm sure that's putting a real wrench in your matchmaking plans, but—"

"Me?" Annie breathed, trying to laugh off the sly accusations and clearly failing miserably, if Rose's flat expression was anything to go by. "Matchmaking?"

"Come on, Annie. I know that it was all your doing. The fake speed-dating night? You thought I was going to buy that?"

For the first time in the conversation, Mynette's face brightened. "Oh, I heard about that. People said it was a lot of fun."

Rose leaned back against the nearby couch, tossing her head with a knowing laugh. "Yeah, it was fun. But it wasn't real. Annie here just set it up because she wanted to get me together with this guy, but I saw right through her and brought everyone I could to come and make sure it wasn't just me and him alone."

Mynette's jaw dropped. Her eyebrows knit closely together as she stared Annie down. "You did that for her?"

Torn between confessing that, yes, it had been her in the library with the candlestick—or, rather, her in the wine bar with the matchmaking schemes—and denying everything even though she'd already been caught, Annie decided on the former. After all, she was trying to turn over a new leaf. Tugging on the ends of a lock of hair that had fallen over her shoulder, Annie played it as cool as she could manage.

"She's my friend. I want my friends to be happy and find love—"

"And maybe one day I will. But let's cool it on the matchmaking, alright? Besides, I heard you'll be pretty busy on your own here."

Mynette chewed another mouthful of taco as she assessed Annie with inquisitive eyes. "What's that supposed to mean?"

Alright. Here was the moment of truth. The moment when she had to decide if she was really going to be herself, be her whole, true, authentic self and tell the truth, or if she was going to hide behind her Annie Martin persona once again. A few months ago, she would have said something sly and secretive, hiding what had really happened in case it made her look foolish or in case someone ran away with this information and sold it to TMZ or something. Now, she looked at the two women sitting across her small living room from her—one of whom, Mynette, was very comfortably lounging with Monster snoozing in her lap—and realized she didn't want to hide anymore. Not from anyone. Not for any reason.

She didn't have to shield herself from the world any longer. She was finally free.

A smile grew wider and wider across her face as the memory of last night reawakened every muscle in her entire body. "I can neither confirm nor deny that yesterday, after much waiting and anticipation and kind of hating him for a while, George Barnett and I finally kissed."

Rose gasped. Now they were getting to the good slumber party gossip. "You didn't."

"We did."

"Where?" Rose followed-up.

"On the lips, where else?"

"No, I mean. Tell me everything."

Annie didn't need anyone to ask her twice. Pulling her knees into her chest, she started at the very beginning—yesterday afternoon and that ridiculous blindfold—and told them all of the details she could remember. The rugged scent of him and the jokes they'd shared and him chasing around the adorable miniature horse and the kisses—*oh, the kisses*. Those sweet moments that Annie wanted to store away in her heart for the rest of time, just so she could go back in there and open them up every once in a while, experiencing them all over again.

"...And then, he just...he kissed me. It was like...it was like for the first time, I really wanted someone to know me. To see me. Like I didn't want to hide anymore."

Her entire being was so full. She didn't know if she was going to be able to contain all of these feelings. She was just...She was just so happy. And happiness was just so underrated, in her opinion.

Rose's hand went to her heart, as if she wasn't sure she could keep it in her chest, either. "Annie, that's beautiful. When are you going to see him again?"

"We don't have firm plans yet, but I'm hoping he calls tonight."

Not that she was going to leave her friends and her sleepover to go and see him, of course, but she suddenly missed the sound of his voice. She'd like to hear it, even if she couldn't go and see him right at this very minute.

"I knew this was going to happen," Rose crooned, leaning back in her chair and kicking her legs up on a nearby coffee table. Annie rolled her eyes.

"You couldn't have known. I didn't even know this was going to happen."

"The two of you were inevitable. Two people so perfect for each other can't exist without eventually falling in love."

The way Rose said it—so light, so easy, so, like she said, inevitable—fisted at Annie's heart.

"Perfect for each other?" Annie asked, her voice barely audible.

Rose contemplated the question for a moment, as if she hadn't expected any follow-up questions to her confident declaration.

"Yeah," she said after a moment. "For example, neither of you are very used to being told no. Neither of you are used to other people getting in your way. But when you're together, you both have to negotiate. Soften. You're like a flower in the perfect soil. You nourish each other. Make each other grow stronger and better. Brighter."

There was a pause, as if Rose was weighing what she might say next. Then, she punctuated her speech. "And... the two of you both seem, no offense, but... kind of lonely. Two people who could really use a family. Who could be each other's family."

Annie opened her mouth to try and brush aside the words—and the emotions that they brought with them—but she stopped short when she looked over to Mynette to see that her face was drawn, pale, uncomfortable.

"Annie," she said, her voice shaking slightly. "I have a confession to make."

"A confession. Sounds scandalous," she replied, completely unworried. What was she going to tell her? That she hadn't liked her before tonight but did now? Something equally fun and exciting? Annie didn't know, but she doubted that anything someone could say tonight would bring her back down to earth. She was too happy to be insulted. Too hopeful to be crushed. "Go on."

"I think you need to know that—"

But her declaration was cut off by the shrill ringing of Annie's phone. Usually, she would keep the thing on silent, but from the moment she and George last went their separate ways, she'd kept it on full blast just in case he'd call or text. She didn't want to miss it. Jumping to her feet, she made a beeline for the front table where she'd left it.

"Oh, just a second. Let me grab that. Maybe it's my boyfriend."

Mynette protested. "No, wait. Just let me say—"

The phone was still ringing, and when Annie picked it up, she realized that the caller identification wasn't coming up with anyone in her contacts. It could be one of the brands she expressed interest in working with during her last call with her Social Media Manager. She didn't want to miss that. A wave dismissed Mynette's sudden desperation.

"I'll be right back!"

Annie ducked through the front door, stepping out onto her top step before sliding the screen to accept the call. Out in her pajamas and without any shoes, she was struck by how suddenly cold it was, like a big weather system was about to move into town. Harsh winds blew goosebumps across the back of her neck. She hugged herself to stay warm.

"Hello?" she asked.

A slightly familiar female voice crackled on the other end of the line. "Yes, hello. Is this Annie Martin?"

"Speaking."

"Wonderful. This is Erica from the *Hillsboro Gazette*; we met when you visited our office a while back. I'm sorry for calling so late, but we're under kind of a tight deadline. Need to get a fact-check to a possible syndication editor. Would you mind answering a few questions on a story we're going to run?"

Chapter Twenty

George

"Hey, Annie. I haven't heard from you. I know you're supposed to wait a day or so before you call a girl you like or whatever, but it's a pretty small town and I kept thinking I would run into you, but…You know, I'm rambling. Basically, I'm just wondering if you might want to hang out? Or if you could send me proof of life or something? So that I don't need to spy on you again." He awkwardly chuckled. "Okay, this is getting weird now. Sorry. Just, uh, if I haven't completely embarrassed myself in this voicemail, could you—"

Nope. This was George's third attempt at leaving Annie a voice-mail, and once again, he'd screwed it up. Dialing seven to delete the recording, he let his phone fall to his side. He was sitting on his usual bench in the town square, eating a bagel and a coffee alone. At his side sat a brown paper bag with another bagel and a second cup of coffee, the sugary kind that Annie had once told him she was obsessed with. He'd been harboring secret hopes that he would see her here, that she'd be strolling by, catch sight of him, and brighten before running over to throw her arms around his neck and kiss him. In those fantasies, sometimes, she would tell him that she'd been called away to L.A. unexpectedly and had lost her phone and had tried to send a telegram and a carrier pigeon letter and a singing telegram, but a series of silent-film-style misadventures had kept all of them from getting to him and, and, and...

And really, he missed her. They'd poured out their hearts and run with the miniature horses and shared secrets and *kissed*. Why the sudden ghosting? He'd never thought of Annie as one of those people who would keep a guy at arm's-length over propriety. She wasn't one of those *absence makes the heart grow fonder* types.

So, where was she? And why was she ignoring him?

Or... Or was something wrong? Had something happened to her? A sudden panic gripped at his heart. Here he was, arrogantly and selfishly thinking that she was just ignoring him, that all of this was about him. But what if she was ill? What if something had happened and she was just too proud to tell anyone?

George checked his watch. He needed to be in the office in half an hour. But if something really *was* wrong with Annie, then it would be worth the talking-to from Erica. Besides, she was just a handful of blocks away. He could causally stroll by, say he was in the neighborhood and wanted to say hi.

Without another thought, George collected his breakfast and started for her house. His heart pounded all the way, uncertainty and fear wrapping around him with the choking intensity of a hungry python. The options that he could stomach were that either she realized she didn't love him or something horrible had happened to her. Neither of those was a particularly comforting scenario.

When he arrived at her house, he wasted no time running straight up to the door and knocking on it, perhaps a little bit louder and more intensely than was strictly speaking necessary.

"Annie?" he called. "Annie, are you in there?"

Just as he was about to raise his hand again to knock, the door swung open, sending him slightly off balance. What waited for him on the other side of the threshold was nothing short of shocking. Yes, it was Annie. No, she wasn't hurt or mortally injured or anything like that.

She was wearing pajamas. A bathrobe. No makeup. Her hair was even tossed up in a messy bun. Her eyes were red, puffy, displaying all of the signs of crying that he could think of.

The sight was nearly enough to rip him in two. When she spoke, her voice barely concealing rage and hatred, though, that finished the job.

"What do you want?"

He reeled back, stunned by the sharp edges of her tone. "Oh, I'm sorry. Are you busy?"

She crossed her arms over her chest and leaned against the doorframe. Not even giving him the privilege of her full attention, she stared down at her fingernails. "Yeah. What do you need? Is your phone broken?"

"I was just..." George swallowed, confused at the sudden shift in her. The last time he'd seen her, she was kissing him and talking about how she never wanted to stop. Now, she looked as if she was annoyed that she'd ever met him in the first place. "I was just thinking about you and wanted to check that you were okay. I hadn't heard from you, so I was worried—"

"And what?" She snorted. It was the first time he'd ever heard her make a noise so derisive, so bitter. "You thought you would just come over here and express your concern in person?"

"Well, I was worried that something was wrong—"

Annie leveled her gaze at him. Cold.

"You know, I have to admire your commitment to the bit, but I think you can do us both a favor and cut it out, okay? You don't have to keep this up anymore."

George knew all of those words, but didn't understand them in the order she'd put them. "Don't have to keep up what anymore? Annie, you're not making any sense."

"George." Annie's mouth pulled down after she'd said it, like she'd just accidentally swallowed a sour candy. She tightened her jaw. "Please. Don't do this. It's just making it worse."

Everything about the way she was in that moment—the hobbled posture, the clench of her jaw, the wobbling of her bottom lip, and the distance in her expression—it all made him want to pull her into his arms, squeeze her tight, and hold her until she realized that everything would be okay. He didn't know what was making her upset, what he'd done to offend her or hurt her feelings, but he wanted to help.

He hated seeing her like this.

"I don't understand what you're talking about."

A wry, mirthless chuckle escaped her lips. "Well, you know what I don't understand? Why you would pretend to be falling for me and make me believe all of this garbage about love and trust when really, the whole time, you had a private investigator searching through my entire life back in Los Angeles."

George felt as if he'd been slapped clear across the face. His jaw hung limp. He fell a step back. That's when he realized that he'd forgotten to call off Eagle. While he was here, swooning over Annie and kissing her like his life depended on it, Eagle had been back in Hollywood, digging through Annie's things and trying to get an angle on a story that George was no longer going to write.

He didn't know what to say. He didn't know how she'd found out about it. All he knew was the pain emanating from Annie's defeated expression.

"Yeah. Not so sweet and romantic now, are you?" she muttered, spitting the words more than saying them.

"I just don't know…I mean…I hired someone for the story, but—"

"You know, you could have saved yourself a lot of money if you'd just kissed me a few more times. I probably wouldn't have even cared when you ran the story. I can't believe I believed you. *Trust me, Annie. It wouldn't be justice, Annie. It would be a tragedy.* What a load of garbage."

She thought that he'd been using her this entire time. She thought that everything he'd said had been a lie just to get a story out of her. The pit of his stomach opened up, and he dropped down into the darkness. He'd asked her to trust him and in return, what had he given her? Nothing but betrayal. Taking a step forward, he tried to help her understand what had happened.

"I'm sorry that I didn't call off the investigation, but you have to believe me. I'm not writing the story, I didn't do anything to try and betray you—"

Annie's eyes went wide. Rage and tears dominated her silvery-blue eyes. She took a step back and briefly glanced at the space between them, as if she was incensed by the mere idea that he could be trying to get any closer to her than he already, disdainfully, was.

He'd been trying to help her understand. But when she spoke again, he realized that it wasn't Annie who'd misunderstood. It was him.

"You're still trying to salvage this? I already got a call from your paper." She separated each word and syllable until she was certain he'd gotten the point. George's heart roared in his ears. "They asked me to fact-check everything. I already know you're a liar and a cruel, heartless man, so don't even stand there and pretend you aren't."

He'd thought maybe she'd heard about the investigator from a friend. He thought that if he explained everything, explained that it was a harmless mistake, that she would understand and see her way to forgiving him. Maybe one day they could laugh about all of this silly misunderstanding.

But that hadn't been the case at all. Someone at the paper had told her, had convinced her that he'd been lying all this time, that he'd been waiting for the right moment to strike and sell her story to the highest bidder.

"What do you mean? I didn't..." He swallowed, hard, and tried to find the words that would help wipe the hatred from her face. "I haven't even written the story. Annie, I love you—"

She flinched. She blinked. Two perfect tears slipped down her cheeks. She wasn't angry. She wasn't filled with rage or heartbreak anymore. Now... now, she was just defeated. Broken. And he didn't know how to fix her again.

"Just go. Please. I can't... I can't do this anymore."

And when she closed the door, leaving him on the other side of it, he'd never felt more alone in his entire life.

George left. His watch informed him that he was late for work, but that was the least of his worries. Rage and concern and betrayal pumped through his veins, pushing him to practically run all the way from Annie's house up to the *Hillsboro Gazette*'s office. Not because he was late. But because he wanted to find out who had done this and what they thought they were doing.

When he reached the top of the stairway, he skidded to a stop when he spotted Mynette sitting behind her desk, her face pale and shocked at the sight of him. A twist pulled at his insides, sending his entire being into chaos. Oh, no. They were all in on it, weren't they?

After a moment of that confirmation, he found he couldn't look at her anymore. Without asking for permission, he went straight for Erica's Editor-in-Chief office, where she sat behind an antique oak desk.

"What the hell is going on in here?" he spluttered, turning the brunt of his brutal anger squarely in her direction. This was probably going to get him fired, but he didn't care. There had been a miscarriage of their duties as journalists today. Annie Martin had cried today. He wasn't going to let that go. He *couldn't* let it go.

Erica looked up, her lips turning into a thin line as she tried to keep her tone cordial and friendly. She kept the receiver of her office phone up to her ear even as she addressed him.

"George. Good to see you. I'm actually on the phone."

"Yeah. I can see that. Hang up."

He felt like a barreling freight train, crushing everything in his path. Never before, not in his entire life, had he spoken to Erica this way. The woman shot him a look, but spoke into the phone instead of to him next.

"Sorry, Mr. Rothschild. George is a great investigative reporter, as I'm sure you know, but he can be quite temperamental." Some noise on the other line. Erica laughed. "Like all good writers, yes! Very good. Let me put you on speaker."

George's jaw dropped. Rothschild was the editor at *The National*, one of the biggest papers in the entire country, a byline that, a week ago, George might have done morally questionable things to get. Now, George didn't want to speak to him. "No, don't—"

But it was too late. Erica had already placed the phone in its cradle, pressed a few buttons, and welcomed the crackling, aging voice of the famous D.C. paper baron into the small office. "George! George, this is Eric Rothschild. I'm with *The National*. We've heard you've done some really great reporting on this Annie Martin girl. Your editor is keeping the exact subject matter and scoop you've gotten tight-lipped, understandably, but we'd like to negotiate some national syndication with you, if you're interested."

The words hung in the air as George stared down his boss. A woman he'd trusted and looked up to for years. Annie's heartbreaking cries still haunted him. This was just a knife plunging deeper and deeper into his chest.

"I'd like to talk to my boss first, if you don't mind. This is all very sudden."

"Of course. Take your time. Just don't give it to anyone else, alright? We got here first."

Erica made quick work on the goodbyes, shuffling the man off the phone as quickly as she could manage without seeming rude. "Alright, Mr. Rothschild. Thank you so much. Goodbye."

Just as friendly and polite as she'd been on the phone a moment ago turned completely in the opposite direction when she hung up and returned to her conversation with George. If he wasn't shaking with his own barely-concealed rage, he might have jumped back when she raised her angry voice at him.

"What are you doing? You could have ruined that deal."

"What deal? What story? What the hell are you doing calling Annie to fact-check a story I haven't even written?"

Erica crossed her arms over her chest. "Your Eagle called the nest yesterday. Told Mynette everything. Mynette told *me* everything because she couldn't get ahold of you. And now, I know that you're sitting on the biggest story in the entire country. Can you imagine what this could do for your career? A salacious celebrity scandal that involves one of the country's most notoriously private tech moguls?"

George's mouth filled with the bitter, acidic taste of blood. He'd been biting the inside of his cheek too hard. "I'm not doing that. It's not a scandal. It's heartbreaking and—"

"And it could make your career."

He knew that Erica was only trying to do what was best for him, which made it all the more important that he explain to her, once and for all, why this wasn't what he wanted *or* needed.

"I'm not writing the story and I can't *believe* that you did this. It's not your story to fact-check and it's not yours to shop around."

"This is what you've always wanted. You've worked hard for your career and I've been there every step along the way—"

"I don't want it. Not like this."

Not if I have to break an innocent woman's heart and life to get it. Not if I have to walk all over her in order to get higher up the ladder. The very thought of it made him sick.

"Why is this any different?"

"Because I'm not going to exploit some woman's tragedy for clicks and a big byline. That's not right."

Erica paused. Assessed him. Then, she clucked her tongue disdainfully, sinking back into her chair. "Ah. But she isn't just some woman, is she?"

That one little question and one matching quirk of Erica's perfectly manicured eyebrow was all it took for the palms of George's hands to start sweating. This wasn't the turn he'd expected this to take. The hairs on the back of his neck stood on edge as he tried his best to dismiss Erica's implications.

"I don't know what you're talking about."

But Erica wasn't buying it. She reeled as her revelation took over her, shaking her head slightly as if she couldn't quite believe it herself. "This whole time, I thought you were dancing around town with her because you were trying to get this story. And maybe that's how it started. But that's not how it ended, is it? You have fallen in love with her and you're letting that get in the way of everything."

"I haven't let it get in the way of anything. I'm trying to do what's right."

"George." Erica's face suddenly slipped into something resembling sympathy. She bit her bottom lip, considering him. Erica had always been a mentor to him, always reminded him of their dedication to this cause. He looked up to her in nearly every way and he'd thought that she had a soft spot for him, too. Watching her as she sat at her desk, conflict written into every shadow of her smooth face, he couldn't help but think maybe he'd been right about that. Maybe she *did* want what was best for him, what would make him happy. But she couldn't give up the other reality sitting before her... All the good that a story like this could do for the paper she'd given her entire life to keep afloat. "I think we're a dying newspaper in a small town and the money that we could get for this story... that would be life-changing. I think it would be wrong to let us drown just because you want to kiss Annie Martin."

"That's not what's happening here," George said, his voice straining.

But now? Now, he wasn't so sure. Was he just protecting her because of their connection? Was he just a boyfriend trying to keep his girlfriend's name from being dragged through the mud? Was he just doing this because he wanted to kiss her forever, and knew that the moment this happened, all hope for him would be lost?

He didn't want that to be true. But Erica had planted a seed of doubt.

"Well. Here's their offer." She slid a stack of neatly bound papers across her desk, which George took but did not inspect. "They sent it over this morning. Why don't you take a look, take a few days, and decide what you think your little crush is worth, hm?"

There were only about twenty pieces of paper in his hand, but, to George, they felt heavier than an entire mountain full of boulders. Erica was right. This was what he'd been working towards his entire life. This was his dream. But on the other hand, there was Annie.

There was justice. There was goodness and everything else he'd ever believed in. He stumbled away from her desk. "Yeah. Thanks."

With every step he took out of her office, every breath he took that didn't end with him screaming that he would never do *anything* of the sort, that he loved Annie and would never let his work hurt her in any way...he became less and less sure of himself.

And by the time he made it back to his own office and caught a glance of himself in the reflection of his glass door, he might as well have been looking at a stranger.

Chapter Twenty-One

Annie

Annie didn't want to see anyone. She didn't even want to look in the mirror. But, at least for now, she couldn't stop acting like everything was fine. She had to go through the motions, had to at least pretend like she was going to survive this. She kept up with her routine. Walks with Monster. Breakfast at one of the cafés on the square. Helping out around Rose's shop.

But for the first time in her life, she found that she didn't have the strength to wear her usual armor. Her mask had slipped, and she didn't know how to get it back.

Eventually, Rose's voice came to her over the shop's counter. "Hey, kiddo, why don't you let me drive you to my place? We can have another girls' night."

Annie's voice flatlined. She couldn't even muster up the slightest, most encouraging of inflections. Her lips didn't curl in a smile. She just nodded. "Yeah. Sure. Sounds good."

Later in the afternoon, after the shop closed and they'd made it back to the Anderson house, Annie tried to do better about at least pretending she was happy to go through the motions of her life. But the problem with having friends, with having people who at least looked out for you a little bit, was that they could always tell when something was wrong. And Rose wasn't the kind of person to let someone wallow for long.

"Annie," she said, when she came down from the second floor of the house to find Annie sitting in the picture box window seat, curled up in a blanket so she could look out over the entire farm. "We're going to have to talk about it sometime."

"Maybe I don't want to talk about it," Annie said, tipping her forehead against the cool glass as though that could stop the raging heat of the tears threatening to break free.

Usually, sitting here, where she could inspect the way the sun hit the flowers growing down the hill in front of the Anderson house, gave Annie good perspective. It reminded her that she was just like one of those flowers, growing and changing and reaching towards the sun. It reminded her that nothing was permanent. That just because you felt like a seedling today, tomorrow you might blossom into an unspeakably beautiful flower.

But today, the clouds hung down low over the farm, filling the landscape with a layer of dense, swirling fog. Annie almost felt like it was crawling towards her, marching ever closer until it would consume her entirely. She didn't turn to see Rose standing there with her concerned expression and her arms full of the board games that she'd gone to fetch in the hopes of changing Annie's gray mood, but she did hear the shifting of creaking floorboards as Rose nervously swayed on the balls of her feet.

"Do you want me to call your brother—"

"No!" Annie said, panic tweaking the back of her neck, sending even more heat rushing to her cheeks. The last thing she wanted was to drag her brother into this. She'd been the cause of so much of his misery; for once, she wanted to handle something on her own. Bear it on her own. If he knew what had happened, what was about to happen, then he'd no doubt rush home from his honeymoon and do everything in his power to stop it. But Annie was too tired to fight it, too tired to once again be the problem in her brother's life. "I don't want him to...I can't...This was my mistake. It was my fault."

"It's never a mistake to fall in love, Annie. Never."

"It's a mistake to fall in love with someone who isn't real. Who never even *was* real. How could I be so stupid? How could I think that I would ever, ever have a love like that?"

Sickness rose up in Annie's throat. These were thoughts she'd been running over and over again for the last few days, but she'd never dared to say out loud. At the end of her bench, she felt the material of the cushion beneath her bend beneath the weight of her friend as Rose came to sit across from her.

"And why wouldn't you?"

"People like me can't be too happy. When we get too happy, the world punishes us."

There it was again, that heat beneath her eyes, begging to be washed away by salty tears. For one brief, shining moment, she'd thought that maybe she was good enough to be loved by someone. That maybe her parents had been wrong when they'd basically rejected her. That she wasn't just this unlovable thing who needed to constantly earn her keep in all of the friendships and acquaintanceships she managed to force her way into. But she'd been wrong. George proved that.

The clock ticked. The wind outside the window shifted. Annie's breath and heartbeat became the most dominant sounds she heard. Rose watched her. She tried not to notice. Then, Rose shifted, pulled a blanket from a nearby basket around her shoulders, and asked a light, easy question. "Can I tell you a story?"

Annie wanted to ask what kind of story she was in for, but she brushed away the question almost the moment it occurred to her. Still, she didn't pull her forehead away from the window. She just shrugged. It was all she had the strength to do right now.

"Sure."

In the glass of the window, Rose's reflected image blew out a long, steady sigh that ruffled her long, loose red hair. Soon, she slumped down enough to mirror Annie's body language, pulling her knees to her chest and leaning against the window as if it was the only thing keeping her up.

Even with all of that, though, she didn't lose her smile. This time, it was a distant smile, soft and hesitant, but it being there despite everything that had happened gave Annie the smallest flicker of hope.

"So, when I graduated from college and opened up my shop, I was so lonely. I'd always thought that once I went to college, even a little community college like the one I went to, that my world would expand and maybe, just maybe, I'd open up my dating pool enough to finally find someone to love me."

This wasn't where Annie had thought the story was going to go. She gulped. Rose continued.

"Annie, I wanted to be loved more than anything. More than I could possibly put into words. I didn't want a big business, like Harper did. I didn't want to see the world like May did. I just wanted a house. I wanted a bread maker. I wanted wine charms and friends who came over for dinner every Thursday night and enough children to start my own basketball team and a husband who loved me like I was the only woman on earth. But I went away to college and you know what happened?"

The question was bait. Annie could have answered it easily—*you didn't find anyone*—but she took that bait instead.

"What? What happened?"

"I didn't find anyone. I had a few dates, but nothing else. Nothing real. So, I started to go online and I started to search and search and, eventually, I found this online pen pal site. There was this guy—Luka—who was just the most handsome, most kind, most intelligent person I'd ever met. He knew how to make me laugh and how to make me *feel* and he kept telling me he'd always wanted to move to wine country."

Annie's pulse skipped a beat in her ears, throwing her completely off rhythm. Pulling herself away from the window, she gave her friend all of her attention. She'd never heard any of this before. Not even when Rose was trying to get her to knock it off with the matchmaking did she mention that she had a guy out there waiting for her.

"But you're..." Annie stammered. "I mean...you didn't..."

It was Rose's turn to shrug. She recounted the twisting knife of the story's climax with all of the nonchalance of a woman describing an expected change in the weather. "It's because he wasn't real. He was a complete fiction. Some guy in Tampa was doing the same thing to about a hundred other girls. We were all on a spreadsheet."

"Rose—"

Finally, her friend turned those stunning green eyes of hers straight to Annie. This time, they were watery. "I've never told anyone. When we started dating, it felt so special and so perfect that I wanted it to just be mine, a secret that I could hold on to, one that I could use to keep the loneliness at bay. And then when this girl contacted me and told me about the whole thing and Luka—sorry, *Gerald*—came clean, I was so ashamed I couldn't tell anyone."

Again, there was silence. Annie picked at the chipping polish on her nails, trying to put the pieces of this story she'd just been trusted with together. She'd always assumed that Rose's life was that of the placid princess, who believed that good things were going to come to her because bad things never had. Now, she knew that couldn't be further from reality. Rose was the way that she was precisely *because* she'd been through hell...and she was grateful to have gotten out of it unscathed.

"Why are you telling me this now, then?"

"Because you seem to think that people who are too happy get punished for it." Rose's teary gaze burned away with the fire in her eyes. "So, then, what did I do to deserve getting hurt like that?"

A rush of righteous rage rushed through Annie's entire being, hotter and more painful than being set on fire. Rose was the best of them, the kindest, most gentle, most wonderful person Annie had ever met. She didn't know how anyone who'd ever met Rose could do anything less than love her with their entire heart, much less offer her the kind of cruelty that this guy gave her. Annie didn't know the man, didn't know anything about him besides what Rose had told her, and yet, if Annie ever had the displeasure of meeting him, she knew without a shadow of a doubt that she would put all of her Krav Maga training to good use. The fact that Rose would think, for even a fraction of a second, that she deserved any of the hatred that had been flung at her by that monster sent her spiraling. "Rose! Nothing! That guy was a jerk. He's the bad guy in that scenario, not you!"

But Rose, as ever, was above spiraling. Above raising her voice. Tilting her head ever so slightly, lowering her voice to the soft volume of a mother giving her daughter soothing but tough advice, Rose reached out to gently touch one of Annie's flailing, emphatic hands, which she wrapped up in her own.

"Right. You would never tell me that I somehow deserved what happened to me. So, why on earth would you think that you do?"

It was equal parts scolding and edifying. At once soothing and shaking to Annie's very core. It was also a question to which Annie didn't have an answer. She'd never thought of it that way, never considered that maybe she would never talk to anyone else in this entire world—especially not her friends and loved ones—the way she talked to and about herself. Rose continued, conviction sharpening her every syllable.

"George Barnett, if he really did this, if he betrayed you and ends up running this story, then he's the monster here. Not you." Rose squeezed her hand. "You deserve to be happy and loved and all of the good things in this world."

Annie tried to smile. Really, she did. She was grateful for the talk and grateful for her friend and she wanted, more than just about anything, to show Rose just how happy she was for her friendship.

But every time she tried to actually display that on her face, her urge to cry only got less and less deniable. She stared at her destroyed nails, inspecting their dull, chipped color and the pale skin beneath. Guilt pooled in her gut.

"I don't feel very happy right now," she muttered, unable to come up with anything else to say.

Half of her expected for Rose to throw her hands up, to pull her off the couch and refuse to talk to her until she stopped wallowing. Part of her thought that Rose might finally be done with her, might finally hate her and want her out of her life just like everyone else seemed to do.

That didn't happen. Instead, Rose just nodded. Slowly. Understanding. Kind.

"I know. But as your friend, I'm going to be here with you, every step of the way until you find your happiness again. I promise."

That settled into the air between them. Annie should have been gun-shy from promises. After all, the last person who'd made her a promise had gone back on it as cruelly as one possibly could. But when Rose smiled at her, she could see the experience of heartbreak in her eyes. She'd been through this before, and when she promised to help, Annie knew that she meant it.

"Now," Rose said, rising to her feet, blanket still wrapped around her shoulders like an elegant flannel shawl. "Should I get you a cup of tea?"

"Yeah. I'd like that. Thank you, Rose."

"Don't mention it. This is what friends are for."

Chapter Twenty-Two

George

George tried to go through the motions. He tried to recover, to rebound, to smile and laugh around the office while he could hear his editor through the walls, talking about syndication and financials and the possibility of future pieces from him.

He hadn't agreed to let them publish the piece. He hadn't even started writing the thing. Every time he sat down at his desk to start, to ruin an innocent woman's life for the sake of his career, the urge to empty the contents of his stomach into the nearest wastebasket became so strong that he almost immediately had to get up and take a walk around the block for some fresh air.

His phone became an extension of his arm. He checked it too often, wondering if Annie had left him a message or sent him a text. He couldn't imagine what in the world she would say to him, but he never stopped hoping that one minute he would look down and see the familiar sight of her contact picture illuminating his screen.

In the years since he and his family parted ways—or, well, when his family disowned him and refused to ever speak to him again—he'd gotten very good at being on his own. He knew how to sit at a bar, alone, for dinner, and order confidently while the waiters made sad eyes at you. Going to the movies solo was always a thrill. Even Saturday nights alone in his house or Hanukkahs spent lighting the candles by himself had their charms. But now that he'd had a taste of love, now that he'd known the true depths of happiness that a real, true relationship could hold...being on his own wasn't nearly so appealing.

In fact, he hated it.

But every time he thought about picking up the phone and calling her, or going out to see her, he just remembered the way she'd looked at him when she'd said she couldn't be with him anymore. Even if he apologized, even if he took the contract and ripped it to shreds, she would still hate him. And she was right to. A man who deserved Annie Martin would have been able to protect her. If he was really so passionate about doing the right thing and justice and all of the junk he always talked about, then he would have been able to save her before she ever even found out she was in danger.

He should have torn up the contract the moment that Erica gave it to him. He should have told the editor in Washington that he wouldn't betray Annie Martin for all of the money and fame in the world. But there was that nagging voice in the back of his head, the one that kept him paralyzed.

Even if he did stop this story, it wouldn't matter. He'd already ruined everything with Annie. Her trust was broken. Her hope lost. And it had been all his fault.

So, he shuffled through his days and tried not to think too hard. One day, hopefully, they would realize he wasn't going to write the story and everyone would forget about it. That's all he could hope for now.

But, of course, Mr. Barnett at the grocery store wasn't happy with his moping. The old man didn't know the first thing about what George was going through, but he was perceptive enough to notice that something was wrong even if George didn't mutter a word of it out loud. As George pulled his cash out to pay for his breakfast, Mr. Barnett tutted under his breath.

"You're feeling a little lean here, Georgie."

Ah, yes. This was the first breakfast in a while where George hadn't also bought something for Annie. A bagel with cream cheese and one of those sugary coffee things she liked. This morning, all he had was a sad bran muffin and a bottle of water for himself. Shaking his head, George tried to play it as cool as he possibly could. He didn't want Mr. Barnett to know what was going on.

"Yeah. It's just me these days, boss."

"And why is that?"

Unfortunately, no matter what George wished, Mr. Barnett was currently holding his bran muffin hostage, and it was clear from the set of his jaw that he wasn't going to let him go until he confessed why he'd suddenly gone from happy-go-lucky, *I've got the world on a string* bagel-devouring joy to misery and bran muffins.

A wave of shame washed over George. It was hard enough knowing he'd failed Annie and would never be able to make it up to her. Now, he had to confess to Mr. Barnett, too?

"Because I screwed up."

Mr. Barnett offered him a kindly, wry smile. The kind of smile he usually gave when he was about to dole out some of that fatherly advice he was so famous for. "Don't you know you can fix screw-ups?"

"Not ones this big," George said, trying to keep the sickness out of his voice. Finally, Mr. Barnett wrapped up his breakfast and handed it over, shrugging.

"You're right. You'll never be able to fix it. Not with that attitude, at least."

An hour and one incredibly difficult phone call later, George found himself at the base of the Anderson family house, standing at the steps leading up to the front porch and barely able to keep his head up. The flower farm's land was still as beautiful as ever, the sprawling acres filled with all of the scents and sights of a full, working horticultural masterpiece. If he'd been in a different kind of mood, the porch might have been the perfect place to sit for a spell and just lose himself in the majesty of the landscape. But, as it was, he had more important things on his mind than absorbing the natural beauty all around him.

He had to fix everything with Annie. And that meant going through Rose Anderson first.

Unlike the first time he'd been here, he was expected. But quite like the first time he'd been here, all of Rose Anderson's attention was focused squarely on him. The weight of her flat, disappointed stare was nearly enough to crush him. When they'd last spoken about Annie, Rose had implored him to be gentle with her, that she was more fragile than she looked. George hadn't known then what she meant, but he'd never even suspected that he had the power or the capacity to hurt Annie, at least not in any way that mattered.

Now, he knew how wrong he'd been. And Rose's stare was the least of the punishments he deserved.

She sat at a small table, set with glasses and a clear-glass pitcher of iced tea. Her fingertips tapped at the glass as she waited for him to say something. Truth was, now that he'd made it here, he wasn't sure what to say. He just knew that this was the right thing to do, that Rose was the right person to start his atonement with. She'd warned him. He hadn't listened. And if there was anyone in the world who could get Annie to open up her heart again, it was Rose Anderson. George swallowed and took the first step up onto the porch.

"Thank you for seeing me," he said, his voice a little weak.

"I wouldn't thank me just yet. Don't forget, I have a wild, bloodthirsty animal that comes whenever I whistle."

Rose nodded her head towards a patch of earth near the flower plants, where Stella—the animal who'd chased George out of a tree during his last visit to the property—sat, watchful and growling. The dark soil staining her snow-white fur did nothing to make her look any less terrifying. His lips tugged upward into a twist somewhere between a grimace and a smile. "That's fair enough. I guess I deserve that."

"So, why are you here? You know I can't absolve you of what you've done or fix it for you."

"No, but I was thinking that maybe you would be able to help me."

It was then that George found the courage to finally look up and meet Rose's gaze. He'd been expecting her to be angry with him and disappointed with his carelessness with Annie's heart, but he hadn't imagined the thinly veiled fury dominating her expression. It was almost enough to make him reel back in surprise.

"You broke Annie's heart. You might have ruined her life and her career. You expect me to help you?"

"Everyone says you're the nice Anderson sister," he reminded her, but the words came out as barely more than a mumble, a half-hearted attempt to get her on his side because of her reputation. Rose wasn't having any of that.

"Being nice is not the same thing as letting myself get walked all over. And it definitely doesn't mean letting people walk all over my friends and their hearts."

George tried to think of a somewhat coherent way to answer that, but he was cut off by the sound of boots coming up the drive-way and a voice from his office—the last voice he ever expected to hear at the Anderson family flower farm—splitting the air. Mynette. What in the world was she doing here?

"Sorry I'm late. I had to finish a copy-editing thing before I could take my lunch break. Deadlines." The woman shuffled up past George without so much as an *excuse me*, and took the only open seat left at Rose's little porch table. She helped herself to a glass of sweet tea. "Continue."

"What are you doing here?"

Rose answered for her. "She called earlier to check and see how Annie was doing. I told her you wanted to come over and she asked if she could, too."

"Why?"

Mynette wrung her hands, but that was the only sign of visible distress he saw in her. She had a remarkable poker face. "Because I feel awful. I feel like this is all my fault."

"It's not. It's mine."

"Right," Mynette agreed, with a nod that told him she didn't quite believe him. He knew that she'd been the one to pass on Eagle's investigation message to Erica, but he knew that the true blame lay with himself for hiring Eagle. Mynette finished a long drink from her iced tea, slammed the glass down, and nodded with an air of determined finality. "Which is why we're going to fix it."

"You want to help me? But I thought you hated Annie."

"No," she said, her voice hushed, repentant. "No, I don't. She invited me over for a sleepover right after I'd told Erica about the investigation and she was so kind and so friendly...I feel awful about the part I played in all of this. It's so easy to dislike someone when you don't know them, you know? So easy to make mistakes when you're just wrapped up in your own little world."

Solemnly, he nodded. The bitter taste of regret flooded his mouth. "Yeah, I know the feeling."

Rose's tapping fingers on her glass made another appearance, pulling his attention back to her. Not even a single muscle in her face had moved or shifted. She was still as skeptical as ever about him.

"George was just telling me about his master plan to get Annie back."

Yes, that was why he'd come here. He needed Rose's help if he was ever going to fix this, if he was ever going to get near enough to Annie to let her know that he was going to take care of everything. But Mynette's appearance suddenly awakened about half a dozen new thoughts and emotions, each one its own path to a new plan.

"Actually... Now that you're here, Mynette, I think I have a different idea."

"*I* still haven't agreed to help out with *any* idea," Rose reminded him, crossing her arms over her chest and gritting her teeth so hard that the words barely made it out.

He knew he deserved everything she hurled at him. He'd hurt her friend, and Rose was loyal to the core. But his heart was on the line here. He needed her help or this would never work. Finally crossing the front porch, George crouched down so he was a little less than eye level with Rose, who was still seated in her stiff-backed chair. Capturing her attention, he pleaded with her in the one way he knew how.

"Rose, I am in love with Annie Martin. I was never going to publish this story about her. I never would publish this story about her. My editor made a mistake. But I am going to fix it. I am going to make sure that this never gets published. And even if Annie doesn't ever even look at me again, much less ever take me back, then it's still going to be worth it. Because I love her too much to see her in pain. I'm not going to let anyone hurt her. Please. Please, help me fix this."

For a moment, she searched his face. Her lips thinned into a hard, straight line, but she nodded once.

"I'll consider it. What's your plan?"

"Well..." His lips turned up in the smallest of smirks as he glanced between Rose and Mynette, his two new partners in crime. "I always believed in the power of the press."

Chapter Twenty-Three

Annie

Annie had thought about moving back into her brother's big house on the hill, but, even though her entire world was ending, she still liked her little house, even if it was full of memories of George.

Memories of him sitting on that couch of hers, with Monster asleep in his lap. Memories of him calling her a shooting star.

God, how had she been tricked so easily? How had she allowed herself to fall for those big, brown eyes of his and for all of his smooth-talking lines?

She should have known better, in every sense. She'd been burned once before by a man telling her she was beautiful and important, a decision that had ruined much of the rest of her life. Now, she'd fallen for the same traps again, only this time, she wasn't just going to lose her life.

She was going to lose her heart, too.

Part of her thought it might be better to go straight to Los Angeles, take up her old life again, and start facing the music head-on. After all, this would be the rest of her life once this story hit all of the papers. If she was ever going to show her face in public again, maybe it was better to rip off the Band-Aid now, to hold her head up high and try to pretend like none of the whispers or the leaked pictures were getting to her.

But every time she moved through her beloved rooms or had a slice of Millie's pie or caught the scent of the Andersons' flowers on the town square breeze, the thought of running away turned sour in her mind. If she went back to Los Angeles, she would be alone. In a city of millions of people, they would all certainly be polite to her face. They would all chatter and gossip and invite her to their parties.

But they wouldn't let her cry on their shoulders. They wouldn't put a cat in her lap and a cup of tea in her hands and let her stare out of the window for hours. They would be near her, but they wouldn't be there for her. Not the way everyone in Hillsboro was.

Still. She couldn't be a burden. Not anymore. Not ever again. Rose had promised her that their friendship meant she would always be there, but the truth of that promise cut Annie to the core. She didn't *want* to be the kind of person that everyone had to protect and look after. She wanted love, but she couldn't stand the idea of being someone's baggage.

Which was why, three days after she got a fact-checking call from the *Hillsboro Gazette*, she was packing up her things.

"Alright, Monster," she said, giving a pointed look to the pup currently resting on her favorite place on the couch. "I know you're not crazy about going on a plane, but don't worry. I'll give you lots of cuddles and after I've had a glass of wine, we can both pass out until we land at LAX."

A whimper from the animal as Annie reached for her suitcase. Annie's heart thrummed painfully, but she tried to put on a brave face. If she couldn't do that in front of her dog, how in the world was she supposed to do it in front of anyone else?

"I know. I don't want to go either. But I'm sure you'll find plenty of other pup friends back in L.A., alright?" Grabbing Monster's leash, Annie reached for her. After a moment of headstrong resistance, Monster finally ducked her head and allowed Annie to loop the harness. Minutes later, they were both on the porch—Annie locking up and Monster in her carrier crate—waiting for the car Annie had hired to take them to the local airport that would fly them both back home.

Well, back to Los Angeles, anyway.

Annie locked the doors to her little house for what felt like the last time, as Monster whined in her carrier. She tried, as best she could, to comfort her.

"That's a good girl. Thank you. We'll be there in fifteen minutes."

But then, a familiar, rumbling voice filled the dead air around her. The sound was both restorative and heartbreaking all at once, a reminder of what she'd lost and how much she'd loved it when she'd had it.

"You know, I heard that you should always tell your animals that you'll be back in fifteen minutes. Animals can't tell time."

Annie didn't turn around to see George Barnett. She didn't have to turn around to imagine how he might have been smirking at their shared joke, at the memory of what they had been before he'd ruined everything and shattered her world. Her trembling hands shook the key ring she held.

"What are you doing here?"

"Just . . . delivering your paper."

That got her to turn around, though she immediately regretted the decision. He was so painfully handsome, so honest looking. The fact that he'd turned out to be just another deceiving jerk of a man despite looking like that only made things worse.

If this had been any other moment, she would have run into him, thrown her arms around his neck, and begged him to take all of the pain she was feeling away. But she couldn't. Not anymore. Not when she knew who he really was.

Sure enough, he was holding a rolled-up copy of the newspaper. In the soft air, she could smell the harsh scent of fresh newsprint. Annie stared at it rather than at him.

"I don't get the *Hillsboro Gazette*. It's a trashy rag that hires tons of unscrupulous reporters."

"Well, think of this as a taster issue. Maybe it will change your mind."

He extended the paper to her once again, this time taking a step forward in her direction. The last thing she needed or wanted was him coming any closer. This was already hard enough as it was. Snapping the paper out of his hands, she shoved it in her purse without a second thought.

A yellow cab came down the street in her direction. She could have kissed it. It was the perfect excuse for escaping this encounter. She didn't know why George wanted her to have this paper so badly, she didn't know why he was so intent on wrecking her life, and, frankly, she didn't want to care anymore. She just wanted to go to a place where she could walk into a crowd and disappear in it.

"Fine. I'll need something to line Monster's cage with when we get to the airport."

George's eyebrows raised, and that's when he finally looked at her feet, where her suitcases and boxes were scattered. Behind him, the taxi parked on the street and the driver made his way up to the curb to help her pack up. "Airport? Where are you going?"

"Back to Los Angeles," Annie said, as breezily as she could manage, flashing a smile at the driver as he took Monster's crate. "I'm going to have some things I have to take care of there soon. Besides, I'm good at being on my own."

That was a lie, and they both knew it. But she wanted him to see how much he'd hurt her, wanted to twist the knife of guilt just like he'd twisted the knife of her shame by showing up here today. It seemed to work. Shuffling his feet, he stepped off her front walkway and gave a wave. A quiet, heartbreakingly simple goodbye.

"Okay. Well, I hope you like the newspaper. Have a safe trip."

That would have been the perfect moment for him to tack on her nickname. *Have a safe trip, princess.* But he didn't.

"Thanks."

He left then, taking part of her with him, a part she tried not to think about as she left her little house and her little town behind. Once she was in the cab, the driver inspected her in the rearview mirror, his gruff voice filling up the quiet, cloistered space of the interior.

"Still heading to the airport?"

Annie didn't have to think twice about that. "Yes, please."

Still, twenty minutes into her car ride, Annie couldn't help it any longer. Reaching into her bag, she withdrew her copy of the *Hillsboro Gazette.* The curiosity rising up in her was just too strong. She didn't have the strength to fight it. Unrolling the paper, the headline, with its bold lettering, practically smacked her.

Annie Martin—Exposed by Those Who Know Her Best

The word "exposed" sent a trail of shivers down Annie's spine, but she straightened to her full height, tilted up her chin, and tried to put on a brave face. If this was "The Story" that would ruin her life, then she'd better bite the bullet and figure out what she was up against as soon as possible. The inset picture was one she wasn't familiar with—it was her running around with Sugar Cube at the miniature horse farm. Annie grimaced, both at the sight of it and at the memory it awakened in her. Back then, she'd been so convinced of her love for George, so convinced that he loved her and that he was worthy of her trust.

She wondered what kind of salacious pictures they would use as the inset picture on page 4 or wherever the story continued. Drinking in a breath, she steeled herself as best she could and carried on reading.

If you happen to meet Annie Martin—an Instagram star who has, over the last few years, taken to splitting her time between her hometown of Los Angeles and Hillsboro—you might not quite understand her at first. I know that I certainly didn't. Our first meeting, she'd caught me trying to spy on her house. The first time we actually spoke was during a wedding dance that ended with both of us storming off in different directions and vowing never to see each other again.

I misunderstood her then. Just as I had done for a very, very long time. When she first moved to Hillsboro with her brother, Luke Martin, almost two years ago, I suspected that this enigmatic woman was up to something. And it turned out, I was right. She was very busy stealing the hearts of everyone in town.

What follows in the editorial below is somewhat unusual and imperfect, and therefore, is the perfect way to introduce the world to Annie Martin, a somewhat unusual, somewhat imperfect woman. In the paragraphs below you will find stories and firsthand accounts from the people who know Annie Martin best—those whose lives she has touched over the years of her life here. In the paragraphs below, you will meet some of these people. And, hopefully, you will come to love her as we have.

Annie's hands were shaking. It had nothing to do with the old road currently taking them towards the highway. She gripped the edges of the paper, trying to get the words to un-blur and come into focus. But the longer she read and the more she absorbed and the more familiar voices came out from the page, the blurrier things got.

Then, the tears began to fall. And she read clearly once again. Just in time, too, because after reading about everyone from the Fire Chief to Mr. Barnett the grocery man to Clarice the dog groomer to Rose to her own brother, she finally made it to page 4, where the story reached its conclusion. Where George got his turn to write.

Over the last few weeks, I have gotten to know Annie Martin. Together, we tried to set up her best friend with a series of slightly ill-advised dates. We attended miniature horse weddings, raised money at bachelor auctions, and even ran our own speed-dating service. All through this time, I wondered when she would slip.

When I would see the real Annie Martin, the one who was secretly cold and cruel and all of the horrible things I'd been taught to believe about outsiders. But, in the end, I was the one who was exposed. She pulled away my defenses and exposed my heart. A heart that I'd somehow forgotten I had.

This was not the editorial I thought I would write when I first decided to pen a piece about Annie Martin. But as a journalist, my first and foremost duty is to the truth. And the truth is this, plain and simple. She is the best friend I have ever had. And I love her.

Annie reread the last sentence over and over again. He loved her. He really, really loved *her*. He'd had everything he ever wanted laid out at his feet. One published story about her sordid past and he would be on his way to the big bylines and the big stories and the fancy Pulitzer dinners. But he'd traded it all for this moment, for this confession.

He loved her.

And seeing it printed out in black and white, in ink and paper, she knew she loved him too.

"I'm so sorry. I need you to turn around," she blurted, folding up the newspaper so she could make desperate eye contact with the driver. Monster yipped worriedly from her carrier.

"What, did you forget something?"

"Yes. Yes, I did," she sniffled. "Can you please go straight to the *Hillsboro Gazette* offices, please?"

"Sure. Yeah," the man said, clearly uncomfortable with the sight of a crying woman in his back seat. "Whatever you say, lady."

Annie clutched the paper to her heart, holding it closer and closer with every passing second, as if she could somehow bring herself nearer to George just by clinging to it.

The moments and the wheels of the tires seemed to roll by impossibly slow, but somehow, finally, Annie made it back to Hillsboro and back to the town square. Practically tossing her wallet at the driver, she begged him to stay and look after her things and to keep an eye on Monster. *Keep the meter running, please*, had been her last words before she threw herself out of the car and sprinted up the rickety stairs leading up to the *Hillsboro Gazette* offices.

She just needed to see him. She just needed to see him. She just—

But then…she threw the office doors open and there he was. Standing in the middle of the press pool, looking over someone's shoulder at a piece of copy, completely oblivious to her presence. Annie's heart stopped.

She loved him. The force of that struck her square between the eyes, setting everything in her world into close focus. Everything else fell away, until he was the only thing she saw.

She'd spent so much of her life believing she didn't belong anywhere. That no one would ever—*could* ever—really want her. But he'd given her a gift today. Not just of showing that she'd been wrong in a romantic sense, but that she'd been wrong in just about every other way, too. He'd given her the gift of knowing she belonged. Of finally believing that she meant something to other people. And that was worth everything to her.

It could have been a minute or an hour that she stood there, but eventually, he must have felt the heat of her stare. He looked up; their eyes met. Her heart sighed at the contact, the kind of sigh you give when you finally slip into your own bed after being away from home for way, way too long.

George didn't say anything. In fact, there was something like hesitation in his gaze, like he wasn't sure what she was going to say or do now that she was finally back here. Weakly, she held up the newspaper currently clutched in her grip.

"I read your article."

"You did?"

Annie was well aware that everyone in the newsroom was currently watching this exchange, but she didn't care. She couldn't care. She was on a collision course with this man, with their love, and she wasn't going to steer away from it. He needed to know how she felt. If she didn't get it out there, she was afraid her happiness and her love were going to consume her.

"And then I read it again. And again. And again. How did you—"

Shoving his hands in his pockets, George walked slowly over towards her, taking his time between each step. "Mynette convinced our editor that publishing the story wouldn't be in our best interest. As soon as Rose even started mentioning your name, my phone was ringing off the hook with people who wanted to talk about you. And today, we all got here at two in the morning to replace the paper's copy with this. We might all be fired by tomorrow, but... but I couldn't not do anything. I had to fight. I had to fight for you."

Now, he was so close that she could reach out and touch him, but she kept her hands to herself. She was afraid if she even blinked too hard, that this beautiful, wonderful dream would come crashing down around her.

George's eyes flooded with emotion. "I'm so sorry about everything. About how scared you must have been and how long it took me to fix it. I wanted to make things right—"

The pain and desperation contorting his face broke her resolve, and she reached out with one newsprint-stained hand to cup his cheek. "You did, George. You did."

When George smiled at her then, a sheepish, hopeful thing that tickled her from the inside out, she felt, for maybe the first time in her entire life, that everything was going to be okay. He reached up and placed his own hand over hers; the contact zapped her with electricity, pulling her in closer as if she'd just touched a live wire she couldn't let go of.

"So, you're not going back to Los Angeles?" he asked.

"I don't want to go anywhere that you're not going to be. Not when I'm in love with you."

George's eyes widened slightly. So did his smile. "I love you too, Annie."

Somewhere in the back of the newsroom, she heard a quiet voice mutter *aw*, which was almost—but not quite—enough to get her to stop asking her next question. Gently, she tipped her forehead against George's.

"Oh, and I do have one more request."

"Anything," he said, and she knew that he meant it.

Annie's eyes drifted to George's lips, and she subconsciously licked her own. Ever since the moment she'd read his article, she'd wanted to do this. More than anything. "Once upon a time, you told me that I should be kissed like I'm the most important woman in the universe. Would you...I mean, if it's not too much trouble..."

"It would be my pleasure."

And when he finally brought his lips to hers, she knew what real pleasure, what real soul-deep happiness, actually felt like.

Epilogue

Annie

Annie had always loved Los Angeles. Despite her fondness for Hillsboro over the last few years, she was always going to be a city girl at heart. She loved the shape of the sky, the way its purple, nightly hue wrapped around the Hollywood Hills. She loved the rattle of conversations over cocktails, the clicking of high heels against stone staircases that gave way to marble flooring. She loved ranch-style mansions and taco trucks and 24/7 delivery. The Egyptian Theater. The Comedy Store. Hollywood Forever Cemetery. The LACMA.

She loved the food and the diversity of languages she could hear spoken any time she stepped out onto the streets. She adored sitting in restaurants with a glass of wine, just so she could people-watch as executives downed bottles of champagne and planned their upcoming slate of films. She loved the city's excesses and eccentricities, the way that it all at once felt like a runaway train and a slow, languorous slip down river.

Los Angeles had a lot going for it, and despite the fact that she now called Hillsboro home, Annie would always be right there, returning to the heart of the city whenever she could, just to experience all that it had to offer.

But one thing Hillsboro had that Los Angeles didn't? Sunday Night Dinners at the Anderson House.

The entire weekly affair of Family Dinner had been put on hold for the last few months. Between the wedding planning and then the honeymoon, along with May and Tom's extended absences as they traveled the world together, there hadn't been a time when the entire family was in the same place at the same time.

And yes, that meant the *entire* family. Because for once, Annie was part of a family again. Family Dinners didn't just include her. They weren't held without her. The table wasn't complete unless she was there, according to the Andersons.

And her week wasn't complete without them. Without some time with her family. Not the family she was born into, but the family she chose and that chose her.

But this week, after a long hiatus, the entire family was back together again and this time... this time, there was going to be a new addition to the crowd. A very nervous, very handsome, and slightly sweaty addition.

"Are you sure I look alright?" George asked, pausing at the front steps of the Anderson house, fiddling with his tie as he did. The golden glow of the house seeped out into the dark, autumnal darkness of California night, a welcoming beacon beckoning them inside. Annie put the pies she'd picked up from Millie's on the square down on the porch so she could adjust his tie for him, gently but firmly moving his hands away for better access to the fabric. She wasn't sure how he'd managed to make it *more* messy while trying to fix it.

Of course, she'd told him over and over again that a tie and jacket weren't necessary for Family Dinner—she, for example, was wearing a T-shirt featuring the words "A Nora Ephron Film" tucked into a pair of her oldest, most reliable pair of high-waisted jeans—but he wouldn't hear of it.

"You look great," she said, gently. "Very kissable."

"Well, I hope the Andersons don't agree with the second part. I wouldn't want to start any drama, princess."

Annie snorted a laugh, but gave him a quick peck on his nose anyway. It hadn't escaped her notice that her boyfriend—oh, what an exciting word, *boyfriend*—was bouncing up and down on the balls of his feet or that his hands were shaking at his sides. All day, he'd been a complete and total nervous wreck, a quirk she couldn't even begin to understand. *She* loved him. And Rose, the Anderson who'd spent the most time with him, already really liked him and had wanted them to be together this whole time. What on earth did he have to worry about? After all, it was just dinner.

"You're going to be great. They're going to love you."

"It's just…"

"It's just *what?*"

She narrowed her eyes slightly, trying to scrutinize his expression for some hint of whatever was going on in that head of his. That was the problem with loving someone so cerebral, so (occasionally) guarded. She wanted to know everything about him, but still was learning how to find the clues to his innermost thoughts lurking in the tiny motions of his expressions.

"It's just like I'm meeting your family for the first time, you know? I want to make a good impression."

The thick shadows of the night surrounding them from all sides suddenly covered George's eyes as he ducked his head. That's when it finally clicked. He wasn't just nervous because this was a new social situation and he was anything but comfortable with those. He was nervous because he was *so much* like Annie. For so long, he'd been without a family, without a community, and now, he was standing at the threshold of one.

He was terrified of rejection, of being left out in the dark all over again. Annie's heart broke for him. All at once, she wanted to throw her arms around him and promise that she would *never* let that happen. As long as she was around, he would always know love, and safety, and the comfort of people who care about you.

But, knowing he'd just end up blushing and stammering and assuring her that he *wasn't* at all worried about rejection and not being loved, she decided not to put too fine a point on it. Instead, she softened the edges of her smile, brushed a stray hair away from his face, and tried to tell him what she wished someone had told her when she was so insecure and so afraid of being alone that she almost didn't go out and make friends with the Andersons at all. It had been two years now, since they'd let her into their world, and she soon discovered that there was no substitute in life for people who actually cared about you.

She wanted that for George. She wanted him to know the happiness she'd known. The happiness of a found family.

"You're right. They *are* my family. And you know what I think?"

"What?"

"I think they're going to love you as much as I do."

Sucking in a harsh breath, George braved a glance at her.

"Really?"

"Yeah. You know the thing about the Andersons that always gets me?"

"What?"

Memories flooded back to her of the times she'd spent with this family. Back when their friendships had just started, she'd been abrasive and demanding, controlling and begging for attention. They'd still loved her anyway. They'd seen that she had a hole in her heart and went straight forth to fill it. That must not have been easy, but still, they'd done it, and in doing so, gave Annie the greatest gift she'd ever been given.

"Their doors are always open, and even if you don't share their last name, you can still become one of them. I promise."

George lifted his face from out of the shadows. That crisp, welcoming light from inside the house illuminated his face once more. His smile—that smile that Annie loved so much—lifted each of his cheeks. "I think I'm ready. Let's go in."

So, together, they went into the warm oasis of the house, where the entire Anderson family—born and chosen alike—were getting ready for dinner. At the sound of the front door creaking open, Harper turned and spotted them, which, of course, started an eruption of introductions and hugs, of welcomes and greetings.

"George, it's so good to see you again—"

"Have you met—"

"I hope you like twice-baked potatoes and—"

"We're so happy to have you—"

"Thank you for coming—"

After hugs were hugged and wine glasses were poured and the most fantastic caramelized Brussels sprouts were covertly tasted before being put on the dining table along with the rest of the traditional Sunday Feast, the entire group sat down at the long, family-style table just off the kitchen.

"Alright, everyone," Mr. Anderson said, offering his hand to his wife and to Luke, who sat at his left-hand side. "Let's all bow our heads and give thanks."

The ritual wasn't necessarily religious—it was reflective. A moment of silence for everyone to link hands, be in communion for one, brief moment, and remember how lucky they all were to be there, together, sharing a meal and their time with one another. It had always been one of Annie's favorite traditions, the time when she felt the most at peace in the entire world, when she finally felt like she belonged.

But when George's trembling fingers slipped into hers, and they laced their fingers together, she knew that it was more than that. A family was more than just a place to be loved and to feel like you belong. It was also a place to make others feel loved, to help others belong.

And of everything Annie had learned in her time in Hillsboro, that was perhaps the most important, the most meaningful. Because when she glanced at George from the corner of her eye, she saw his small, secretive smile…a smile that told her everything she needed to know.

They didn't just belong here in Hillsboro. They didn't just belong here with the Andersons. They belonged together.

Acknowledgments

When you start to write a longer-running series, you build a community of folks who become as important to you as the books themselves. With each story, you grow your bookish family, and here are a few of mine. My mom, as always. The entire team at Bookouture. Karina Longworth. The wonderful team at the Healdsburg Museum and Historical Society in Healdsburg, California. In particular, though, this book wouldn't have been possible without the brilliant guidance of two of the most incredible women I know—Emily Gowers and Kelsie Marsden.

I also have to thank Katharine Hepburn and Cary Grant, without whom Annie and George could never have existed.

And, of course, as always, I have to acknowledge Adam, who, aside from being my husband and my best friend and the man who makes sure there's always cold Coke Zero in my glass, always rescues the dinner from getting burned whenever I get distracted by a book idea.

Reading Group Guide

A Letter from the Author

Dear Reader,

Thank you so much for joining me on a retreat to *The Perfect Hideaway*—I hope you enjoyed. When writing this book, I found my own perfect hideaway in Turner Classic Movies and the novels of Jane Austen, so I love to think of this story as my marriage between the screwball comedies of the 1930s, like *Bringing Up Baby* and *The Philadelphia Story*, with notes of Jane Austen's *Emma*. A fan favorite since her debut in *The Magnolia Sisters*, Annie was a delight to write for—and finding her perfect love story was a journey I will always cherish!

Frequent visitors to the town of Hillsboro will know that I create an original pie recipe for every book I write, and *The Perfect Hideaway* is no exception. In the story, George and Annie attend the wedding of two miniature horses, so I created the Apple of My Eye Wedding Pie to celebrate the equine nuptials. Combining barnyard treats like sugar, apples, honey, and oats, this pie comes together to create a farm-warm classic apple pie. To give it that signature Alys Murray twist, I also added almonds in a nod to the marriage traditions of my hometown. In New Orleans, our wedding cakes are almost exclusively almond flavored, so much so that if you go somewhere and see "Wedding Cake Flavor" on the menu, you know you're getting a delicious almond-based sweet. In short, this is the perfect pie to take as a gift when you next get an invite to a miniature horse wedding!

Again, thank you for reading *The Perfect Hideaway*! I love connecting with readers, so please find me on TikTok, Twitter, Facebook, Instagram, and BookBub.

Until we meet again in the pages of another great book,

Alys

"Apple of My Eye" Wedding Pie

This is a horse-themed twist on a classic apple pie.

Note: I love baking almost as much as writing, but the one thing I have never been able to master is the perfect pie crust. If you're a whiz with cold butter and flour, absolutely make your own! But if you're as lost with a pastry cutter as I am, I'm going to give you the advice of the immortal Ina Garten: "Store-bought is fine."

For the pie:

8 Granny Smith apples
1 tablespoon lemon juice
1 teaspoon almond extract
¼ cup honey
¼ cup granulated sugar
½ cup brown sugar
¼ cup all-purpose flour
3 tablespoons cornstarch

1 teaspoon pumpkin pie spice

¼ teaspoon cinnamon

1 premade pie crust of your choosing

For the topping:

½ cup all-purpose flour

⅓ cup brown sugar

1 teaspoon cinnamon

A pinch of nutmeg

A pinch of allspice

4 tablespoons unsalted butter

½ cup old-fashioned oats

½ cup sliced almonds (Toasted or untoasted is fine; I prefer toasted, but don't stress if you don't want to take the extra step in your baking process!)

To start, preheat the oven to 350 degrees. Thinly slice apples, and then toss with lemon juice, almond extract, and honey to preserve.

Whisk together all remaining pie ingredients except for the crust. Add in the apple mixture, and toss to combine.

Place a large pan over medium heat. Once the pan is hot, pour the apple mixture into the pan and cook for roughly five minutes or until the mixture is slightly thickened. Remove from heat, and allow to cool completely—you can use this time to make the crumble!

In a second large bowl, combine the flour, brown sugar, and spices. Using a pastry cutter or sturdy fork, cut the cold butter into the mixture until fully incorporated. If you prefer, you can make this step a little easier by placing the flour, spices, and brown sugar into a food processor and slowly adding the cold butter. Once the butter is incorporated, stir in the oats and almonds. (Tip: Spread the mixture for the crumble over a nonstick or presprayed baking sheet and bake for 5–10 minutes at 350 degrees for a simple, snackable treat! Stir in dried fruits, extra nuts and seeds, or chocolate chips before baking for extra pizzazz!)

Line your pie tin with your pie crust; then fill with the apple mixture. Top the apples with the crumble. Set in the preheated oven, and bake for 45 minutes to an hour, keeping a close eye in the last 15 minutes for any signs of burning. Pie will be ready when a tester smoothly slides into the pie and out, demonstrating that the apples inside are completely cooked through and soft.

Allow to cool for 20–30 minutes; then slice and serve to enjoy—I recommend topping with ice cream!

Questions for Discussion

1. The title of this book, *The Perfect Hideaway*, never appears in the story. What do you think the title refers to? If your life was turned into a book with that same title, what would *The Perfect Hideaway* be referring to in your own life?

2. Because of her brother's marriage, Annie is now facing a new chapter of her life—one where, for the first time, she will be living on her own. Have you ever had to begin again, maybe by going to college, becoming an empty nester, or moving to a new city? What was the experience like?

3. One reason Annie enjoys matchmaking is that it distracts her from her problems. Do you think this habit is helping or hurting Annie? What might you have done differently in her situation?

4. Annie defends her job as an influencer by pointing out, "Just because men don't like it doesn't mean it's not valuable." Do you think it is true that traditionally female pursuits and interests are denigrated in our real world? If so, where? What steps can you take to address these beliefs in your everyday life?

5. As a small town, Hillsboro has an understandably small dating pool. Rose points out that you can't just fall in love with

someone because they're there and they're convenient. Do you agree with that sentiment? What is—or was—your own dating pool like? What would you change? What would your ideal situation look like?

6. A central theme of this story is protecting the people you love. Annie and her brother are both very protective of each other, and George chooses to protect Hillsboro over his biological family because of his love for the townsfolk. Do you agree with the choices they made when it came to protecting their loved ones? Do you agree with the *ways* they protected them?

7. Romantic gestures, like the grand one George makes for Annie, are a common trope in romances. What's the most romantic thing a person has ever done for you? Or, what's your all-time favorite romantic gesture from a favorite book or movie?

8. When George challenges Annie on her matchmaking scheme, she says, "I believe more love in this world is always a good thing, even if it takes a little meddling to get there." Do you agree with her? Why or why not? If you do, should there be limits?

9. Annie and George attend two unique weddings during the book—one where a bridesmaid throws a groomsman's phone in a punchbowl and one between two miniature ponies. What's the weirdest wedding you've ever been to? What makes it stand out in your memory?

About the Author

Alys Murray writes novels for the romantic in all of us. Born and raised in New Orleans, she received her BFA from NYU's Tisch School of the Arts and her Master's in Film Studies from King's College London. She loves black and white movies and baseball games that go into extra innings.

You can learn more at:
AlysMurray.com
Twitter @WriterAlys
Facebook.com/AlysMurrayAuthor
Instagram @WriterAlys